Mickey and Michael Andrews

Myrtle Beach
A Body Found

CEDAR CREEK BOOKS

SAVANNAH, GEORGIA, USA

www.cedarcreekbooks.com

Myrtle Beach: A Body Found
By Mickey and Michael Andrews

Published by
Cedar Creek Books
Savannah, Georgia 31405
www.cedarcreekbooks.com

2006021257

ISBN 0-9785852-0-8

First Edition

9 8 7 6 5 4 3 2 1

Cover Design and Photography by Michael Shortt, Copyright 2006

Printed in the United States of America

Foreward

This book is a work of fiction. The authors do not intend for anyone to believe the characters or events portrayed herein are true. However, the authors were influenced and inspired by many real events, including but not limited to the railroading of a totally innocent young black man for the rape and murder of a white woman and the murder of an individual who's body was found in the trunk of his new Cadillac at Myrtle Beach, South Carolina. It is the purpose of the authors to use fictional accounts to show how the rich and powerful are able to control and manipulate the judicial system at their bidding to the exclusion of the poor and powerless.

No one was ever prosecuted despite overwhelming evidence, for the murder of the white man whose body was found at Myrtle Beach. The innocent young black man, Darryl Hunt, spent nineteen years of his life in prison from a conviction based upon contrived evidence.

The same corrupt judicial system is responsible for both miscarriages of justice. The authors see little change in the corrupt system to this day. Injustice is not acceptable and can be prevented.

The authors challenge those in a position to bring a more just judicial system, especially the media to do just that, especially by digging into the why's of both of these cases.

Prologue

I'm Michael Spears. This is my story. People ask me what kind of story it is. Is it an expose of corruption? Is it a lesson in the law? Is it pornography? Is it a fantasy? Is it a love story? I don't know. You be the judge.

I was thirty years old when it began. I am now sixty years old as I close the story.

It is the story of a young lawyer whose character and personality were formed in America in the 1950's. It's about a lawyer who grew up wanting to be his heroes, Superman and the Lone Ranger: who did good and then rode off with their only reward, knowing they had helped the helpless.

I grew up in Winston-Salem, North Carolina, the tobacco capital of the world. The drug that made my city rich has killed more people than any other drug the world has ever known. The money from the drug has corrupted my city and state. Tobacco drug money bought the Democratic Party. When I was growing up it was said the Democratic Party was so powerful that if you knew the right Democrat, you could raise the dead. This belief was fortified at every election when we saw how many dead people voted Democratic. It was also said that if you knew the right Democrat, you could get away with murder. Read this story and judge for yourself.

For me, the story I tell you began in August 1975 at Myrtle Beach with… a body found.

Chapter 1

Sunday evening, early August 1975, Winston-Salem, NC

Big Head had just finished a supper of steak and potatoes and beer at the Elks Lodge on Old Plank Road. Steak and potatoes was just about all he ever ate: the steak rare, the potatoes fried. Beer was about all he ever drank.

As he left the Elks Lodge, he casually mentioned to the barkeeper that he was going to pick up the "Fly" and probably drive to Myrtle Beach.

As he got to the end of the driveway, he saw Darlene, the 23-year-old girlfriend of James Crow.

"Gimme a ride to James's place."

"Get in," Big Head said, knowing that James's gambling house was only about a quarter mile up the road and there would probably be a party crowd waiting for the results of the score and thus their bets on one of the West Coast pre-season games.

"I been out at the lake sunning all day and got burned. I need a shower and some fresh clothes," Darlene complained as she pulled her tank top down to show Big Head her tan line.

Big Head pulled into James's driveway. The house was several hundred feet off the road and was shielded by a bunch of pines that kept people passing on the road from seeing anybody or any cars parked around the house. There were no cars taking up any of the ample parking.

"Everybody but me stayed down at the lake to watch the end of the game. They won't be back before midnight, if then," Darlene said as she got out of the car.

"Come on in and keep me company," she said as she unlocked the door to the house. Big Head sat down on the living room couch after turning on the television to the football game. He had fifty dollars on it, so he had some interest.

"I'm gonna run, Darlene. Me and the Fly's thinkin bout drivin to Myrtle tonight."

4

"Stick around, Big Head, while I take a shower. You'll get to Myrtle soon enough," Darlene told Big Head as she handed him a Budweiser. "Drink that; it'll make the drive easier."

"You need any help with your bath?" Big Head asked, disregarding the possible danger of anyone returning to the house.

"Naw, I can wash up by myself, but I might need you to put some sunburn lotion on me after I get cleaned up."

Hot damn, thought Big Head. Here he was in his old friend/acquaintance James's gambling house with his friend/acquaintance James's latest squeeze just about to get lucky. He had an eye for young girls and would take chances to be with them. Everybody knew that, including Darlene.

"How'd you get back from the lake?" Big Head asked thinking he had better do some checking. After all, a feller could get killed messing with women like Darlene. Big Head knew James was on his way to prison for a drug conviction, but he wasn't there yet and wouldn't be until his appeals had run out.

"Joe Wrench drove me back up. I had started to the Elks Lodge when I saw you."

"Where's Joseph?"

"He went on up to One-Eyed Jack's."

Darlene had cracked the door to the bathroom, so they could hear each other talking. Big Head could barely see Darlene as she removed her clothes. His excitement was mounting. Darlene was twenty-three years old, about 5-foot-two, and 105 pounds and had long black hair.

Big Head was only thirty-nine years old but drank beer all the time and never got any exercise except for sex, which he amazingly got a lot of. He thought of himself as a lady's man and had no trouble picking up women.

He turned the television on in part to distract himself from staring at the beautiful young girl apparently making herself so available to him. The game was over. Regular Sunday night programming was on. Nothing interested him but the girl. He could see her through the crack in the door. The shower door was clear glass. Suddenly, their eyes met. She knew he was watching her. Now, ashamed of himself, he glanced away, She was in control. He thought to himself how unfair it was, the way a woman could control and manipulate a man with nothing more than a flash of a breast or her butt or pubic hair.

She had turned the shower off. He could no longer see her. She must be drying herself.

She came out the door wearing just a white towel.

"Did you like what you saw, Big Head?"

"Sure as Hell did!"

"Well why don't you put some of this sunburn lotion on me?" Darlene asked as she handed Big Head the tube of lotion.

"I can't reach my back with that lotion. How red's my back?" Darlene asked as she let go of the towel and let it drop to the floor.

"Your back ain't too bad that I can't make it feel better," Big Head said as he rose to follow Darlene to the bedroom.

By the time Big Head got to the bedroom, Darlene was lying on her back.

"Big Head, why don't you take a shower yourself? I like it that way."

Big Head started undressing, first taking off his shirt, all the time staring at the beautiful nude girl lying on the bed waiting for him. He sat on the side of the bed and removed his pants and shoes. Just as he threw his second shoe to the foot of the bed, he heard footsteps.

Into the room walked Joseph Wrench with a .38 drawn and cocked.

Darlene jumped up off the bed and hurried past Joe through the door.

No sooner had Darlene left the room than Jerry McGee walked slowly into the bedroom. Big Head was shocked. Of course, he had been caught with other men's women before. This was different. He'd been set up and he knew it. Something told him that this wasn't about a woman (at least not Darlene).

Without a word, Joseph raised the .38 toward Big Head's chest. Big Head dropped from the bed to his knees. "Don't kill me, Joe! Please don't kill me! I'll pay you. I'll give you anything you want!"

Joseph straightened his arm, again pointing the gun toward Big Head's chest.

Big Head held his right hand up to shield his body from the gun.

"Please God...." The first bullet passed through Big Head's hand and into his heart. There were two more shots, but they weren't needed.

Chapter 2

Two Weeks later.

"3:00 PM, August 17 on the Grand Strand. Time to turn so you don't burn," he heard as he passed by the kid's boom box. "God, I thought only nigger kids had them noisy things," he thought out loud.

The seventy-year-old fisherman walked off the pier behind the Seaview Motel at Myrtle Beach and on toward the parking lot separating the motel from the pier. Two teenage girls passed him going into the shop at the entrance to the Pier. They were wearing the new string bikinis. He couldn't believe they were legal here in the Bible Belt. Ten years earlier, even strippers at the fair wore more than those two girls.

As the fisherman walked behind the brown-on-brown, 74 Coupe de Ville, he saw that the gas was leaking onto the pavement. He also saw that the left rear tire was flat. He decided to tell Mark, the manager of the Seaview Motel.

"Ju know gas is leakin from that Coupe de Ville, Mark?" he asked as he entered the motel lobby.

"Naw," Mark responded. "That's Big Head Rains's Cadillac. He brought it down to show it to me when he bought it. It's been parked there two weeks without being moved."

Mark and the fisherman walked on out to the Coupe de Ville. The car stunk to high heavens. Mark remarked to the fisherman that Big Head must have left a bucket of fish rotting in the trunk. Mark checked the driver's door, which was unlocked. He opened the glove box to push the trunk release. The trunk release would not work.

"I'm going to get a Myrtle Beach cop to come get this car out of here," Mark told the fisherman.

"I got stuff to do. I'll see ya tomorrow, Mark," the fisherman mumbled as he walked away.

Mark walked to the front desk of the Seaview Motel to phone the Myrtle Beach Police Department. He was especially concerned about the apparent gasoline leak coming from the rear of the Coupe de Ville. Within thirty minutes an officer arrived to check out the car. Mark waved the officer toward the car located in the right rear corner behind the hotel.

The cop tried to jimmy the trunk, but the odor was so bad that he gave up. He radioed for a locksmith to come open the trunk.

"74 Cadillac Coupe de Ville" the cop said into his mike to the locksmith.

Within fifteen minutes, the locksmith arrived.

"Stinks, don't it?" Mark said to the locksmith.

The locksmith didn't bother to answer. He just inserted a key and the trunk lid flew up.

The sight and the odor overcame Mark. He began to wretch uncontrollably.

The cop and the locksmith had better stomachs. They just stared down into the trunk. Big Head's eyes stared back out of his bloated face.

The cop raised his radio: "Myrtle Beach…a body found…."

Chapter 3

It was 9 o'clock on a Sunday morning, a week after the festival. I had decided not to go to church, but I was awake, purving on what I had seen the previous Sunday morning.

Three beautiful girls had come walking out of the water: a blonde, a redhead, and a brunette. All three completely nude. The redhead and the blonde showed no tan lines; the brunette showed distinct tan lines. They had crawled up the 40-degree embankment, passing within arm's length on my right, each of them nodding as they passed by, just a mere hello.

The phone rang, disturbing my reverie. It was Glenda from the answering service (she often called me on Sundays just to talk since it wasn't a busy time for her and the other girls at the service).

"Whatcha doin?"

"Oh, just thinking about the festival."

"You made alotta money, didn't you, Michael?"

"Actually, no, I lost money, but I had alotta fun. Now its back to the boring practice of law."

"Did you hear about that body that was found at Myrtle Beach?"

"No, I've been too busy with the festival to spend much time reading the paper."

"Anyway, Michael, the reason I bring it up, I know the dead man's children, and they need a lawyer. Would you be willing to talk to them?"

"Tell me something about the case."

"Well, he left everything he had and a million dollars in life insurance to his girlfriend and didn't leave anything to his two children."

"How old are the children?"

"Linda is sixteen and Harry is fifteen."

"Well, I'm not supposed to ask for business, but if you want to have them give me a call tomorrow morning, I will be glad to talk to them."

Glenda and I talked for another thirty minutes and then we said bye to each other. I didn't give much thought to the dead man found in the trunk of his car and was able to get back to thinking about the three gorgeous girls back at the festival.

Chapter 4

The next morning when I walked in my office, my secretary told me that she had made an appointment for Linda and Harry for 2 o'clock that afternoon. Linda and Harry showed up early for their appointment. Linda was a good-looking sixteen-year-old girl and Harry was a handsome fifteen-year-old young man. Their mother had come with them, and she was a very attractive woman in her late 30s.

As with most all of my clients, I asked that we all be on a first-name basis, if they were comfortable with that. They all seemed to like the idea. I tried to get to know them personally a little bit before I got into the business side of things, as it seemed to make clients more comfortable and honest.

"Tell me about your former husband, Doris."

"There's not much to tell. I married him on the rebound. My first husband had just died. We had met at Chandler Raceway Stadium where he had hung around the racing pits. He was a good man, but he had a drinking problem. I needed somebody, and he seemed to be the answer to my prayers."

"Who was your first husband?"

"Buddy Long."

"Not the Buddy Long?".

"Yes, he was killed in 1955 when he went into the wall at Darlington."

"My God, Doris. Buddy Long was one of my first heroes while I was growing up as a child. If he had lived, he would have been bigger than Lee Petty or Junior Johnson. He and his brother Billy were the first racecar drivers backed by Chandler Tobacco Company. They built NASCAR and The Winston Cup. So your marriage to Rains was a rebound after you lost Buddy?"

"Yes."

"Now go ahead and tell me about Rains."

"Well, for one thing, his nickname and what all his friends called him was Big Head."

"Why did they call him Big Head?"

"Because when he was a child, he refused to grow a neck," she said, laughing. "He was just one of those people whose heads appeared to come directly out of their bodies without a neck, and it made his head look bigger. He was raised by his grandparents, who had owned a lot of rental property in Winston-Salem, all of which he inherited when they died. He never really had to work and pretty much just played all the time."

"Was he a good father?" I asked.

"Yes, or at least he tried to be. But he had a drinking problem, which always concerned me about him being with the children, especially while he had them in the car with him. I asked him to choose me or his beer, and he chose his beer."

"What did this do to the relationship with Big Head and the kids?"

"Our daddy did the best he could until that woman came along," Harry said, interrupting. "I 'member how she made him stop takin me to the race track so he could spend all his time with her. Since she came along, I hardly ever saw him, and when I did, she was by his side draggin him away. Before Henrietta came along, Daddy would take me and Linda to Wake Forest basketball games in the winters and just about every stock-car race in North Carolina in the summers. But, like I said, after Henrietta came along, he didn't hardly even ever speak to us again."

"Linda, tell me about yourself."

"There ain't much to tell. Daddy was good to me and Harry before he met Henrietta, and it ain't fair for Henrietta to get all that money my daddy had."

"Oh, I agree Linda. Harry, tell me about yourself."

"There ain't much to tell about me, neither. I just go to school and try to help Mama best I can. And, like Linda said, it ain't right for Henrietta to get everything Daddy had."

"I agree with you, Harry, and I will do what I can to get as much for you as I can, but y'all are going to have to help me out by telling me something that we can use in the law to get some of your father's estate for you."

"Henrietta killed him," they all three said with anger and hate.

"Henrietta killed him?" I had been working so hard on the music festival for the past three months that I had been out of the loop. I hadn't read newspapers, listened to the news, or even talked to any of my legal colleagues to know what was happening in the real world for the past three months.

Doris qualified her statement: "She didn't kill him herself, but she had him killed for the insurance and everything that he owned."

"How do you know that? As a lawyer, I have to have evidence."

"Everybody knows it," all three of them added.

"Please, Michael, you are the fourth lawyer we have met with, and nobody will take our case."

I was dumfounded; I didn't know what to say. So I sat there a few moments and said I would get back to them within the next day or two.

After the three family members left, I walked across the hall to an attorney whom I considered to be my mentor, Lester Payne, and told him what had just happened in my office. Again, I was shocked by his immediate response.

"That woman killed Big Head, and like your clients say, everybody knows it. The problem is there is a cover-up in progress to protect her by some of the most powerful people in town, maybe in the state."

It was like I was getting more information than I could process, and I walked out without asking the obvious questions: who is doing the cover-up of this murder and why? But I knew I had a challenge here that I was not going to refuse. Those two children had lost their father, and they deserved someone to fight for them.

Chapter 5

The evening after meeting with Linda, Harry, and their mother, I had dinner with another friend/business partner, Reggie Scott. Reggie and I had planned to meet to discuss whether we were going to re-do the music festival that had just ended in August of '75. Both of us had lost a lot of money in the fiddler's convention music festival, but we had had a lot of fun doing it. We both saw potential for the festival to grow and to become profitable if we stuck with it. Reggie was an interesting person, having served as president of the ACLU for Northwest North Carolina and the champion of many civil rights causes. The only thing he enjoyed more than helping the weak receive justice was forcing the powerful to accept it. He and I had come to know each other at a time when I was organizing for the NAACP in Union County North Carolina and before I had become an attorney. His attacks on the corrupt law-enforcement officers had given him strong connections with the honest policemen on the force. I was hoping these connections would help me get inside information into the Big Head Rains case.

"Reggie, do you know anything about the murder of Big Head Rains?"

"I know that Henrietta Handy had him killed for an insurance policy of one million dollars and for all of his property, which included a shopping center on the west side of town."

"Look, Reggie, everybody, including Lester Payne, is telling me that Henrietta Handy had this man killed. What do you know, or have you been told, that gives any support to this allegation?"

"Michael, do you know who her lawyer is?"

"No."

"It's Charles Powers."

"So?"

"Do you know who he is?"

"No, I don't."

"He's a king-maker who has always wanted to be a king. Remember, Michael, it's often better to be a kingmaker than a king. Charles has run for judge several times and each time he should have won, but for some reason, each time he ran, some fluke prevented his winning. Remember in 1966 when all five of the Democratic judges were thrown out of office and five totally incompetent Republicans were put into office by the people of the county?"

"Yes, Reggie, I remember that year when our family attorney, Floyd Harding, was elected judge."

"That's exactly my point, a lawyer who was the joke of the county and was abused and humiliated by every judge whom he appeared before was given by the voters themselves one of the most powerful and prestigious positions in the county. That man had run as a Republican and had the courage to put his name on the ballot in just about every election since 1930. He had often been the only local Republican on our ballots, and indeed the Democratic Party made him pay for that personally and professionally."

"I understand now why every time anybody in my family went to court in, say, a landlord tenant case or a simple 37 in a 35 speeding ticket, it seemed the judge had it in for us. Now you're telling me the judge didn't have it in for us, he was punishing our lawyer through us?"

"Bingo. After three years of law practice, Michael, you're beginning to see how the system really works."

"Okay, what happened in 1966?"

"Somehow, and no one really knows how to this day, the people of the county decided to throw the Democratic crooks and cronies out of office, even if it meant replacing them with five incompetents, three of whom weren't even competent enough to pass the NC State Bar. Apparently, you don't even realize how this county has been run."

"Reggie, I do remember my criminal law professor at NC Central telling us that the legal system of North Carolina was controlled out of Winston-Salem."

"You don't even begin to realize the power of some of the families in this town. Did you realize that at one time Allegheny and Forsyth County North Carolina were one judicial district?"

"That's hard to believe. They aren't even adjoining."

"Bingo. For the only time in the history of the entire state from the 1920s until the 1960s, the North Carolina State legislature created and maintained a judicial district where the only two counties were not contiguous. The result was that the district attorney, the magistrates, the justices of the peace, and the judges for both counties were both appointed, and for the most all lived, in Forsyth County, and the people of Allegheny County had little to nothing to say about their judicial system."

"That seems really unfair to the people of Allegheny County."

"That's what they thought, too."

"Why was this done?"

"Up until 1900, Winston-Salem and Forsyth County had been a backwoods North Carolina town and county. Charles C. Chandler had come down from Mount Airy before 1900 and started the Chandler Tobacco Company. Chandler Tobacco was dwarfed by the Great American Tobacco Company out of Durham, up until Teddy Roosevelt came along and busted up the monopolies Standard Oil, U.S. Steel, and the Great American Tobacco Company just after 1900. This gave old Charles C. Chandler and Chandler Tobacco Company the opening they needed. With the federal government holding American Tobacco down, Charles Chandler built his own tobacco monopoly.

"By 1920, Charles Chandler was making money and spending it like a modern-day Columbian drug lord. He had so much money, he couldn't even spend it all. He and his family built mansion after mansion in Winston-Salem and Forsyth County. They could afford to, so they began to buy politicians. Within, no time they controlled every politician in Winston-Salem and Forsyth County. These Tobacco Barons didn't care who they hurt. They became accustomed to having their way.

"They bought everybody in their way, and if they couldn't buy somebody, they bought somebody who would move the person they couldn't buy their way. They bought judges, sheriffs, the North Carolina legislature, U.S. Congressmen, and Senators.

"Charles C. Chandler decided he wanted an old medieval fiefdom, so he bought 20 square miles of mountainous Allegheny County.

"Chandler ran into a roadblock up there. He couldn't buy the sheriff, the district attorney, or the local judge, so he ordered the N.C. Legislature to make Forsyth County and Allegheny County one judicial district. That way, Chandler could control Allegheny County from Winston-Salem. Since Forsyth County and Winston-Salem had many times the population of Allegheny County, the district attorney and judges would henceforth all come from Winston-Salem. If the sheriff of Allegheny County wanted to prosecute Chandler or anyone in Chandler's family for an alcohol violation (remember Allegheny County was a dry county until the 1960s), he had to get the approval of the district attorney and judge from Winston-Salem. In other words, he had to go to a district attorney owned by Charles C. Chandler and the Chandler Tobacco Company.

"Charley Chandler used to joke about an episode that took place at the only stoplight in Allegheny County. Charley said he was drunk one night. He was doing 70 mph in a 25 zone in his 1936 Packard convertible and couldn't stop for the light. Charley said he rear-ended an Allegheny County family of rednecks in a Model T Ford and drove them clean through the red light. There were six of them in the Model T: a daddy, a momma, and four kids.

"Charley said Bud Wolf of the N.C. Highway Patrol came up to investigate. Charley said he wasn't worried, that Forsyth County District Attorney Mac Fowler would do whatever Charley's daddy, Charles C., told him to do to get Charley off.

"Charley said Highway Patrolman Bud Wolf was just all over himself apologizing for having to bother Charley with questions about what happened. Charley said he was so drunk he couldn't even walk, but he knew Bud Wolf didn't have the guts to charge a Winston-Salem Chandler with drunk driving 'cause the governor would have his job the next day.

"But Charley almost lost it laughing when he related the only question Bud Wolf asked him: 'Charley, how fast you reckon them hillbillies was going when they backed into you?'"

"That's incredible, Reggie. I don't know how I had never known that before."

"Chandler Tobacco owns or controls everything in Winston-Salem. Even the largest law firm in this state was founded to serve Chandler Tobacco."

"You mean Forbes-Grundy?"

"Yes, Forbes-Grundy even has a secret section called 'The Project' that is housed in an old Chandler Tobacco warehouse. The exclusive purpose of 'The Project' is to clean up old Chandler Tobacco documents and prepare for the government attack that is inevitably going to try to put Chandler Tobacco out of business because of the damage tobacco is doing to America's health.

"Now, let's get back to attorney Powers. Do you know who the district attorney of Forsyth County is?"

"Yea, Tod Linstrom," I said.

"Do you know who put him in office?"

"Sure, the voters of Forsyth County."

"Oh, you poor, simple person. You don't know that Tod Linstrom had very little to do with winning the office of district attorney" he was handpicked by a small group of elite Winston-Salem powers, led by Charles Powers. As a matter of fact, Powers was so sure of himself this time that he allowed himself to be listed as Tod Linstrom's campaign manager. Now Charles Powers is representing Henrietta, who I am told by confidential police sources used Powers and Linstrom's names in soliciting known criminals to murder Big Head Rains. I'm also told Henrietta showed James Crowe stuff that convinced him if he helped kill Big Head, he wouldn't have to go to prison, you know, on that charge and sentence he's out on appeal on."

Chapter 6

The next day, I called Doris and asked her to bring Linda and Harry in the following day for us to sign a retainer agreement.

When the three of them came in, I had the agreement already prepared for them. We talked briefly about the terms of everything. It was the standard agreement: 25% of whatever recovery from the estate of Harold Stennis Rains to me, the attorney, in the event of a settlement without filing suit, and a third of any amount recovered should it be necessary to file suit. The two children seemed to be delighted that we were on our way, but I cautioned them that in the law, there are no guarantees, and at that point, I couldn't give them any prospect as to either a chance of winning or an amount of recovery. When they left the office, I had as good a feeling about my relationship with my clients as I had ever had.

I had normal business at the courthouse, so I walked over there. As I entered, an individual whom I had never met before stopped and asked if he could talk to me for a while. He introduced himself as Rick Stanton, the criminal reporter for the *Winston-Salem Early Edition*. Rick was a pleasant fellow, about thirty years old, clearly a capable and intelligent reporter. I liked him immediately. Rick surprised me by asking me if I wasn't the attorney for the Big Head Rains's children. This particularly surprised me since it had only been days since I had first met with my clients and had only within an hour of meeting Rick signed a retainer agreement with them.

Rick started by asking me, "Can we talk confidentially?"

"Certainly," I said. "But first, Rick, let me ask you, how on Earth did you know that I was representing these kids this early? I've only just now signed the retainer agreement."

"This is one of the most interesting and possibly the most explosive cases that I have ever investigated as an investigative reporter. I've been on to it since the AP first reported possible body of Winston-Salem man found in trunk of Cadillac at Myrtle Beach."

"Rick, I'm sure you know a lot more about the case at this point than I do."

"Probably." He paused and then asked, "Have you eaten yet?"

"No."

"Where would you want to go to eat?"

"How about the 'New Deli' across the street?"

"I'd rather not; too many court people there who might hear us talking. Let's go to the Beef Eater. It's only a block farther."

We went on over to the Beef Eater and found a booth that was pretty much isolated.

Rick began, "I've already spent three weeks on this case. I'll bring you up to where I am as much as I can. The Winston-Salem Police Department is leaning toward believing that the murder took place in South Carolina. The Myrtle Beach Police Department is leaning toward believing the murder took place in Winston-Salem. In other words, both police departments are avoiding responsibility for the case by saying that the other city has the primary responsibility to investigate. I guess you could make an argument that an experienced criminal defense attorney planned this murder knowing that by killing someone in one city and state and depositing the body in another city and state, you would create a situation where neither department would assume responsibility." Rick snickered as he said this and then went on. "As you probably know already, Henrietta Handy is a primary suspect, if for no other reason than that she stands to inherit several million dollars, giving her the primary motive for the murder. An interesting note you might remember is that this body was found at a very public place, as if put there to draw attention so it would be found."

"You're right, Rick. It does seem like someone put the body there deliberately, placing a rotting body in a public parking lot at a beach in August, even though it is in the trunk of a car. Sure does seem like somebody wanted that body to be found.

But why does anybody kill somebody and then deliberately, or, let me correct that, not just kill somebody, but brutally murder them, and then place the body where it is obviously going to be found?"

"Michael, use your head. If you want to collect on a million-dollar life insurance policy, what do you have to show to the insurance company?"

"A dead body."

"If Big Head's body had not been found, it would have been at least two years before Henrietta could have established proof of death, and there's a possibly she could have never established proof of death knowing the kind of unpredictable person Big Head was. There is a good possibility, if not a probability, that Henrietta would have never collected that million dollars if the body had not been found."

"Are you saying she has collected that million dollars?"

"Yes, she was paid within ten days of the time the body was found. I know you're the fourth lawyer those kids have talked to. I knew you would take the case 'cause everybody knows you're crazy."

"But, Rick, I don't consider it to be that big of a challenge."

"Michael, for one thing, consider if you win, how are you going to get paid? The other lawyers considered this."

"Well, I mean, my God, Rick, a million dollars in life insurance and all of the other property Big Head had."

"Now, Michael, don't you think that Charles Powers is already telling Henrietta how to hide that money and get rid of all that property? That was a major factor in the other three lawyers refusing the case. But, in addition to the fact that you may never get paid, something is going on here that I can't put my finger on in the power politics of this state and town. Do you know Blaine Cromer?"

"No."

"He's the best detective on the Winston-Salem police force. In fact, I would say he is the most professional and best detective I have ever met. Blaine grew up out in the Stanley Station area with Big Head and demanded to be given the case when he heard about the Winston-Salem connection. He's been stymied at every turn. He tried to talk to Henrietta, but she refused to talk to him and referred him to her attorney, Charles Powers. He's tried to talk to Tod Linstrom, but Linstrom refused, saying that the murder obviously took place in South Carolina and it's South Carolina's responsibility."

"Do you know if South Carolina is doing anything about it?"

"If anybody in South Carolina is assuming responsibility for the investigation, it would be SCLID, their counterpart to the North Carolina State Bureau of Investigation, and they have tried to talk to Henrietta, but she has refused to talk to them and referred them to Charles Powers. Did you know Charles Powers was Tod Linstrom's campaign manager?"

"Yes, I learned that last night."

"Have you been told that there is information that Henrietta used Powers and Linstrom's names with individuals she solicited to murder Big Head?"

"Yes, I was told that last night by Reggie Scott."

"Listen to Scott; he has an ear to the ground and knows a lot of what's going on. Talk to detective Cromer; you'll be impressed."

Chapter 7

I didn't want to, but if I was going to serve my clients, I had to do what I had to do, talk to cops and be nice to cops. You see, to avoid the draft during the Vietnam War, I had gotten a job as a chemistry teacher at an all-black school. I, myself, had grown up the son of mill-hands who lived from hand-to-mouth, always not more than one or two checks away from being street people. Fortune had shined upon me, and I had managed to afford a college degree and eventually a legal education.

While teaching at the all-black school, I learned what it was to be less than poor, to be black and poor. I had begun organizing for the NAACP in Union County North Carolina, a stronghold of the KKK and intimidation of black people. I had decided to go to law school and become a great civil rights lawyer. From my experiences growing up poor and working with, and for, poor black people, I had come to see the police officer as the enemy of the poor man. It was in this context that I knocked on the door of detective Blaine Cromer.

The man who held his hand out to shake mine was the portrait of an SS officer, tall, blond, handsome, blue eyed, and approaching 60 years old, still standing straight as an arrow. However, his appearance, for whatever it would mean to you or me, did not describe the honest and sincere man I would come to call a friend. Even worse still, though, after Blaine said hello and I told him I would be representing the children and thus we were legally on the same side of the law, Blaine insisted that I meet his partner.

"This is Donnie Drake," Blaine said and told Donnie that he expected the three of us would be working together in the time to come.

I had never met detective Donnie Drake, but I certainly knew his name and the reputation he carried. He was known as the meanest, baddest, kick-ass detective in the history of the Winston-Salem Police Department. He had a reputation for setting people up on drug charges and beating up prisoners when he took them into custody. I knew that Donnie knew of my representing many prisoners in federal civil-rights suits filed against police officers for beating up prisoners.

Nevertheless, the three of us sat down and began talking about the murder of Big Head Rains. The more Blaine talked, the more I liked him.

"Michael, I fought for freedom and for this country in World War II, and I fought for everybody's freedom," he said as if trying to let me know that he did not resent my civil rights activities. "There's been more politics in this case, though, than I have seen in a long time. We've probably seen more political interference in this case than any since Raymond Chandler's body was found at the boathouse over at Lake Helen at Chandler Gardens. Ain't that right, Donnie?"

Donnie just smiled and nodded in agreement.

"I'm just short of retirement but want to stay and see this case brought to a conclusion. I came on the force in '47, and in those days, I can remember it seemed like every Saturday night, being sent over to east Winston-Salem to bust a drink house. If we had any legal problems and had to call DA Mac Fouler, you know where we'd find him, Michael?"

"No."

"Drunk at the country-club with all the Chandlers. What's the word for it, Donnie?"

"Hypocrisy, Blaine."

"Donnie knows all those big words, Michael. If you talk to him for long enough, you'll find out he's got a lot more. Anyway, my point is, there we were, breakin down doors on all those black people's houses for doin the same thing that the people runnin the town were doin the same night."

My thoughts were that this man cares as much about civil rights and doing the right thing as I do, and I felt extremely honored that he was sharing this one example of the hypocritical use of power.

Blaine went on to say, "On Sunday morning, the paper would show how the police department, working closely with the district attorney, had conducted a raid that produced so many gallons of illicit alcohol and so many black men and women had been netted and taken off the street in the process. Now, you didn't come here to hear me rant and rave about injustice in society. Let's talk about my old friend, Big Head Rains. I grew up over around Stanley Station where my dad still lives, and you might want to talk to him. If any former police officer could be called a saint, it would be my dad. Yes, my dad still lives only houses away from where Big Head grew up."

"So your dad must go back to the 1920s in the Winston-Salem PD."

"Sure does," Blaine said as he pointed over at a photograph from 1927 of the Winston-Salem PD and pointed out which of the officers was his dad. "Yeah, I knew Big Head growing up. He was younger than me, but I knew him. I guess you could say he wasn't a good person or a bad person, just the kind of person who drank too much beer and never seemed to hafta work. I never heard of him getting in any fights. I never heard of him using drugs. So far as I know, he never even drank liquor, always beer. He would regularly get in his Cadillac with the Fly, and the Fly would drive him to Myrtle Beach while Big Head would consume as much as a case of beer on the way there."

"The Fly?" I asked.

Blaine laughed. "Willy 'the "Fly' Choate. Big Head and the Fly were always together. So far as I remember, Big Head never even had a drunk-driving charge because the Fly was always driving him around when he was drunk."

"Have you talked to the Fly?"

"No. For whatever reason, we've been pretty much put on hold. We wouldn't know nearly as much as we do about the case, except we've had a slew of calls come in to volunteer information, and I'm amazed we haven't been blocked from receiving that by whoever wants to put a lid on this case."

"Can you tell me any of the people who've called you?"

"I don't see why not. At least nobody at this point has told us not to give you information like that. One person who probably could tell you more than anybody else I know is Barbara Jean Duncan. She goes by Jean. Jean was living at Jack Turner's gambling house over in Surry County at the time Big Head was killed."

"What can you tell me about this Duncan woman?"

"Michael, I don't mean to be short with you, but I think it would be a benefit to both of us if you tried to talk to her and see what she tells you, and then let's compare notes."

"Can you tell me how to get in touch with her?"

"I don't see why not. Donnie, you got her number there in your file?"

Donnie wrote down a telephone number for me and said she was living with her mother and father in Lewisville at that number as far as he knew. As I stood up to leave, I told Donnie and Blaine that I enjoyed meeting and talking with them and that I appreciated their time. As I shook hands with both men, I told them I would be back in touch after I talked to the Duncan girl.

Chapter 8

I couldn't decide: should I call Barbara Jean Duncan, or should I go to her door unannounced? I learned where she lived, which was not all that far from where I was living myself. I decided to call first and go ahead and tell her that Donnie and Blaine had given me her number. Our phone conversation was pleasant enough, so I went on to tell her that I worked best while eating and asked her if I could take her out for a burger. She agreed, and within an hour, I was picking her up at her parent's home. She was small, being only about five feet tall and probably not weighing more than a hundred pounds. She was attractive with that rough West Virginia kind of beauty.

As we began to talk, I learned that she and I were products of the Forsyth County public schools, both having graduated from high school in 1963. Jean readily opened up to me, telling me about her whole life as if we were old friends. Jean had first married while she was a senior in high school. Jean had spent the last four-plus years as a gambling-house groupie and was living at the gambling house of One-eyed Jack Turner at the time Rains was murdered.

We sat down in a booth in a little greasy spoon a half a mile away from Jean's house. Jean insisted upon sitting so she could watch the door.

"Detective Ransom taught me this," Jean said. "He said you would never get shot in the back if you always faced the door while eating."

"You know alotta cops, don't you, Jean?"

"I sure do. I guess that's how you and me ended up sittin' here today. They threatened to revoke my probation for a little liquor violation they caught me with."

"Probation? What's your probation for?"

"Drunk driving. I figured you knew. People say I have a drinking problem, and part of my probation is alcoholics anonymous and therapy."

"Did you know Big Head Rains?"

"Yea, I had known him for at least ten years."

"What did you think of him?"

"Not a bad man, but he was like me, he drank too much beer. I'm not sure I ever saw him completely sober."

"I understand you were living at Jack Turner's gambling house when Big Head was murdered."

"Yes, I was. I was living with Jack, and Joe Wrench was staying there, too. Jack's poker night was always Thursday, and Joe was his bouncer. Just like in Vegas, the house furnishes all the beer, liquor, and snacks the customers can take. The drunker the customer gets, the more he loses and the more the house makes."

"I had never heard of these gambling houses before. You said Jack's night was Thursday. Are there other gambling houses around?"

"Yes, there are five in and around Winston-Salem, and they all work together so that nobody has their night on the same night as his buddy. Besides poker and blackjack, they all handle numbers and sports."

"Don't the cops know about these gambling houses?"

"Yea, but they look the other way, the way they do with the prostitutes. Anyway, Big Head was a regular at all of the gambling houses."

"Do you know anything about Big Head's murder?"

"I know that Joe Wrench told me and Jack that him and Jerry McGee killed Big Head.”

"Was he drunk when he said that?"

"No."

"Do you believe it?"

"Yes. Joe has bragged about killing other people, too."

"Would you be willing to testify to that?"

"Yes."

"Have you told this to Blaine and Donnie Drake?"

"Yes."

"Well, why hasn't Joseph Wrench been charged with the murder?"

"What I hear is there's a cover-up going on."

"A cover-up of a contract murder? That's really hard to believe."

"Michael, wake up and smell the roses. You grew up in this town and you know that there are some people who can get anything they want."

"But, Jean, Henrietta Handy, the woman charged, runs a self-cleaning operation in Rains's old shopping center. How could she possibly have the pull to manage the cover-up of a contract murder?"

"All I know is what I've been told, and what I've been told is Henrietta used her lawyer, Charles Powers, and District Attorney Tod Linstrom's names to get Joe and the others to help her kill Big Head."

"But why would a powerful lawyer and the district attorney help a nobody like Henrietta Handy?"

"Big Head himself told me that Henrietta had taken a million-dollar life insurance policy out on Abner Stitt last year. Big Head said that Henrietta then went around lookin' for somebody to kill Abner Stitt so she could get that million dollars."

"Who was Abner Stitt?"

"He had some kinda business with Henrietta over at the shopping center where her laundry is."

"Well, was he killed?"

"No."

"Well, what happened?"

"Henrietta had gone to Pricey Meyers askin' Pricey to find somebody to kill Abner Stitt. Pricey went straight to detective Dwayne Best."

"Whoa, whoa, Jean. Are you talkin' about the same Pricey Meyers who ran the prostitution ring used by Chandler Tobacco Company to entertain Japanese and European businessmen and make them more agreeable to signing one-sided contracts in favor of Chandler Tobacco Company after a night with one of Meyers's girls?"

"That's the Pricey Meyers I'm talkin about."
"You know that Best deserves a medal for exposing the business prostitute connection. He was a simple but honest police detective who tried to expose that ring for years, but the powers that be in Winston-Salem, including the district attorney, refused to prosecute. So Best went to the newspaper, and not the Winston-Salem newspaper, but the Greensboro paper. Even at this, it was only Pricey and Pricey's girls who were ever prosecuted. None of the big corporation fat-cats or city officials or even judges faced any prosecution whatsoever."
"Ain't that the golden rule? Those with the gold make the rule. Anyway, Best called Abner Stitt, and the life insurance policy on Stitt's life was canceled and Stitt's life was saved. But Henrietta ain't been charged with shit after nearly two years. You know if that was you or me, our ass would be in Raleigh servin' thirty years and servin' as Bubba or Beaula's bitch. I gotta go, but you call me anytime you want to."

Chapter 9

"Blaine, you busy?"

"No, they got me and Donnie on ice. Donnie's sittin across from me, shootin' rubber bands at the wall."

"How 'bout I hang up here and come on down, tell you 'bout my meeting with Jean?"

In fifteen minutes, I had walked from my office to City Hall, where Blaine and Donnie's offices were.

"She's a little fireball, ain't she Michael?" asked Blaine.

"She sure is; she's not afraid of anybody."

"She has shot two men in the past ten years, one of which was a husband of hers. If you'd checked her pocketbook the day you saw her, you woulda found a thirty-eight police special, which she wouldn't hesitate to use, and everybody who knows her knows she'd use it."

"Don't you guys ever prosecute anybody like her for concealed weapons?"

"Forget all that stuff that you see on TV about guards protecting witnesses and people whose lives are threatened and stuff like that. We know they hafta protect themselves. And in a case like Jean, we know she's not gonna hurt anybody who's not plannin to hurt her."

"Let me get my notes out here. She told me that Joseph Wrench bragged about him and Jerry McGee killing Big Head."

"Yea, she told us that. She said that both her and One-eyed Jack heard it, but Jack says he didn't hear it. He doesn't deny that Jean mighta heard it, but he says that he didn't hear it."

"Why hasn't Joseph Wrench been charged with the murder?"

"District Attorney Linstrom says Jean's word is not credible."

"Now, Jean told me another incredible story. She said that Big Head had told her about a plot to kill a feller named Abner Stitt. She told me that there was a million-dollar policy in '73 or '74 on Abner Stitt's life and Henrietta tried to get different people, including, and this is the part that's the most incredible,

Pricey Meyers, to do the murder of Abner Stitt. Anyway, to make a long story short, Jean says that Pricey told detective Dwayne Best about Henrietta's attempt to kill Abner Stitt and that Best put a stop to it."

"Let's correct one thing about that story. Best told Stitt about Henrietta's wanting to get him killed for the insurance, but it wasn't Best that put an end to it, it was U.S. Magistrate Tarleton Blevins."

"How did U.S. Magistrate Tarleton Blevins put an end to a contract murder plot?"

"Blevins and Stitt had grown up together and graduated from Glenn High School together. When Stitt discovered the plot to kill him, he called Chandler Insurance Company and demanded they cancel the policy. They refused to cancel the policy, even though Stitt told them it was to be used as the motive for his murder. So in desperation on a Saturday, Stitt called his old friend, Tarleton Blevins. At 11 o'clock on that same Saturday night, Tarleton Blevins reached Armand Chandler at the county club and demanded that the insurance policy be canceled. Chandler apparently knew about the situation and had been part of the refusal to cancel the policy. However, within thirty minutes of the time Tarleton Blevens reached Armand Chandler, that policy was canceled, and Stitt is still alive."

"Have any charges been brought over the Abner Stitt episode?"

"No, none whatsoever."

"Why not?"

"Again, District Attorney Tod Linstrom says there's not enough credible evidence for an indictment."

"Whatda you and Bobby think?"

"We both think we do the investigation and we turn it over to the district attorney and that's all we can do."

Chapter 10

Adam, Angie, and Cindy came out of the house on the south side.

"Gimme the Goddamn keys," Adam said to Angie.

"Fuck you mother fucker," Angie replied. "You're too damn drunk to drive. Ain't that right, Cindy?"

"Neither one of y'all is fit to drive; give me the keys," Cindy said, grabbing Angie by the arm.

"No, I'm gonna drive the Goddamned car," Angie said as she broke away from Cindy's grasp.

All three of them staggered on toward the car. When they got to the car, Adam grabbed Angie, this time by the throat, and started choking her, yelling at her, "I'm drivin' you mother fuckin' whore!"

Cindy grabbed her brother, Adam, and managed to pull him off Angie. After several more minutes of screaming, cussing, and fighting, the three of them got into the car. They drove east on the four-lane highway, which was the opposite direction they intended to go. After driving for a few thousand feet, they all three realized they were going in the wrong direction. They were already up to a hundred miles an hour when they decided to take the exit. Of course, they couldn't stop when they came to the intersection at the top of the exit. Still doing at least 80 miles an hour, they sailed past the stop sign and T-boned the nurse who was driving home after her second shift at the nursing home.

Chapter 11

"2 o'clock in the morning, it's gotta be some drunk calling me to tell me that after throwing back bourbon and water at a bar for six hours, some cop mistakenly saw him swerve and knock over a mailbox and just assumed he was driving drunk," I said to myself.

"Hello," I answered, not trying at all to indicate that I was not pissed about being awakened at 2 o'clock in the morning.

"Michael, are you awake?"

"What the hell do you think? I wasn't until you woke me."

It was Jean.

"Michael, Adam is in Forsyth County Hospital."

"Adam who?" I asked.

"Adam McGee, Jerry McGee's brother. They're gonna charge him for killing his sister, Cindy. There was a wreck. Adam's sister, Cindy, and a black nurse were killed. There were three people in the car, and they're going to charge Adam with driving it. With his record, if Adam is convicted of this, he'll never get outta prison. If you can help Adam get outta this, he can help you with the Rains case."

I crawled out of bed and drove over to the hospital. The admitting nurse was Stevie, an old friend of mine from high school. Stevie let me go in to see Adam. He had a broken neck and had four metal prods drilled into the top of his skull (which was shaved) to stabilize him and provide traction.

"Adam, this is Michael Spears. He's a lawyer and a friend of mine."

Remarkably, Adam was as alert as anyone you would ever talk to.

"Michael is the lawyer representing Big Head's boy and girl. If he helps you, will you help him?"

"I'm gonna need a lawyer, that's for damn sure. That nigger cop, Hairston, has already brought an arrest warrant for me for drivin the car," Adam said as he pointed to the table beside his bed.

"Do you want me to represent you, Adam?"

"I guess so."

I took the papers up and saw that they were charging Adam with two counts of death by motor vehicle: one count for the death of his sister, Cindy, and one for the death of the nurse. One thing struck my eye as I looked at the arrest warrant. It listed Angie Snow, Adam's girlfriend who had been in the car also, as a witness against Adam.

"Adam, I want you to concentrate on getting yourself well right now. I'm glad I came tonight. You can't start preparing a defense too early. You get rested, and I'll see you tomorrow sometime."

Jean and I walked into the hallway. I told Jean we should walk over and see if we can see Angie Snow. We walked down the hall to another section of the hospital to where we knew Angie's bed was. I asked at the desk if we could see her. The nurse said, "Angie Snow is on a machine that is breathing for her, and she is in a coma."

Chapter 12

Later on that morning, I called Blaine and Donnie.

"Donnie, I have some new information, or at least a new source."

"Whatcha got?"

"It's really sensitive. I'd rather come down and talk to you fellows."

I walked on over. Blaine's door was open. Donnie was sitting in there with him.

"Can I shut the door, Blaine?"

"Sure, go ahead."

"Jean has turned out to be a real bonanza. She called me at 2 o'clock this morning and asked me to meet her at Forsyth County Hospital. You guys will never guess what it was for."

"We already know," said Donnie. "You met with Adam McGee. We got a call from the DA's office wanting to know what you were doing there."

"Damn you guys. Is the CIA in on this thing, too?" We all laughed.

"The DA wants us to tell you to back off."

"What for? They don't have any right to tell me who I can represent or who I can talk to."

"The DA says you're interfering with a criminal investigation, and they want us to tell you to stop."

"What investigation, fellas?"

"You know, the one we're not doing either because it's the business of the Myrtle Beach PD."

"Well, you fellas gonna tell me to stop?"

"Donnie, you tell him to stop and we will have done what the DA wants us to do."

Donnie looked at me and said, "Stop it, Michael." We all laughed.

"I'm going on over to talk to Adam now. I'll keep you guys posted."

Before I left, Blaine said to me, "Michael, I'm not going to tell you what to do, but I am going to give you some advice. Be careful around these people you're dealing with. As I've already told you, Jean has already shot two people, and Adam McGee was once shot at least five times by Fred Burke. I don't think I hafta tell you that these people will kill you if they begin to think you're a threat to them. We all know that they have killed at least one person, that person being Harold Stennis Rains. And before you go, we just got back the autopsy report from South Carolina." Blaine opened his briefcase and handed me a thick brown folder. "The first picture you see there is Rains's Coupe de Ville sitting behind the Seaview Motel."

I looked at the picture and noticed that the left rear tire of the Coupe de Ville was flat. As I held the glossy 8x10, Blaine said, "We found out from our investigation so far that this tire had been leaking for at least a month, and I know from the investigation we've done, and from knowing Big Head as a boy, that he was the kind of person who would never really fix a flat tire, but rather have somebody pump it up when he saw it was low. Also, he was the kind of person who would buy a get-up of clothes, shirt, pants, underwear, and wear that same get-up for a week, then buy another one and throw the old one away. In other words, hygiene wasn't one of his higher priorities." The next 8x10 that I looked at was pretty gruesome. It was a picture looking down into the open trunk, with Big Head's bloated body lying there with his face toward the rear of the trunk. I then looked at the autopsy report itself. White male, 39 years old, 5 10", 220 pounds, cause of death multiple gunshot wounds piercing the heart. The next page showed a diagram of the body with three points of bullet-entry in the region of the heart. In addition, the diagram showed a bullet wound, which had pierced the victim's right hand. As I looked at the diagram, Blaine pointed out, "The one that went through his hand probably is the one that killed him. We often find that people hold up their hand to fend off a gunshot."

Chapter 13

As I drove toward the hospital, I couldn't help but think about all of the intrigues that were intertwining in this case. Of all of the powerful political, social, and economic forces involving the tobacco company and other industries that had grown up from it in my hometown of Winston-Salem. As I walked into Adam's room, I was amazed to see that he was already sitting up with a huge cast on his neck. He was that kind of redneck who was gonna do what he was gonna do, even if it killed him, or in this case, possibly would leave him as a quadriplegic. The hospital staff all avoided him the way they would a madman or wild animal. I was comforted by the thought that my mentor, Lester Payne, had once burned in my mind: "Michael, just remember this: the client always needs you more than you need him." Certainly, Adam had had enough time dealing with the North Carolina criminal justice system to know that he needed me more than I needed him. Adam was a little older than thirty. He had been handed from foster home to foster home, and the only relative he was really close to was an uncle who lived up in rural Stokes County. Adam had learned the trade of breaking and entering as a child, having been first convicted in juvenile court at age twelve. No one had ever cared anything about him, and he had never cared anything about anybody else. He had once been married and had two young sons. He had once walked in on his wife screwing another man who had shot him no less than six times, and yet Adam still lived. He had spent half of his adult life in prison, having first been sent to prison at age fifteen, when North Carolina didn't even send fifteen-year-olds to prison. He had told the cops when they picked him up that he was eighteen years old, and although by the time the trial was over for the B and E, everyone despised him, including his own lawyer, the judge listed him as an eighteen year old and sent him away as an adult, noting that the prisoner had advised the police officers that he was eighteen years old. You could actually say that he had become institutionalized in the sense that when he was in prison, he lived the healthiest of anytime in his life. In prison he would get good food on a regular basis, receive medical and dental care, and get regular exercise in the prison yard. It could fairly be said that a man like Adam actually felt more secure and at peace inside than outside. Both Blaine and Donnie had told me that he was a model prisoner and never gave any trouble while confined.

"How you doin', Adam?"

"What the fuck do you think?"

"Adam, I guess you know they have you charged with killing both your sister and that black nurse."

"Yea, that's what that nigger cop, Hairston, said when he brought them papers to me."

I didn't quite know how to handle the fact that Adam was charged with killing his sister, Cindy, but I had seen no indication of remorse or sadness or any other human emotion when I mentioned he was charged with killing her. Nevertheless, I went on.

"I'm sorry about your sister, Cindy, Adam. I understand they're gonna bury her tomorrow." I still saw no reaction from Adam.

All he said was, "I sure ain't gonna go to no Goddamned funeral tomorrow."

"Adam, we hafta prepare a defense. So I'll get right into it. Were you driving the car?"

"Fuck no, I wasn't drivin' no Goddamned car."

"It was your car, Adam. Who was driving it?"

"Cindy was drivin' the mother fuckin car and I'm sorry she got killed."

"Adam, I'm gonna go to the junkyard and look at the car. I'll be back with ya."

I left his room, not really believing him when he said Cindy was driving the car, but actually believing that Adam had been so drunk that he really didn't know who was driving. I walked down the hall to intensive care to see if I could talk to Angie

Snow. When I got to the desk, the nurses refused to let me see her and told me that she was still in a coma. I walked down to her room and looked in. Angie was lying on her back with the breathing tube passing through her nose into her lungs and the machine breathing for her. This woman clearly couldn't tell me anything today.

I drove on over to the junkyard. I'd always been fascinated with junkyards and the people who worked in them. I wasn't mechanically inclined myself, but I really enjoyed sitting around a garage watching my cousins take apart and put together motors and transmissions as if they were giant three-dimensional grease-covered puzzles. I asked Jim Hunt, an old buddy from high school, if he could tell me where to go in the yard to find the '66 white Ford coupe that had been towed in from the wreck a couple of nights back.

I walked down through the piles of wrecked cars on either side of the North Carolina red dirt road toward the bottom of the junkyard. When I got to the Ford section, it was easy to spot the '66 white Galaxy involved in the wreck. The front end of the car had been smashed and radically pulled to the left. The car was a two-door coupe. The driver's door had been jammed shut as a result from the impact, whereas the passenger door had been clearly torn open and appeared to me to have provided the perfect exit from which any passengers would have been thrown. I didn't yet have a copy of the accident report and would have to have this to do my job defending Adam. I took several pictures of the car and made about a half a page of notes to myself to suggest what I thought the police report might show. As I was leaving the junkyard, I stopped to say good-bye to Jim Hunt; we reminisced a while about our old days in high school. Jim told me he was building racecars and was a regular winner at Chandler Raceway Stadium. I joked with him, telling him that one day Chandler Tobacco would be backing him and he would be up there with Richard Petty and Junior Johnson. Jim had had a really rough life, and racing was about the only way that the boy was gonna get out of taking parts off cars in a junkyard.

I went on back to the police department and picked up the police report on the accident. Officer Hairston's report said that Angie Snow had told him at the scene of the accident that Adam was driving the car. Hairston's report also said that Angie had repeated the statement that Adam was driving the car when he interviewed her forty-five minutes later at Forsyth County Hospital.

I decided to call my friend, Stevie Hunter, whom I had seen at the hospital the night Jean had me come over to meet Adam.

"Stevie, whatcha doin' tonight?"

"I don't hafta work, if that's what you mean."

"Let me take you out for Chinese."

"Sounds great. What time?"

"Pick you up at 6:30?"

"I'll be waitin' with bells on."

I drove on over to her house.

"You sure look pretty."

Stevie was a beautiful blond nurse. I had a weakness for blondes and nurses.

"Where's Marty?" I asked about her eight-year-old son.

"He got off the bus at his grandparent's house and asked if he could stay the night, which worked out just fine."

"How about Hong-Kong City? I really like the duck they serve."

"I don't know about duck for me, but Hong-Kong City's my favorite Chinese."

Stevie and I made small talk. It was really fun having an old girlfriend who I'd grown up with to talk to. We talked about how the community had changed and how our parents were beginning to have the aches and pains of old age. She talked about her son and how well he was doing in school, and we talked about our exes and how they had done us wrong.

She said it had been good to see me the other night at the hospital and wondered how I could pay that much attention to every client I had. I began to tell her about Jean and how Jean had gotten me to the hospital that night. I began to tell her about the murder of Big Head Rains. She was impressed and intrigued as I told her bits and pieces of how the case appeared to be developing.

"What about this Adam McGee?" she asked.

"Jean tells me his brother took part in the murder itself, and Jean believes that if I can help Adam, Adam will help me. I looked at the car today, and then went down and got the police report. I want to talk to Angie Snow as soon as possible. Officer Hairston says in the report that Angie told him that Adam was driving the car."

"That's a lie."

"What do you mean?"

"You saw her."

"What do you mean?"

"The woman's in a coma. She was in a coma when the ambulance brought her to the hospital. She had a machine breathing for her when she got to the hospital, and a machine has been breathing for her from that time 'til now. That woman hasn't been able to tell anybody anything, whether she knows it or not. Michael, I'm an RN with a specialty in running these machines that you laymen would say breathe for people. I took her in, and as per doctor's orders, I shot her up to keep her in a coma so that she couldn't talk."

"Why do you keep her in a coma?"

"It's not likely that she would have come out of a coma to this point, but if she had without the drugs I gave her, if she attempted to talk, it would have destroyed her vocal cords and caused bleeding that would probably have killed her."

"So you're saying this police officer is lying?"

"Call it what you will. If he said Angie Snow gave him a statement the night I took her in to Forsyth County Hospital, he is not telling the truth. But you don't have to take my word for it; talk to Dr. Patrick Sparks, who attended her at the accident site and saw her again with me at the hospital the same night."

Stevie and I came back to my house that night and had a really good time talking about old times and all of the people we'd grown up with, including Jim Hunt, who had only lived a few houses from her. Stevie knew much more about Jim than I did. She and many of the nurses were racing fans and were following his career. She said she believed he was the next Richard Petty. We went to bed about midnight, made love, woke up, talked about old friends again, made love, and then finally slept through the rest of the night.

The next morning, I woke up before Stevie, and being the perv that I am, I couldn't resist pulling the covers off her nude body. I woke her up by kissing her body and devouring her huge breasts. We kissed when she woke up and I couldn't resist saying to her, "Stevie, you're more beautiful now, even after having a son, than I ever remembered you being, or ever thought you could be. But I hafta ask you: I really like that bright red pubic hair, but why do you dye it?"

"You big silly, don't you remember I was that skinny little redhead who lived down the street from you? The blond is what's not real, and these breasts, they were paid for. I'd be as flat as a pancake, except for modern medical miracles."

Chapter 14

Stevie and I had breakfast at Shoney's. Both of us had worked off quite a few calories, so we felt the indulgence of the breakfast bar wasn't really excessive.

As I dropped Stevie off at her home, she told me not to forget to call Patrick Sparks. I just went back home to call Dr. Sparks. I had never actually met Dr. Sparks, but since he was the medical examiner, I knew of his work and had seen him testify several times. His secretary put me through when I told her I was an attorney.

"Hello, Michael Spears. It's good to talk to you. How's the investigation in the Rains case coming?"

"Very well, Dr. Sparks. How did you know I had that case?"

"It's a very interesting case, if for no other reason than the way the body was found down at the beach at Myrtle, and it's become the talk of the town."

"Dr. Sparks, I talked to an old friend, Stevie Hunter, who told me to say hello from her and suggested I talk to you. I'm representing Adam McGee, who has been charged in the death of his sister, Cindy, and a black nurse in a car wreck from a few nights ago. I understand you helped with the victims of that wreck."

"Yes, I did. I got there with a rescue team the same time the police arrived.

"Stevie says you treated Angie Snow."

"I did."

"I have wanted to talk to Angie Snow, but Stevie tells me Angie has been hooked up on life support since the night of the accident. Now, Officer Hairston, the officer who investigated the accident and wrote the report, has written in his report that he talked to Angie at the scene of the accident and at the hospital within an hour later and that Angie told him Adam was driving the car. Can you tell me anything about that?"

"He's lying, and if he repeats it under oath, it's perjury."

46

"Dr. Sparks, I really appreciate this. It helps my case and helps my client, but how do you know?"

"When I arrived on the scene, the first person I saw was Cindy, and it was clear I couldn't do anything with her. She had been decapitated. So I went immediately to Angie, who was lying within twenty feet of Cindy. Angie's windpipe was fully obstructed, and I immediately performed a tracheotomy and put her on life support at the scene. She was comatose, so there was no need for anesthetics. It was impossible for that woman to have made a statement to anyone after that accident. At least, until now."

"And Hairston says he went to the hospital and she repeated her statement."

"Michael, I don't know how I can make it any more clear, and I'm not going to equivocate: Hairston is lying when he says Angie Snow has told him anything. Because of my work as medical examiner and my close work with the PD and the sheriff's department, I am a sworn law officer, and it upsets me when a fellow officer lies. There is no excuse or justification."

"Dr. Sparks, I know you pick a banjo every now and then and make it to the Union Grove Fiddler's Convention every year. Had you heard about the New River Jam Fiddler's Convention I had up near Galax this summer?"

"Yes, I did, and I heard you had the best of the talent that had attended Union Grove this Easter. Are you going to hold it again?"

"My partner, Reggie Scott, and I hope to, but we lost so much money this year that we're undecided right now."

"I hope you do it again. From everything I've heard, your festival site was as nice as any site in the U.S., and everybody had a really good time."

"Yes, one of the benefits that we really have is a lot of water. Our festival site has a beautiful mountain stream running through it, and it's always seemed to me that, at least beginning with the Woodstock festival, the opportunity to see and be seen naked was a major attraction of music festivals."

Dr. Sparks laughed and told me he had seen a lot of pictures of some of his pretty nurses in that stream up at Galax.

"I really appreciate your talking to me, Dr. Sparks."

"No problem. And keep me posted on both your cases there and how and what you're gonna do about your festival."

Chapter 15

Reggie Scott walked into my office.

"Michael, we've got a lot to talk about. Let's go for lunch."

"Beef Eater sound good, Reggie?"

I ordered my usual open roast-beef sandwich. Reggie ordered a salad. When my sandwich came, you couldn't see the beef, there was so much gravy.

"Michael, even at your age, your arteries have got to be so clogged with all the gravy you eat. But the way you're going, you're gonna die the way Big Head did anyway. So go ahead, eat that gravy. Within a week's time, you've pissed off more people then Stoneman did in 1865 when he rode through here freeing all the slaves those pacifists in Germanton owned. I've never heard of a case that stirred up so much talk."

"Reggie, I need help with this case. Would you like to join me as co-council?"

"I sure would. I think it would be more fun than I had suing the North Carolina State Board of Elections the day I was admitted to practice."

Reggie had filed a re-districting petition against the State Board of Elections in the North Carolina legislature on the day he was sworn in to practice law to force North Carolina to obey the American Constitution. Before that time, Congressional districting had been done so that, in some cases, white Congressional districts were able to receive double the representation in Congress as poor black districts.

"Michael, bring me up to speed on where you are with the case right now."

"I'm working with Blaine Cromer and Donnie Drake."

"Now, that's a joke. The civil rights lawyer teams up with the ultimate pig. They could make a cartoon book series out of that one and call it the Ultimate Crime Fighters."

"Reggie, both Blaine Cromer and Donnie Drake have the interest of the average Joe first in mind."

"In a way, I guess that's true. Do you know about Donnie and Forsyth Hyde?"

"No, I don't."

"The Winston-Salem PD got a tip that Forsyth Hyde was going to break into Smith Drug Store and steal drugs. Donnie Drake was ordered to look into it. Every cop in Winston-Salem, PD, Sheriff's Department, even security guards, knew who Forsyth Hyde was. Hyde was more or less a petty thief who never worked, would steal people's lawn mowers and sell them, break into the garages and steal their tools, chain saws, weed eaters, little stuff like that, but stuff that for the average working man is a day to a week's salary to replace. Then Hyde would fence it for pennies on the dollar so he could get drugs and liquor, and then when he would get drugged up or liquored up, he'd pick fights with anybody and everybody, but mainly older folks who he knew he could take, and even kids. He'd go out in the street cussin' and yellin' loud enough to wake the whole neighborhood. Anyway, what I'm saying about him is he was just the kind of worthless person who everybody would like to get rid of, but the legal process doesn't have any provision to handle. Well, anyway, when Donnie got the tip Hyde was gonna break in Smith's Drug Store one night, Donnie laid in wait in the store. And, sure enough, here came Forsyth Hyde, and as he started to climb over the counter into where the drugs are kept, Donnie let go with a 12-gauge shotgun. Donnie didn't shoot him in the back, but few people doubt that Donnie couldn't have taken him alive. Michael, I don't know myself how to judge Donnie's actions. He did eliminate a human parasite, but, after all, the man was a human being."

"Reggie, Donnie and Blaine both believe they're intentionally being prevented from developing the Rains case. Linstrom is refusing to talk to them and telling them that it's Myrtle Beach's problem. They have put me on to one individual, Barbara Jean Duncan, who is being really helpful. She was living at One-eyed Jack Turner's gambling house across the

Yadkin River at the time of the murder. She says that One-eyed Jack's bouncer, Joseph Wrench, told her and Jack that he and Jerry McGee killed Rains down at James Crow's gambling house on Old Plank Road and that they carried the body to Myrtle Beach. Jean also put me onto Adam McGee, who is Jerry McGee's brother. Adam has two charges of killing two women while driving drunk. I'm representing Adam in that case and believe I'm going to be able to get him off."

"Michael, you know how hard it is to get anybody off of drunk driving anymore. Just how do you think you're going to be able to get this Adam McGee off?"

"To begin, Reggie, I don't believe the guy really knows whether he was driving the car or not. I think he was so drunk that he was probably passed out in the back seat. Among other things, he was the least injured in the accident, although he did get a broken neck. The real kicker in this drunk driving case is that the black cop who investigated the case has made up evidence. He's fabricated a statement from a witness saying Adam was driving the car at the time of the wreck."

"Michael, just how do you think you're gonna prove that before a jury of twelve Forsyth County citizens who assume that no cop would ever lie and are going to be instructed by a Superior Court Judge that a police officer has no motive to lie?"

"Aha, just good investigative lawyering," I said as I threw my trump card on the table. "Reggie, the statement the cop supposedly took was from Adam's girlfriend, Angie Snow, who was in the car and in the wreck at the time. I have statements from Dr. Patrick Sparks and the head nurse of intensive care who treated Angie Snow on the night of the accident."

"Head nurse? Is that the one that gives head?"

We both laughed.

"What do they say, Michael?"

"Both of them say that Angie Snow was rendered unconscious by the accident and that she was put on a machine that breathed for her first at the scene of the accident and then again in ICU and has not been able to talk to anybody up until now. Reggie, they don't equivocate. They both say the cop is lying, and I don't mean stretching the truth, they say lying. It really disturbs me to have a sworn police officer with the power to put a man away for the rest of his life to so deliberately lie to put that man away."

"Michael, wake up and smell the fuckin' roses. I'm not gonna say it happens every time, but it should never happen anytime, cops lie. You've only practiced law for three years now, but you've been in traffic court at least a hundred times. Have you ever heard a traffic cop when asked by the District Attorney "can you identify the man who you clocked doing 45 in a 35" say "no sir, I can't."?

"No, I have not."

"Consider the facts. That cop gave out twenty, fifty, maybe even a hundred tickets that day to people he had never seen before in his life, and it's been at least two weeks since he saw the defendant, if not six months in many cases, and he's given out maybe as many as five hundred, or possibly a thousand tickets since then. Do you think he's going to be able to remember that person's face? The pivotal word is NO. And, Councilor Spears, what is your legal conclusion as to the testimony of that traffic officer sitting up there that day?"

"It's perjury."

"So, Michael, when you tell me this cop is lying to put your client away, shock is not one of the emotions that comes to my mind. But now, just how is helping this Adam McGee going to help us, and I do consider myself to be a part of the Rains murder case investigation, in our case?"

"I guess it's a long shot, but Jean says if I help Adam, Adam will help me. At the very least, with me being so close to a class-A source in Adam, it puts some pressure on the murderers. Reggie, what do you want to do about the New River Jam?"

"I'd like to do it again. I can honestly say I've never had that much fun losing money. Seeing hundreds, if not thousands of nubile young women cavorting around naked in that beautiful stream of yours gave my libido a tremendous boost. I think if we put more time and money into it and if we look at it as a long-range project, it can show promise of profit in the future. But it's only the first of September, so we've got several months to decide where we're going with the New River Jam. Let's concentrate on this Rains case right now."

Chapter 16

When I got home, I checked my messages. The first that came up was Jean. I gave her a call back.

"What's up, Jean?"

"Let's go to Myrtle Beach."

"When?"

"Right now."

"What for?"

"Let's find Jerry McGee."

"How do you know he'll be there?"

"It's Friday night. He's a bouncer at a titty bar."

"Jean, won't it be dangerous trying to talk to Jerry."

"I'll take care of ya, Michael."

We both laughed, and I said, "You don't give me much notice before you move, do ya?"

"Why should I?"

"I'll see ya in thirty minutes, Jean."

As I pulled up in front of Jean's mother and father's home, I laughed to myself about what she would say when she saw what I was driving. Ironically, a court reporter friend had called me asking if I would want his '73 brown on brown Coupe de Ville. He was in a pinch for money and had offered it for half of book value if I could get the money to him today. I did and was now driving a car that I knew people would assume was Big Head's car. I figured it couldn't hurt. I went to the door to see if I couldn't help Jean with her stuff. Jean's dad met me at the door and I met her mother when I came inside. Her parents appeared to be in their seventies and I learned that they had been mill-hands and had worked for the same mill where my mom and dad had worked. I told her folks that we needed to go if we wanted to check into a motel at Myrtle Beach before they all closed. I took Jean's suitcase, and we walked out the door. As I opened the door to the Coupe de Ville, Jean gasped.

"How in the hell did you get this?"

"I got connections, Jean. Naw, really this one is a '73. Big Head's was a '74."

"You know Big Head bought Henrietta a sedan the same day he bought this one."

"You mean the one that looked like this one?"

"Yea, right. I'm still in shock. Do you know where he got the money to buy it?"

"No."

"It's a long story. I can tell you while we ride. Big Head told me that Henrietta had drugged him and tried to burn him alive about a year before she finally had him killed."

"Whoa, Jean. Where? What? When?"

"You don't know shit, do ya?"

"I guess not."

"About a year before Henrietta finally got Big Head, there was a fire at Big Head's house on Indiana Avenue. You know, the house where he was raised just up from where Blaine Cromer's daddy lives. Somehow, Big Head woke up and crawled out of the house. The firemen were already there, so when he collapsed in front of them, they were able to give him oxygen and save his life. Big Head told the cops at that time that Henrietta had tried to kill him for that insurance money, but the fool still went back to her and used part of the insurance money he got for the house to buy him and her Cadillac's."

"Jean, why do you think he went back to her?"

"I just don't know."

"And, Jean, she was trying to kill Big Head for insurance money about the same time she was trying to kill Abner Stitt for insurance money, wasn't she?"

"That's exactly right. Henrietta was acting like she could kill anybody she wanted to, pretty much as openly as she wanted to, and didn't have to worry about anybody charging her with anything."

For me, it's about a five-hour drive from Winston-Salem to Myrtle. Jean and I made small talk for the rest of the way down. It gave us a great chance to learn a lot about each other. As we neared Myrtle, I saw it was already after midnight.

"Jean, got any idea about where we might stay the night?"

"The Seaview. Don't you wanna get a feel for this case?"

"I guess. I've said it before and I'll say it again, you ain't afraid of nuthin. Show me the way."

The Seaview was within walking distance of the famous Myrtle Beach Pavilion. It was one of the older oceanfront motels, with no parking in front, but a lot of parking in back between the motel and the pier itself. There was a restaurant/bar/tackle shop/gift shop at the entrance to the pier, and none of these were open after midnight. The motel was only five stories tall, which was short compared to most of the oceanfront motels.

"Room 209," Jean said. "That's Big Head's room."

September was off-season, so there was plenty of parking and we were able to park right next to the building. I walked around the building to the front desk and tapped the bell. A middle-age man immediately walked from the adjacent room and placed a card before me. At first, I started to use a fictitious name, but I decided to go ahead and use my name since this was a business trip and I would be using my expenses for tax purposes. I asked for and was given the key to room 209. When I got back to the car, Jean was gone. I assumed she was going to meet me up at the room. I got my suitcase and took the steps up to room 209, where Jean was waiting at the door.

"I'm gonna take a shower," Jean said as she opened her suitcase and removed a few toiletries.

She left the door open, and I could watch her undressing. When she was nude, she bent over to start the water and checked it with her hand to find a comfortable temperature. She then started the shower and stepped into the tub.

She shouted out, "Come wash my back."

Being the gentleman I am, I didn't make any excuses, but

immediately forced myself out of my trance and started tearing off my own clothes as I walked to the bathroom.

"Hand me the shampoo; it's on the sink."

I grabbed the shampoo and stepped into the tub at the end opposite the shower. Jean was standing under the showerhead facing me with her eyes closed and her head leaning back, with her hands running through her hair to get it thoroughly soaked. I poured a glob of shampoo into my left hand and reached up to put it in her hair. I pulled her close to me with my right hand and began to gently work the shampoo into her hair. At 5 feet tall, she was nearly a foot shorter than me. She took both hands and grabbed my sides for stability. I drew her body close to me and her ample breasts touched my abdomen. I pulled her head gently against my chest and held her as if she were a delicate doll. She seemed to enjoy letting her cheek rest against my chest as I gently massaged her scalp with the shampoo. I gently pushed her head back under the shower and let some of the shampoo rinse out. I then filled my left hand with another glob of shampoo and continued to gently massage her scalp. When the shampoo was thoroughly worked into her hair for the second time, I reached for a bar of soap, lathering my hands with the bar of soap, and then gently beginning to cleanse her, first her forehead, then her cheeks, then her neck. I took the bar of soap in my right hand and began to rub it along her back and then pushed her slightly away and began to caress her breasts with the bar of soap. I had her hold her hands against the back of her head so that I could caress her armpits and sides with the bar of soap. I then took the soap and began to gently caress between her butt cheeks with it. I then began to caress and soap her pubic area. At this point, she held on to my shoulders with her hands and put her right foot onto the side of the tub, opening her nether-regions to my wanting and willing hands. As I touched her vagina with my soapy hand, she gave a mild shudder and sucked in a deep breath.

"You're so gentle. I'm not used to that, but I like it," she said.

"You look good enough to eat," I said to her.

"Thank you, kind sir, I hope you mean that," she said as she rinsed herself, getting ready to step out of the tub.

I watched her as she toweled herself and then dropped the towel on the bathroom floor and walked out of my sight to the bed, wiggling her cute little butt for me as she walked. I finished my shower and quickly brushed my teeth. When I stepped into the bedroom, Jean was lying on her back with her eyes closed and wearing nothing but a great big smile.

"Put some oil on me, if you don't mind. It softens my skin."

I took the fragrant scented oil in my hand and began first on her legs, working my way up her thighs with the oil as I kneaded her flesh.

BANG. BANG. All of a sudden, there was a terrible rap at the door and somebody tried to twist the doorknob to get in. It scared me so bad I thought I pissed myself as I jumped up off the bed, looking for some clothes. I tried to say something, but I tripped as my feet hit the floor. Jean jumped off the bed, ran naked to the door, and threw it open.

"Well hello, darlin'," the big redneck standing in the doorway said as he looked down at Jean's naked body. "That'll be eighteen dollars, and I'll accept your flashing me as my tip."

"You got a twenty, Michael?"

"Yea," I said as I reached into my pant pocket for my wallet and handed it to her. The big redneck fumbled for change, but I said keep it as he handed the pizza to Jean. Taking one last look at her naked body, he stuffed the twenty into his shirt, turned around, closed the door, and left.

"What were you thinking?" I asked, my voice still quivering. "He could have raped you."

"Honey, don't nobody get a piece of me lessn I want'em to. I was hungry and you ain't fed me since we left Winston-Salem."

The pizza was a supreme and I was hungry, and this little woman sure could give a feller a lot of excitement, I thought as we sat on the bed eating the pizza we had just received.

Chapter 17

After I finally got over the shakes from the experience with the pizza deliveryman, Jean and I curled up in bed spoon style, with me holding her with her back to me. I had never been with a woman like Jean before. To me, she represented freedom with her devil-may-care attitude. Rather than sleeping, we began to make love again and continued well after dawn. It was well after 2 p.m. before we finally got up.

"My pizzas run out," Jean said.

"Let's get a picnic and take it down to Brook Green Gardens." I suggested.

"What's that?"

"It's an old English-style garden with beautiful sculptures and other pieces of art spread out over hundreds of acres of walking paths."

"What do they grow? Stuff like tomatoes, corn, and squash?"

I laughed. "No, it's an English-style garden, much like Chandler Garden in Winston-Salem. It's a garden that grows flowers, shrubs, and trees which are sculpted and landscaped beautifully and artistically."

"I ain't into that artsy-fartsy stuff," Jean snickered.

"Indulge me, Jean. Let's get a picnic and take it down there, and if you don't like it, we'll leave."

"Okay, if you promise me we'll leave if I don't like it. I don't guess it can hurt nuthin to go down there."

I found a place in the yellow pages that offered picnic baskets and included wine, cheese, and French bread along with the food. On the way down from Myrtle, I told Jean that speakers were strategically placed along the paths of the garden and played classical music continuously.

"Oh, good," Jean said. "I ain't like most of my friends; I really like classical music."

I was a little bit surprised to hear Jean was a fan of classical music.

"Good, I'm glad that you like classical music. Until recently, Richard Wagner was my favorite classical artist, and I especially liked the 'Flight of the Valkyries,' where the German angels carry the dead German warriors to Valhalla. But within the past few years, I've really become primarily a fan of Wolfgang Amadeus Mozart and enjoy his soothing peaceful music much more. I also like Maurice Ravel's 'Bolero.'"

"I ain't ever heard of them musicians. When it comes to classical music, my favorites are Hank Williams, Sr., and Patsy Cline. They really know how to hitcha right in the heart."

I suppressed a laugh, not wanting to embarrass Jean, realizing that classical music to her and to me were two very different things. To me, classical music meant the great artists who had passed the test of time and whose work people listened to, not because they were made to or because it was "the thing to do," but rather because of it's spiritual and moving beauty. To Jean, classical music meant the great artists of country music whom her parents had listened to when they were our age. Both kinds of music had their beauty, value, and purpose.

When we got to the gardens, I gauged Jean's reaction.

She said, "Oh, I've been by here many times before. I just thought it was where a bunch of rich people lived."

"Naw," I said. "Nobody lives here, and all of it is open to the public."

We walked for a ways through the gardens, looking at the various statues located along the walkways. Although she didn't appreciate them as much as I had hoped she would, she really wasn't negative in her reaction to these works of art.

"That music ain't what I expected, but I've heard it before and it's real pretty."

As we listened to Johann Pachelbel's "Cannon in D," I said, "Jean, a lot of the classical music we will hear here will be familiar to you because it has been used as background music in a lot of the movies that you've seen."

"That's real pretty what we're listen'n to, Michael. Whatda say it was?"

"Johann Pachelbel's 'Cannon in D.'"

"Taco Bell's Canyon in D?" she said, laughing.

"The title does sound like that, Jean, yes," I said.

We crossed over a little footbridge and could see an alligator swimming beneath us. We walked back to the car to get the picnic basket. Instead of using a picnic table as provided, I spread a blanket under a magnolia tree and we had our meal. We stayed until nearly dark and then went back to the Seaview. I told Jean that I wanted to talk to the manager at the desk and see if he was Mark Goodwin, who had called the police in to open the trunk. The tall thin man behind the desk said that, yes, he was Mark Goodwin and that he had known Big Head for years before he was murdered. He said that Big Head would come down, usually arriving after 1 in the morning and never making reservations. Big Head would often check himself in, always taking room 209 when available and always parked in the same spot, where his car was found eventually by the police. Big Head had brought down the Coupe de Ville a day or two after he bought it and showed it to Mark. Mark asked me how I got Big Head's car; not realizing my car was the model from the year earlier than Big Head's. Mark said that he didn't remember exactly when he first saw the car the period of time when the body was found in it's trunk, but he believed it had been there for two weeks. But since Big Head was a regular customer, he hadn't considered having the car towed until that fateful day when the fisherman pointed out to him what they both believed to have been a gas leak, but which turned out to be bodily fluids draining from Big Head's decaying body.

Mark said, "When the cop popped the trunk, the odor and the sight hit me in the face all of the sudden, and all I could do was turn around and puke."

Mark said that he came back into the Seaview, cleaned up, and then went back out and watched the SCLID cops as they took pictures and prepared the car to be towed to the coroner's office. He said the only alteration, other than popping the trunk, was that they pumped up the tire before towing the Coupe de Ville away. I thanked Mark, and Jean and I walked over to our motel room.

"Let's get cleaned up before we go to the titty bar to see Jerry tonight," Jean said.

I agreed, knowing full well that I was going to get to take another shower with Jean. We left the motel about 9, stopping to have a couple of sandwiches before going on to the strip club. I was apprehensive about walking into a murderer's place of business unannounced, but somehow I knew that Jean would handle the situation. As we walked into the darkened club, our eyes had to adjust. South Carolina law did not allow total nudity, so the dancer on the stage as we walked in was completing her show wearing a G-string. I looked around the room and couldn't see any women in the room other than the dancers and the waitresses. All of the fifty or so men in the room immediately diverted their eyes toward Jean. We sat down at a table not more than three feet from the stage. When the waitress came around, Jean and I both ordered Budweiser longnecks. A new girl was taking the stage. She was dressed as a cowgirl. The disk jockey introduced her as Daisy, the cowgirl. Daisy began her dance, taking off a piece of clothing every one to two minutes until she was down to her G-string. She paid special attention to Jean, and Jean paid special attention to Daisy. I gave Jean about ten one-dollar bills, and Jean walked up to the stage. She leaned against the stage, which put the top of her stage about even with her belly button. The dancer had obviously noticed me hand the dollar bills to Jean. Daisy squatted down with her right knee touching Jean's left elbow and with her left knee touching Jean's other elbow. Jean pulled the front top of Daisy's G-string away from Daisy's body about six or seven inches. Jean slowly slid a dollar bill down the front of Daisy's belly, allowing the backside of her hand to caress Daisy as she slid it down toward her honey-spot. The rules in South Carolina don't allow a man to touch the dancer, but that didn't seem to apply to girl-girl touching. I looked around to see if anybody was going to interfere. A new bouncer had just taken a seat on a stool next to the entrance to the titty bar. He was staring intently at Jean and Daisy, but I caught his eye as I glanced at him. He just smiled, clearly enjoying the show as much as everybody else in the bar. It was clear he had no intention of stopping the show. Jean leaned forward and, with her tongue, lifted the belly-ring in Daisy's navel.

Daisy jumped up as the Bachman Turner Overdrive song "Let it Ride" began to blare out. "Ride, Ride, Ride, won't you let it ride," Daisy danced, pretending to ride a wild pony. Jean motioned with her finger for Daisy to come back to the edge of the stage. Daisy, instead of coming toward Jean, turned her backside to Jean and did a shuffle, gyrating her butt back and forth as if riding a horse or performing the sex act. Daisy slapped her own butt cheek and turned again to face Jean. As Daisy was turning to face Jean, she motioned with her finger for Jean to join her on the stage. The crowd went wild. Someone said "Go," at which point the men in unison began chanting "Go, Go, Go, Go." Jean jumped up on the stage, and the two women slammed their bodies into each other. This is what dirty dancing was all about. Daisy straddled Jean's right thigh and continued humping to "Ride, Ride, Ride, won't you let it ride." The song ended. Jean went to her knees and one-by-one put all of the dollar bills I had given her in Daisy's G-string, slowly caressing Daisy each time she pulled the G-string out and slid the dollar bill in, circling Daisy's body with each individual bill. Jean then stood up and Daisy moved toward Jean to give Jean the little kiss on the cheek that would be the reward to a man for his money at a titty bar. But instead of a little peck on the cheek, their lips met, and Jean grabbed Daisy's exposed right butt cheek, forcing the two women together in a passionate kiss. The crowd went totally wild. Jean sashayed down the steps off the stage and over to our table. She leaned over and shouted (over the noise the crowd of men were making) in my ear, "That's Jerry McGee at the door. I'm gonna go talk to him."

Jean walked over to Jerry, who had clearly recognized her while she was dancing. She gave him a big hug like they were old friends. She pointed back at me and said something to Jerry. Then she waved her arm, motioning for me to come over.

"This is my friend, Michael. We're down here for a few days." Jerry shouted over the noise, "Lets go back to the office. We can't talk in here."

We went through a back door and into a small, dingy office. Jerry shut the door.

"You gotta wild woman on your hands there, Michael. It is Michael, isn't it? With all that noise, I couldn't tell for sure."

"Yes, Michael is right. I'm pleased to meet you, Jerry."

"Jerry, Michael is representing Adam. If anybody can get him off, Michael can."

"Adam's been in trouble his whole Goddamned life. I ain't sure he don't belong in prison, and I ain't sure he didn't kill Cindy."

"Jerry, Adam says he didn't do it, and the black cop who's charged Adam has made up evidence to try to convict him. The cop says that he took a written statement from Angie Snow that Adam was driving the car. I've thoroughly checked it out and have concrete proof that Angie was unconscious at the time that she' was supposed to have given her statement to the cops. If your brother didn't kill your sister, it would be seriously wrong for him to go to prison for doing it. I've checked Adam's background, and it's clear to me he's never had a break in life. It's also clear to me that your brother's as mean as a snake. But I can't say that I wouldn't be too if I'd been raised like him."

"Michael also represents Big Head Rains's younguns."

Son of a bitch, I thought. Talk about droppin' a bomb. This woman gets right to the point. I fully expected Jerry to grab

64

that sawed-off shotgun not so well hidden under a corner of the desk and blow me and Jean, or at least me, away. But instead, I saw this big redneck showing fear. He wasn't becoming angry and mad and blushing. Instead, the color was clearly draining from his face. Jean saw it, too. She glanced over at me and we read each other's mind. This woman had bigger balls than any man I had ever known, and she knew how to read people.

"I don't know nuthin bout Big Head Rains." Jerry spoke rapidly, his voice dropping so many octaves that he sounded like a little kid who just got caught after setting his granddaddy's barn on fire while play'n with matches. "I didn't have nuthin to do with kill'n' Big Head Rains."

"Damn, Jerry. Nobody said you did. But I just figured you woulda heard sumthin since his body was found not more than a half a mile up the road from where we are now."

I couldn't stand the tension. I didn't know where Jean was going, but I couldn't take it anymore. "Jerry, I know it's a hard time for ya. And we didn't come here to talk about anything in particular, even Adam. Look here fella, it's been good meet'n' you, and Jean and me will probably be down here again later, and maybe after you've had time to get over Cindy's death, you and me and Jean can just sit down and let me listen to y'all talk about old times. Jean, lets run on back to the motel."

"We're stay'n at the Seaview. Like Michael says, I reckon we'll be down here again in a few weeks. We'll come on back down here to the bar again. If you get to Winston-Salem anytime soon, give Michael or me a call. Give him one of your cards, Michael."

I reached in my wallet and pulled out one of my business cards and laid it on the desk for Jerry. I held out my hand. Jerry stood up and shook hands with me with what was a cold, clammy, and shaky hand. Jean walked around the desk and hugged Jerry as he stood there like a zombie, not reacting to her hug, a clear opposite of the warm hug he had given her not thirty minutes earlier. As I got in and sat behind the steering wheel, I looked at Jean.

"I told you Joe said him and Jerry did the murder. You believe me now?"

"I always did, Jean. As a lawyer, I knew you didn't have anything to gain and a lot to lose when you first told me. I'm sorry I broke things off so abruptly with Jerry."

"That's okay, Michael. I guess we got exactly what we came for. We didn't get a confession, but you and I don't have any doubt now that he did it.

Chapter 18

Jean and I spent the better part of Sunday and Monday on and off the beach and on and off each other. We returned to Winston-Salem late Monday night. I saw the Myrtle Beach trip as a mixture of business and pleasure, and, certainly for tax purposes, it was all business. But I have to say I received far more pleasure and never in my life had I enjoyed a beach trip as much as this one. Whatcha gonna say: how much sex, sun, and terror (as I remembered the pizza delivery on our first night) can a man stand in three days?

On Tuesday morning, I parked my car on Trade Street in the lot beside Sammy's Shoe Store and started the two-block walk to my office.

"Michael, come here," someone shouted from the doorway of Nathan's Haberdashery. It was Simon Epstein, now known to all of his friends as the Sage. Simon "the Sage" Epstein was probably the most intelligent and most intellectual person I had ever known. The Sage had earned an undergraduate degree in American government and then a Masters as well as his Doctorate in American government from American University during the late '50s and early '60s. The Sage had fancied himself becoming the first Jewish-American president and had been heavily involved in Democratic politics and the civil-rights movement in the '60s, a time when it was neither popular nor fashionable to champion the rights of black people. He had been in burning Mississippi with Cheny, Goodman, and Schwerner, and I often wondered why the Klan hadn't buried the Sage in that dam with those three civil-rights heroes.

"Big Head's case is now off the front page, Michael. Have you seen this morning's paper?"

"No," I answered. "I've been at Myrtle since Thursday."

"The body of a twenty-five-year-old girl was found down at the bottom of the hill yesterday morning."

"Was she a hooker?" I asked, knowing that that area was where both black and white hookers paraded up and down the sidewalk advertising their assets.

"Oh no, oh no, oh no, this woman was an assistant copy-editor for the *Winston-Salem Evening Post*."

"Whoa, Simon, you bet that's big. Now can the Sage look into his crystal ball and tell me who did it?"

"No, I don't know who did it, but write this down and open it in two months or less: the pressure's gonna be so great from the power structure that owns that paper that the cops are going to pick some brother off the street and charge him with it, whether he did it or not."

"Simon, I'm gonna call Rick Stanton and see what he knows about the girl's murder."

I walked into my office, and the first call I made of the morning was to Rick Stanton.

"Rick, I've got a lot of new information in the Rains murder. I can have lunch and bring you up to speed, but wanted to see if you might not be too busy because of that copy editor whose body was found on North Trade Street."

"No, I've got time. I'm working on the girl's murder, but our paper considered that case important enough to put three reporters on it, so I'm just one of the three. How about 1 o'clock at the Beef Eater?"

"I'll see you there, Rick."

This would give me several hours to catch up on some of my bread and butter work. I had divorces, drunk driving, contracts, and wills to write. All of this work seemed so mundane compared to the exciting life I was living with the Rains case, but all of it had to be done. There was a secretary to pay, an office to rent, law books to read; those expenses didn't stop for me to take a trip to Myrtle Beach.

At 1 o'clock, I met Rick at the Beef Eater. I told him as much as I felt I ethically could about what the detectives had told me. I told him about going down to Myrtle Beach, looking over the parking lot where the body was found, and even staying in the room that Big Head normally used. Rick was anxious to talk about the assistant copy-editor's murder. The way he described it, half of the staff and energy of both his paper and *The Evening Post* were being devoted to finding the girl's killer. The autopsy wasn't in yet, but all indications were that the girl had been brutally raped and stabbed multiple times.

"Who was the girl, Rick?"

"Her name was Charlotte Pendleton. She had only been with *The Evening Post* a few weeks and was apparently walking to her office from the parking lot when she was grabbed. All of the women of the paper are terrified now, and we've begun having a man walk every woman to and from her car. I know it shouldn't be, but everyone is assuming it was a black man who did it. As you know, that area is full of street people who will walk right up to you and demand money for a 'sandwich.'"

"Rick, this will give a legitimate reason to the DA's office to downgrade what the PD is doing to find Rains's killer."

"There's no doubt about that. Did you know Chandler Tobacco owns *The Evening Post*?"

"No, I didn't."

"Let me tell you a little bit of history about *The Evening Post*. Have you ever heard about the East Winston-Salem riots of 1947?"

"Yes, I've heard older people, including my father, vaguely refer to the East Winston-Salem riot."

"Do you know what precipitated the riot?"

"No, I don't."

"After WWII, the Tobacco Worker's Union sent organizers to Winston-Salem to organize Chandler Tobacco Company. The organizers were mainly Jews and blacks. The organizers targeted the black community, believing the blacks would be the most receptive to a union for a number of reasons. The blacks did the hardest work and were the lowest paid. The blacks did what, for lack of a better term, and I think you will understand when I use the term, did what was called 'Nigger work.' There was no chance for advancement for the blacks, no matter how hard they worked. They weren't even allowed to use the 'white water-fountains' or eat in the 'white cafeteria' or use the 'white bathrooms.' To say they were treated unfairly would be a gross understatement. After two years of work, the union had signed up 90% of the blacks and had started to make gains among the white workers."

"Rick, as you know, my parents were mill-hands, and when I asked them why they went to work during WWII for the mill rather than Chandler Tobacco, they said that at that time Chandler and the mills paid the same salaries, all of which were low, but it beat working on the farms they had come off of."

"Yes, that's true, and a real benefit of the union organizing was that the Chandler Tobacco Company raised its salaries, making it much more attractive to work in tobacco than a textile mill."

"My mother told me that while she was making clothing for the army during WWII, she was only making ten dollars a week."

"And most of the mill-hands don't even make a hundred dollars a week now."

"But I digress. Rick, go ahead and tell me more about the union."

"In order to bust the union, Chandler Tobacco hired an FBI agent who was working in the area and actually doing surveillance in 1947 for J. Edger Hoover on the union."

"What did they hire him to do?"

"They hired him to bust the commie union."

"Oh yea, I remembered my father talking about the communists stirring up all them Niggers."

"Michael, as you know from history, a lot of the union organizers were in fact socialists, and many of them during the '30s and '40s saw communism and socialism as being the salvation for the American working man. Even before the McCarthy era began in the '50s, J. Edger Hoover had his agents concentrating on the communists within the United States. So Chandler Tobacco Company recruited this FBI agent to become a reporter to slander the commi union and portray it as un-American and to turn the black and white Chandler workers against each other."

"Rick, how did he ever get an FBI agent to give up that government salary and retirement program and become a reporter? No offense, but everybody knows that with the exception of a handful of people like Woodward and Bernstein, you guys are, well, to put it delicately, not paid very well."

"No offense taken, Michael, and as one crusader to another, there are things that make getting up in the morning worthwhile in life to some people other than money. But I'm not saying that the fellow we're talking about here (the FBI agent) was a crusader. No, money, prestige, and security is what they offered this man. They offered him a permanent job with the paper, which he holds to this day, and he still draws a salary to this day."

"Are you saying that whether he strikes a lick or not, he gets paid still to this day, over twenty years later?"

"That's exactly what I'm saying, Michael. And by his destruction of the commi union with the articles he wrote, he earned every cent of it and more. Chandler Tobacco Company considered that investment in that FBI agent a total profit. It was an investment that paid for itself many times over, and it wouldn't stop there. Chandler also bought many of the black organizers who are also on the tobacco company's payroll to this day. Eventually, the tobacco company had managed to turn public opinion in the white community so much against the union that they felt they had a free hand to use whatever means they chose to complete their destruction. Under the pre-text of just another drink house raid on a hot summer night in 1947, a group of Winston-Salem PD went after the house in East Yadkin where the union was holding its meeting. Without a warrant or any legal authority, they knocked down the door looking for the leaders of the union. The cops grabbed a Jew and five black union organizers and charged them with operating a drink house. Some liquor was found, most of which the people present claimed was brought in by the police informant who had tipped the cops off to the meeting. The cops had been backed up by a group of 'auxiliary officers' who turned out to be clansmen from Union County. Word of mouth spread throughout East Yadkin, and within an hour, a crowd of over a thousand black men had formed, blocking the street. The mayor ordered the chief of police to disperse the crowd. By the time reinforcements got there, several white-owned businesses, including a lumberyard, were burning. The police opened fire, but the number of killed and injured was kept secret, and no reporter for either paper had the guts to report the truth of the incident. Michael, your town has been run until this day like the fiefdom of Chandler Tobacco Company, and I don't see any change coming, except that the tobacco industry as a whole is under the attack of health groups that eventually may put them out of business. Chandler Tobacco controls this town like drug cartels control Columbia, and they will until the government puts them out of business."

"I'm afraid of that, Rick, and when it comes, the rich and powerful will have sold their stock and reinvested their profits elsewhere, and the people who will suffer will be the workers who didn't see it coming or weren't able to do anything about it to protect themselves anyway, when the government finally clamps down on tobacco."

I couldn't help but recall what Blaine Cromer had told me about being forced to go on those raids in the black community and to liquor houses. I couldn't help but wonder if he, himself, hadn't been part of that raid on the union meeting back in 1947, and if it wasn't that that he was trying to tell me about at that first meeting I had with him. Blaine was clearly a man of conscience, and I couldn't help but wonder if his conscience didn't still bother him about that night in 1947, if he had taken part in that raid. I also couldn't wait to get back to the Sage and get his perspective on this phenomenal story that Rick was telling me. To find that in the 20th century, one company, a tobacco company at that, would have the power to so thoroughly pervert the political and economic process to its advantage was incredible, although I didn't doubt the truth of what Rick was telling me and wondered if it might not even be worse than what he was telling me. All my life, I had seen the rich and powerful turn the poor black man and the poor white man against each other and against their own individual interests as totally and completely as if the poor black man and the poor white man were nothing more than puppets being marinated by the giant hands of powerful forces that left them without the power or ability to begin to control their own destiny, either future or present. I had seen the Vietnam War used the same way. While the poor black man and the redneck were sent to fight and die, the rich and powerful had been able, in most cases, to avoid the war altogether through college deferments, job deferments, and doctor-created disabilities. They were the folks who supported the war, but not to fight in it. They wouldn't hesitate to send a poor black man or a poor redneck to die in their place. These people were willing to fight to the last man, whether it was the last poor redneck or the last poor black man. There had been the John Kerry types, who enlisted and fought when it was the thing to do. But when it was no longer the thing to do, the John Kerry types miraculously, like St. Paul on the road to Damascus, were stricken by a vision that showed them the war was wrong. It seemed the only time the rich and powerful had had to make any sacrifice at all during the Vietnam War was as weekend warriors with the National Guard, which had become a country club for the rich and powerful during the Vietnam War. I had heard stories of National Guard units spending their weeks or weekends of duty on camping trips in the woods drinking beer and partying like a bunch of grown-up boy scouts. Everyone knew that during the Vietnam War it had taken connections to get into the National Guard and thus get your deferment from becoming a "real soldier." At bar association meetings, it was by far the exception to see the lawyer of Vietnam War age who was a veteran of Vietnam, and I found myself admiring the lawyers who were Vietnam veterans, especially the amputees.

Chapter 19

After Rick and I parted, I decided to go over and pay an unannounced visit to Blaine and Donnie. I felt especially honored that these two fellows I was coming to so greatly admire had taken me into their confidence. When I got to Blaine's office, I found him working with the door open.

"Blaine, if you're busy, just tell me so. Your time's more valuable then mine."

"Naw, come on in. I needa break."

"Where's Donnie, Blaine?"

"I guess you could say he's been reassigned."

"What to?"

"He's been put on that Charlotte Pendleton case like every detective I know and even traffic control people. I thought the Rains case was political, but this one even beats that. I have never seen the pressure being put on the PD the way it is on this one."

"Who's doing it, Blaine?"

"Well it seems like everybody in town who's got any political power at all is pushing us to arrest somebody, anybody, in this case. The DA has called for twice-daily briefings from the PD, and they're under as much pressure as we are. But it's mainly that Chandler Tobacco Company owned newspaper that's pushing for this case to be solved. All those liberals over at that newspaper are call'n for us to bring every other black man in Winston-Salem in for questioning. The paper's already got a hundred-thousand-dollar reward offer out there for the arrest of whoever did it. And like I say, all these liberals want us to take shortcuts in the Charlotte Pendleton case. I can't do it, and I won't do it, if for no other reason than that I don't want to catch whoever did it and have some appellate court let em walk because of a civil-rights violation. With this kind of pressure, I'm mighty afraid that an innocent man is gonna get charged. And with the atmosphere surrounding this case, the DA knows anybody we charge they can convict in this town."

"I don't reckon you're gonna have much time for the Rains case until this Charlotte Pendleton case is solved."

"No, as you know, we were held back in the Rains case anyway, and any time we spend on it now would be considered time taken from the Pendleton case. Michael, it's out of my hands, but I'll do what I can for ya."

"Let me fill you in briefly what I've done so far. Jean and I drove to Myrtle Beach this past weekend, checked out the motel, and approached Jerry McGee."

"He didn't tell you nuthin, did he?"

"No, but I have a feeling I might get some help from him in the future."

"Did you talk to the Myrtle Beach PD?"

"No."

"Did you talk to SCLID?"

"No, but I'm expecting to."

"Let me suggest one thing to you, Michael. If you can do what you can to take the money away from Henrietta, I think that might give both of us some leverage."

"I'll see what I can do. Blaine, I'm gonna get out of your hair. Good luck with that Pendleton case."

I left Donnie's office and went back and called Reggie Scott.

"Reggie, let me fill you in on what I've done so far on the Rains case."

I told him about the trip to Myrtle Beach with Jean and my conversation with Blaine. I asked him to help me draft a petition asking the court to take the estate out of Henrietta's hands.

"Under normal circumstances, I would say we have enough to take it away from her and put it in the hands of the public administrator. But in this case, it wouldn't help us a bit if the estate were put in the hands of the public administrator. Now, Michael, this is one to ponder: consider the statement I just made and guess why the public administrator won't help us in this case."

"Don't talk in riddles, Reggie. Go ahead and tell me what the problem is with the public administrator."

"Charles Powers has already checked us on this one. I spoke to him at the courthouse this morning, and he told me he had retained Jeffrey Beamon, the public administrator, as co-council to represent Henrietta. Another thought, too: Charles Powers drafted that will for Big Head and is a probable witness to prove the validity of the will. What I'm saying it is a conflict of interest for him to represent Henrietta, but no Forsyth County Judge has the guts to remove him."

"Damn, Reggie, Powers don't miss a trick. He's a step ahead of us before we even begin considering taking the step."

"Michael, let me give it some thought because we do need to do something. Otherwise, we can guarantee all of the money will be gone, and it might be gone already. You know, of course, the way Henrietta had that life insurance policy drawn, it didn't pass through Big Head's estate and she was free to dispose of that immediately when she had it in hand."

"Reggie, I'll call you in a day or two. We can have a meeting and talk."

Frustrated, depressed, I can't describe the way I felt. Blocked at every move. I left my office early and started walking back toward my car. The Sage was standing in his doorway, so I thought no better way to pass some time then a conversation with him.

"Simon, it looks like that forecast you made in that copy-editor case was right-on. I just came from City Hall, and it looks like to me they're gonna grab up the first brother off the street and send him to the gas chamber for killin' that girl, guilty or not. It's also put the Rains case on the back burner to the extent I'm afraid it makes a cover-up even easier. On another subject, Rick Stanton told me about Chandler Tobacco Company owning *The Evening Post* and how they had done things that led to the riot of '47. Do you know anything about that?"

"Oh, sure, they hired an FBI agent for the sole purpose of destroying the commi union. When I was a boy, my dad owned a paper stand across from factory 41. I used to see those men come out of there in the summertime so soaking wet in sweat that they looked like they'd passed through a shower on the way out. I would also see the mill-hands coming out of the cotton mill the same way. The difference between the two groups was the lint-heads out of the textile mill would be covered with white cotton lint, and the tobacco workers would be totally brown, head-to-foot covered with tobacco dust. If people ever needed a union, it was those folks. My dad knew Joel Silver, the Jew who was trying to organize the tobacco workers. Joel would sometimes attend temple with us and would sometimes come for dinner at our home. I was a child at the time but have vivid memories of Joel talking about the harassment tactics the police, even Hoover's FBI was using to break the union. But in spite of everything they did, until Alton Handley began slandering the union organizers in *The Evening Post*, the union was making progress with black and white workers."

"What were some of the tactics they used, Simon?"

"Well, for instance, Joel would get a permit to picket in front of Chandler Tobacco, but all it would take would be a call from Charley Chandler and six squad cars would show up to arrest five union organizers, permit or no permit. Joel would appear before a justice of the peace, the same justice of the peace who had issued the arrest warrant, and, of course, the justice of the peace would find that Joel and the others were guilty of trespassing in front of the Chandler plant. And although Joel might be found innocent two weeks later on appeal, he would have spent a night in jail and been tied up away from organizing for two weeks or more. But, like I say, in spite of this, or maybe even because of it since a lot of people admired the sacrifices the union organizers were willing to make, the union was making progress until Chandler hired Alton Handley and Alton painted the union as a bunch of commies under the control of Moscow

Chapter 20

Tired, frustrated, not really knowing where to go or where to turn, I drove on home and got there just in time to catch the beginning of the local news. The local TV station was owned by the same family that owned the Winston-Salem newspaper, and you could always count on them to portray the Tobacco Company and the tobacco interest in a positive light and to color any group that might question the tobacco industry and/or its power over Winston-Salem as anti-American, anti-freedom, anti-Southern, and anti-Winston-Salem. Their lead story tonight was the Charlotte Pendelton case, and they had three different stories with three different reporters with film footage discussing different aspects of the case. The autopsy report by the medical examiner in Chapel Hill had come back, and just like Blaine Cromer had said, the Pendelton girl had been raped and stabbed multiple times, with a laceration to the throat being the cause of death.

The next reporter was standing in front of City Hall interviewing the chief of police, who was saying that no stone would be left unturned to find "the sleaze bag" who had committed this "horrible crime."

A third reporter was filmed in the parking lot where Charlotte Pendelton had left her car before beginning her walk to her job as assistant copy-editor. The reporter was interviewing a co-worker of Charlotte Pendelton from the newspaper.

"What do you remember about Charlotte Pendelton?" the reporter asked.

"I remember her smile. She always had a smile on her face. And she was a Christian. I know she's in a better place now, but I hope they catch that animal who did this to her. I believe in the sanctity of human life, but I wouldn't hesitate to pull the switch on that animal, cause people like that don't deserve to live."

"What, if anything, has been the reaction of you and your co-workers of the newspaper to this brutal murder?"

"Well, for one thing, when any of us come to work, a man will meet us in the parking lot and walk us into the paper. When we leave work, a man will walk us from the paper to the parking lot. A woman just can't be too careful these days. All us girls are scared to death and were even before Charlotte Pendelton got raped and murdered, of all this trash hang'n' around here," she said while indicating turning her face in the direction of a black man, apparently a street person shuffling down the sidewalk about a block away.

The camera panned toward the black man, who was dressed in rags, walking down the sidewalk, occasionally stopping to take a sip out of a bottle in a brown paper bag.

My God, I thought. This TV station isn't even pretending to be subtle in working up and taking advantage of a racial situation.

"Clearly, the women who work in downtown Winston-Salem are justified in their fears following the brutal murder of Charlotte Pendelton. Back to you, Matt."

"The newspaper has put up a one-hundred-thousand-dollar reward, and anyone having information about the murder of Charlotte Pendelton is urged to call the Winston-Salem Police Department and/or here at the station, where we're giving top priority to this case. Our prayers go out to the family of Charlotte Pendelton. Now to Diane with the weather."

"Matt, I sure do hope they get that animal. It was a beautiful day today in Winston-Salem. The next few days promise to give us more of the same."

The telephone rang. It was Jean on the phone.

"How was your day?"

"Good news and bad news."

"What's the bad news?"

"The Charlotte Pendelton case is gonna take all of Blaine and Donnie's time. They're not gonna have any time to give us, maybe until that whole case is over."

As usual, Jean was able to turn a sow's ear into a silk purse. "That's great. The people who would keep us from getting anyplace are gonna be spending so much time and energy on that newspaper girl's case that they're not gonna have time to keep us from doin' what we need to do. Whatcha doin' tonight?"

"Jean, I gotta get some sleep and rest. You wore me out this weekend."

"Ha, I wore you out. I don't remember you ever call'n' a stop to anything. But I'll let you go anyway. Lets get together tomorrow and maybe go see the Fly."

"You know where he lives, Jean?"

"Yea, he lives up in Elkin, and his health is really bad, so I figure he'll be home most anytime we wanna go see him."

"Don't we needa call him first?"

"Far as I know, he doesn't have a phone. Lives in a shack up there without running water. Not sure if he's even got electricity."

"Okay Jean, I'd like to do it. Let me give you a call, or it won't be any problem for me to just pick you up sometime, will it?"

"Naw, I'll be here anytime. See you tomorrow."

"Bye."

I was really beginning to like that girl.

Chapter 21

I woke up refreshed. I had really needed the rest that the twelve hours had given me. I first called into my office and told my secretary that I'd be working out of town for the day and to reschedule all of my appointments. There wasn't anything really pressing, but my bread-and-butter cases were suffering from a lack of attention. My mentor, attorney Lester Payne, had once described the practice of law as feast and famine. You're a small businessman whose total income depends upon yourself. You may work for years on the same case and end up settling and receiving absolutely nothing off that case while you're working on it for those years, then you settle the case, earning thousands, or tens of thousands, of dollars in a settlement that you really could have, and should have, made with the defense attorney within days of the time you got the case. During these years that you spent on the case, you danced around with the big law firm that represented the defendant in the personal injury case.

The defense attorney doesn't really represent the doctor whose negligence resulted in the brain-damaged child or the woman whose right breast was removed when it was really the left breast that had the cancer. The defense attorney represents the insurance company. It's not up to the doctor to decide when or whether to pay a claim; it's up to his insurance company. And yet North Carolina law will not even allow the jury to be told whether or not the doctor or the truck driver who injured your client has insurance. This is the case even when the insurance adjuster or the insurance executive is sitting as close to the defense attorney as the doctor or truck driver himself. Thus, if the defense attorney can create enough sympathy for the doctor himself, he can convince the jury to give the injured person far less money than they deserve if the jurors fear that the payment will come out of the pocket of the doctor. After Chandler Tobacco, the doctors have the most powerful lobby in Raleigh of any group. They buy politicians with political contributions and otherwise right and left, and the politicians pass laws that restrict not only the amount of recovery the injured patient can get, but the legal process by which the injured patient seeks his recovery.

When I had applied to law school, I had intended to fight for right justice and the American way and all of that other stuff that I had admired as I watched the Lone Ranger and Superman fight for when I was a child. My first murder case after being sworn in and admitted to the bar had been an eye-opening experience. My client had taught me far more about criminal law than I had learned in law school. He was an indigent, and thus the state paid for his defense. I suppose you could say he was truthful with me, but in a perverted sort of way. He was brilliant, a very young twenty-year-old man who had been raised in Canada. He had already killed a man in Canada, but he had been found not-guilty for that murder. He had learned a lot about how to defend himself from his first trial for murder. The judicial system does not require me to disclose nearly as much about a criminal defendant to the district attorney as the district attorney and police are required to disclose to me.

In my first conversation with the young man, he made his disdain, distaste, dislike, and lack of respect for lawyers clear to me. I didn't like him then and grew to dislike him more and more as my representation of him continued. He considered lawyers to be technicians whom he was free to use and manipulate as he saw fit. To him, lawyers were nothing less than hired guns. One of the first things he said to me was what billionaire H. L. Hunt had once said: "I don't hire a lawyer to tell me what I can't do. I hire a lawyer to tell me how to do what I want to do."

My client went on to say, "You lawyers are just modern day witch doctors. You use magic incantations that ordinary folks are not supposed to know and, by your rules, aren't allowed to use."

"What do you mean?" I asked him.

"I'll give you a few, Michael. Res ipsa loquitor, res jestai, res judicata. By using magic incantations like this, you lawyers have the magic ability to turn a poor man into a rich man, to turn a rich man into a poor man, to turn a free man into a slave of the state, and to turn a slave of the state into a free man, and the ultimate ability that you lawyers have that no doctor in America has: you lawyers have the right and ability to take the life of a perfectly healthy living man."

This client was smart enough to question me about the law without disclosing what had happened in this murder and to tailor the facts to create a self-defense case that eventually got him off. The only other witness to the scene of the crime had been the dead man, and, as we all know, dead men tell no tales. It was in this context that I now contemplated the powerful lawyers and the force they had behind them as I worked to recover their father's estate for Linda and Harry.

By the time I picked Jean up, I was bursting to tell her about this client. On the way up to see the Fly, I told this story to Jean. She listened patiently and courteously, understanding what I was saying as if she herself were a lawyer. She had been in and out of the courts helping friends seeking child support and in a multitude of criminal cases where she had been a witness, in defense of herself, and on behalf of friends for fighting, insurance fraud, and just about everything that I had appeared in court for as a lawyer. She said that she had had many of the same thoughts about the court system that I was expressing to her but had never put them into words the way I was doing.

I couldn't help but wonder with her quick mind and the proper circumstances if she couldn't have been a far better lawyer then I would ever be.

When we reached Elkin, Jean directed me along several turns past the town and out into the country. We ended up on a dead-end road at an old shack on the banks of the Yadkin River. Jean hopped out of the car and yelled, "Yo, Willy," and ran up the rotten steps and onto the porch of the shack. As I followed up the steps, Jean pounded on the door, yelling over and over again, "Yo, Willy, its Jean." After several minutes, a tall, skinny, bent-over man opened the door. He had one of those clear plastic tubes around his neck with two protrusions just under his nose. Attached to the plastic tube was a small cart with a green three-foot bottle of oxygen.

"Damn, girl, it's good to see you."

Jean grabbed him and hugged him.

"Willy, you're getting skinnier all the time."

"I ain't long for this world, Jean," Willy said as he shuffled back to take a seat. Jean grabbed his hand.

"Willy, lets go sit on your porch. It's too purdy to be in here."

"You gonna wear me out, girl," Willy said as he attempted to stand back up with Jean's help

"That's what all the boys say. Ain't that right, Michael?"

"It sure is, Jean. I don't know 'cause I can't speak for all of 'em, but you sure wear me out."

"Aww, shush. Y'all just gonna give me a big head talkin' like that."

"Now that's a double entendre, Jean."

"A what?" Jean said.

"It's a word or phrase that can have two totally different meanings."

"Willy, ain't he smart, use'n those big words? I keep tell'n' Michael, with all them big words he knows, he ought to be a lawyer."

As Willy came through his doorway with Jean's help, Jean said, "Willy, this here's my friend, Michael." And in her way of getting straight to the point, she said, "Willy, my friend, Michael is a lawyer. As a matter of fact, he's representing Big Head's younguns, Linda and Harry."

"Is that a fact?"

"Sure is. I really do think they ought to have sumthin from Big Head's estate," I said.

"I'll agree with that," Willy said, nearing the side porch overlooking the rapids of the Yadkin River.

"This is a beautiful view. How'd you ever find this place, Willy?"

"I grew up here, and my momma and daddy left it to me. I was disabled from the Korean War and ain't never gotten my health back."

"Willy, you got power yet up here?" Jean asked.

"Yea, when I got that fancy machine in the house that makes my oxygen, the government run the power lines down here to run it."

"Willy, I'm gonna formally introduce you to my gentleman friend: here is Michael Spears, esquire. And Michael, my other gentleman friend here is Willy "The Fly" Choate. They call him "The Fly 'cause when he got back from the Korean War, he'd lost so much weight that everybody said he looked like with a little breeze he'd fly away. Willy, what can ya tell us about Big Head get'n killed?"

"Well, the last time anybody saw him alive was when he had supper down at the Elks Lodge over on Old Plank Rd. He called me from there and said he would be over to pick me up in an hour or two, and that was about eight o'clock. I was down at my cousin's house down in Winston-Salem, and I waited for him, but he never came. I just figured he got hooked up with a woman and forgot about me, and I didn't worry none until I hadn't heard from him in over a week. I got my cousin to bring me on back here, and it was about a week after that that I heard they had found Big Head's body behind the Seaview down at Myrtle Beach. What's the strangest to me about it is, and, Jean you know this too, Big Head never drove to Myrtle Beach. I would say for the last ten years he didn't go to Myrtle Beach without me goin' with him."

The Fly leaned back in his chair. Each breath was coming easier now since he had had a while to sit. He sort of leaned his head on his left arm, with his left hand propping up his head as he stared out into the river and at the occasional fish jumping out of the water and then splashing back. Willy seemed lost in his thoughts. It was a sad look on his face as he reminisced about his old friend. He began talking again.

"Jean, you know that Big Head didn't like to drive to Myrtle Beach, and he didn't like to drive while he was down there 'cause he was always drink'n beer and didn't want to hafta worry about be'n' pulled over for drunk driving. We would always drive down together, always park in the same space if there weren't nobody else in it, and always stay in 209 if it was available, and he'd get me a separate room if he had a woman. It didn't matter to me what room I stayed in. But Big Head had a pattern that he sort of lived by. Has anybody told y'all that about a year before his body was found, Henrietta tried to burn him up to kill him for that life-insurance money?"

Jean responded, "Yea, Big Head told me that while I was stay'n' up at One-eyed Jack's."

"How's One-eyed Jack doin'?" Willy asked Jean.

"I don't know, Fly. Things weren't the same between One-eyed Jack and me when Big Head went missing, even before his body was found. I wasn't told to move out, but I just moved out on my own. Joe Wrench told Jack and me that him and Jerry McGee killed Big Head so Henrietta could collect a million dollars in life insurance. Whatda you think, Willy?"

"Henrietta had some kinda power over Big Head. I don't know what it was. I couldn't believe he went back with her after he said she tried to kill him with that fire. He said she cried and told him she loved him, and he said when he accused her of try'n' to kill him for that million dollar life insurance policy, she said money didn't mean nuthin to her and she'd have that policy canceled if he wanted her to and lose all the money that they'd paid on the premiums. But a man woulda had been crazy to believe Henrietta after her attempt to have both Abner Stitt and Big Head killed. But she was able to convince him that she had nuthin to do with no plan to have Abner Stitt killed for insurance money and that she had wanted to cancel the policy on Abner Stitt before the insurance company had canceled it. Did y'all know that her lawyer, Charles Powers, sued the insurance company for the premiums that had been paid after the Abner Stitt policy was canceled?"

"No, I didn't know that, Fly. I'll check down at the courthouse to see what happened to that case."

"I reckon you knew that each one had a million-dollar policy on the other. I reckon the two of 'em lived such wild and dangerous lives, neither one of them figured they was gonna live long anyway, so the one that was left after the other died could get rich off the first one dyin'. Right after the fire, he was scared to death of her, and the way he first told me about that Abner Stitt mess was Henrietta tried to get Pricey Meyers to kill Abner Stitt for a life-insurance policy. The woman would do anything for money. From the time Big Head met Henrietta 'til he died, he was a different man. He used to be a good daddy to them two younguns, and I believe if he coulda quit drink'n', him and Doris coulda stayed together. After he met Henrietta, he quit visit'n them younguns all together. In the wintertime, he'd always be takin Linda, and sometimes Harry, to Wake Forest basketball. In the summertime, the three of them never missed a stock-car race on Saturday night at Chandler Raceway Stadium, unless there was a Winston Cup race at Charlotte, North Wilkesboro, Martinsville, or Rockingham, and they always talked about drivin to Daytona, but I woulda dun the driving to go that far, and I just never was up to it. Lots of times I would go to them basketball games and races with Big Head and his younguns, and, believe it or not, he wouldn't do no drink'n, or at least he'd cut back. He was a different feller when he was with them younguns. But as soon as Henrietta got her claws in him, he up and quit them younguns altogether. By that time, they was teenagers and they mighta started lead'n their own lives anyway, but things changed when he met Henrietta."

"Fly, did you say Henrietta offered to cancel the policy on Big Head after the Abner Stitt episode and after the fire that nearly killed him?"

"Yea, that's what he told me. Now, wait a minute. Seems like he told me she told him she did cancel that policy. Otherwise, he wouldn't gone back with her. My mind jus don't work like it used to. I reckon I just don't get enough oxygen to my brain no more. And I am get'n older. Let me just sit here a minute and think."

"Fly, I've always loved comin' up here lookin down at the river. It sure is one pretty place," Jean said as we all three gazed down at the river and listened to the slight roar of the minor falls below us. This was the kind of place where a man could be at peace and spend the rest of his life just sittin' on this porch, rarely ever having contact with other people.

"Jean, I just, I'm thinkin' here." Willy started to stand up, and Jean came over and pulled him by both hands to his feet. "Let me go in here a minute, Jean." Jean and the Fly walked back into the house. It gave me great pain to watch Willy's difficult steps. My own father was on oxygen, and that could have been him passing in front of me. I stayed seated on the porch at peace with my thoughts and enjoying the company of my two new friends, Jean and Willy "The Fly" Choate. After several minutes, Willy came shuffling back out with Jean's help. He was pulling the little cart with his oxygen bottle. Jean held his left arm with her right hand to help him walk. Clutched in her left arm was a small cedar chest, the kind mountain people keep their important papers in, such as deeds, love letters, and letters from the boys who were away at war to their mommas. Jean helped Willy sit back down between the two of us and then picked up the cedar chest that she had put in her seat so she could help Willy take his. Willy took his time getting settled back into his seat and catching his breath.

"Jean, open that cedar chest there. Look through them papers." Jean opened the top of the little cedar chest. The chest was just big enough to hold letters and papers. The first thing on top of the stack was a picture of a mountain man and woman standing in front of this very house.

"That's my momma and daddy," Willy said.

"Your momma sure was a pretty woman, and your daddy a handsome man. You take after him, Fly," Jean said.

"Yea, I miss 'em. Keep on goin' down in that chest. I'm thinkin I might have a letter Big Head give me." Jean continued, carefully lifting the papers one by one, even finding a birth certificate for Willy. Then, she came to what appeared to be an 8-½x11 letter, twice folded. Jean unfolded the letter and began reading it.

"Dear Mrs. Handy. As per your request, we are this day notifying you that the life-insurance policy in the amount of one million dollars owned by you and made payable to you on the life of Harold Stennis Rains was terminated and its cancellation made final effective November 22, 1974. Signed Armand Chandler, Chief Executive Officer Chandler Life and Indemnity Corporation."

"Whoa, Fly. That letter says that policy on Big Head's life was canceled more than eight months before he died. The policy was canceled, according to that letter, more than eight months before he died and yet Henrietta's still been paid the million dollars in insurance money. And who does it say signed that letter, Jean?"

"Armand Chandler, Chief Executive Officer Chandler Life and Indemnity."

"Can I see that?" I asked.

Jean handed me the letter for me to look at it. It was on Chandler letterhead paper addressed to Henrietta Groom Handy at her address in Lewisville and the reference showed: "Re: Cancellation life policy WS123G8000006 Harold Stennis Rains $1,000,000," signed by the same Armand Chandler who had canceled the policy on the life of Abner Stitt under pressure from the United Sates Magistrate. This was a bombshell.

"Fly, how'd you say you got this?"

"Big Head brought it to me, handed it to me with a big grin on his face, said there weren't any reason he couldn't trust Henrietta and him and her was getting' back together."

90

"Fly, Chandler has already paid Henrietta a million dollars on the life of Big Head."

"Seems like I'd heard somebody say that, Michael."

"Jean, you and me need to run and make a copy of this if it's all right with Fly. Fly, ride with us to someplace where we can make a copy of this thing."

"I just don't feel like ridin' no place, Michael. You and Jean take that thing and keep it. It ain't gonna do me no good, anyhow. I'd like to ride in Big Head's car one more time, but I just don't feel up to it."

Jean and I both laughed. "That ain't Big Head's car, Fly. Look at it. That one's a year older model. It does fool everybody, though. It even fooled me. Fly, me 'n Michael could take that thing and make a copy and bring that one back to you."

"Y'all don't hafta go through that trouble."

"Fly, I ain't no lawyer, but I know this thing is big, and we sure do appreciate you diggin' it out."

"If it can help them younguns, y'all do whatever you want to with it. I'll just wait here and sit on my porch 'til y'all come back."

"Can we get'cha anything, Fly?" Jean asked.

"Ahh, I reckon I got everything I need right here, but I 'preciate the offer."

Jean and I drove several miles into Elkin, stopped by a 7/11 that said "copy's 10 cent apiece." We made about ten copies of the letter. I figured we couldn't have too many copies. I had so many things on my mind, I wasn't watching where I was going and nearly backed into a fellow who was sitting next to the road. If Jean hadn't yelled for me to stop, I would've hit the man's car. I finally got my composure back, and we headed back toward the Fly's.

"I ain't no lawyer, but I know this thing's important, Michael. Big Head would still be alive like Abner Stitt if that life insurance policy had been canceled like that letter says."

"Jean, I've got so many questions to ask that only Armand Chandler can answer. I need to get in touch with Reggie Scott and the two of us figure out where we go from here."

"Don't you owe me a hamburger and a little bit of your time first, Michael?"

"I'm sorry, Jean. I'm just so exited about this letter, I wasn't thinking about anything else. I think I owe you a steak dinner."

"I'll take you up on that steak if we can get a twelve pack of Bud and cook it back at your place."

We took the letter the Fly had given to us back to him and spent another hour or so sitting on his back porch. Jean and the Fly talked about old times, mainly about the gambling houses and the characters the two of them had known and funny incidents that had occurred over the ten or so years the two of them had known each other. There were times the Fly showed emotion in talking about his old friend, Big Head, and the times the Fly and Big Head had spent with Big Head's children. The Fly had served primarily as Big Head's chauffeur, driving Big Head here and there while Big Head sucked down Budweisers. But, clearly, the adventures that the Fly and Big Head had had together had filled a void in the Fly's life. I don't recall the Fly recounting any negative experiences that would have reflected badly upon Big Head, other than the risks Big Head would take with some of the dangerous company he liked to keep around the gambling houses. Maybe it had been a fascination with the strong independent ways of Henrietta, although she was clearly totally self indulgent, that made her attractive to him and kept them together. I couldn't help but reflect that I found something of this kind of attractiveness in Jean, although it was absolutely clear to me that Jean had no interest whatsoever in the material world and being rich or owning property. She took each day one day at a time, enjoying the moment and not thinking about the next day. As we started to get in the car to leave, I caught a glimpse of a car turning around at the last curve just before the Fly's house.

"Jean, that sort of looks like that car I nearly hit at the 7/11."

Jean turned to look in the direction of the car, but all we could see was dust as the car sped away.

When we started our drive back to Winston-Salem, Jean told me that she didn't know I could be so quiet. I told her I had been enjoying the moment sitting there on the Fly's porch. Jean said that she needed to stop by her mom and dad's to get a few things and to tell them where she would be. I had the feeling there was gonna be a sleep over at my house.

We stopped by Krogers for some T-bone steaks, baking potatoes, and a couple bottles of White Zinfandel. When we got to my house, I put the White Zinfandel on ice and walked out to start my grill.

"Jean, I use charcoal, so it will take me a while to get the grill started. You make yourself comfortable."

I started the grill blazing with starter fluid and stepped back into the house. Jean had made herself comfortable, all right.

"My name is Jean. I'll be your waitress tonight. If you'll take a seat, sir, I'll pour you a glass of this fine wine."

Jean was dressed in a white maid's outfit with a little white tiara on her head, a white lace French bra with her breasts hanging over it and her nipples fully exposed, a white lace garter belt, semi-transparent white hose, a pair of white high-heeled shoes, and nothing else.

"I ain't never had service like this before," I said as Jean stood not three feet from me, facing me, and, yea, I forgot to tell ya, white laced gloves, that kind without the fingers being covered.

"Where is your china, sir, so that I may set the table?"

"The china cabinet in the next room," I said as I started to get up.

"Oh no, sir, keep your seat," Jean said as she turned to go through the French doors to the china cabinet.

"I was just gonna get some candles and placemats," I said as I followed her cute little naked butt as she passed through the French doors.

"I'll get them, sir," Jean said, twisting her body with her head turned toward me but her butt still facing me. She had already learned that's my favorite part of a woman's body.

I gotta be the luckiest man in the world, I thought as I watched Jean bend over to pull the drawer open. She pulled out the placemats, two candles, and two silver candle-stands. What the hell, I thought. Here I am, thinking I'm the luckiest man in the world.

"Jean, I'm the luckiest man in the world," I said.

"I know that, sir. But it's awfully nice of you to say it." She put the placemats down, one in front of me and the other where she'd be sitting. She put the two candleholders on the table and put the candles in them. She walked over to her purse, got a cigarette lighter, and lit the two candles, all the while moving and performing so exquisitely for me and at the same time clearly enjoying every moment of the appreciation she knew I had for her and her beautiful body. I watched her as she went back to the china cabinet and brought two plates to the table and then went back to get the silver place settings for us. As she finished placing the silver before me, I said I had to get up to put the meat on the grill.

"I'll let you do that, sir. I know the gentleman prides himself on his grilled steaks."

After seasoning the steaks with my secret seasoning, I took them out and placed them on the grill. As I turned to go back into the house, there stood Jean right there in my backyard under the evening stars with a glass of wine in each hand.

"What if the neighbors see you, Jean?"

"Well, I just reckon that would make us the talk of the neighborhood, wouldn't it?" Jean said, cocking her head to the side, batting her eyelashes, and smiling.

Oh, what the hell, I thought. With the hedges surrounding my backyard anyone would have to be going out of his way to really see and know what was going on over here, so why not enjoy the moment? I pulled up two patio chairs and took my glass of wine from Jean. We both sat out there, not really saying anything significant, just sipping our wine for the ten minutes or so the steaks cooked to rare. When the steaks were done, Jean insisted upon getting the plate to put them on. I deferred.

We enjoyed our meal by candlelight, and when we were finished, Jean walked around the table to me.

"Follow me, sir, and I will give you that dessert you enjoy so much."

I won't go into detail describing my dessert, but I enjoyed it way into the early morning hours.

Chapter 22

"Jean, it's 9 a.m. I gotta get up. I wanna see Reggie Scott. You're welcome to stay here all day if you'd like, or I can take you back to your mom and dad's, whichever you want."

"I'd better go back to mom and dad's and spend some time with them. When can you and I see each other again?"

"I'll call you this afternoon, and we can decide then."

"You had a shower yet?"

"No, ma'am, but we sure could save alotta water if we took one together. You know I sure believe in saving our resources. Get your lazy ass outta that bed." Jean jumped up and beat me to the shower.

"I really enjoyed last night, Jean, and I thank you for your help," I said as I kissed her at her parents' doorway.

"Oh, I'm gonna send you a bill," Jean said.

I hurried to my office, briefly stopping in to say hello to the Sage before I got there. I called Reggie Scott, and we made plans to meet for lunch. As soon as we had ordered and the waitress had left the table, I handed Reggie a copy of the letter the Fly had given me.

"Do you realize what we have here?" Reggie said with excitement I had never seen in him.

"For one thing, Reggie, I believe it to be the closest thing to a goldmine that I've ever seen or will see in my lifetime."

"Tell me how you got this."

"Jean led me up to Elkin and then down a dirt road to a shack on the banks of the Yadkin river where she introduced me to Willy 'the Fly' Choate. The Fly said that Big Head had given him that letter to prove that Henrietta loved him and there wasn't any need to be afraid of her."

"But the policy wasn't really canceled. As a matter of fact, I don't know if I've told you this or not, but the policy was shown to some of the hoodlums who Henrietta wanted to kill Big Head so they would accept the job."

"I had already heard that, Reggie. I think Blaine and Bobby may have told it to me. Reggie, this letter was written around the same time that same man Armand Chandler canceled the policy on Abner Stitt's life."

"Do you have any plans for tonight?"

"I was sort of hoping to spend the evening and night with Jean."

"Bring her on over to my house tonight, if she wants to come, and we'll draft a complaint."

When I got back to my office, I called Jean and told her Reggie and I were going to work together on the Rains case and if she wouldn't be bored, I'd like her to join us.

"I don't really have a life anymore outside you and the Rains case, so why not."

"I'll pick you up at six. We'll get some burgers and be at Scott's by 7:30."

Scott had converted an old stone gristmill into the most unique house in Forsyth County. The original two-hundred-year-old water wheel that had been brought over from England still worked. The house sat on a thirty-acre millpond. From the kitchen area where Scott and I always worked, you could hear the steady sound of the water cascading over the spillway of the millpond dam. Scott had a gismo beside his kitchen window that could divert the falling water over the waterwheel so you could see it spin. Scott lived in the house alone like me, having been divorced for about three years. He would often pull out a picture of two new Mercedes sitting in his driveway and point to the Toyota Corolla that he now drove to show what his divorce had done to his life. But he still had that house.

"How on Earth did Michael ever find anybody as pretty as you?" Scott said as he met us in his driveway, and he opened the door for Jean. "Now, you know that an older, more experienced gentleman can show you a whole lot better time than a boy like Michael."

"Michael's the best I've ever found," Jean responded with mental jousting. "Not only does he go good, but he goes long."

"Well, if you ever see he ain't got all you need, you just come on and spend some time with this old miller and his old gristmill. Come on in and I'll show you my house, and we'll get down to work." Scott gave Jean a quick tour of the house, pointing out as old as the house was, it was still in excellent condition since the only wood used in the house had been oak and walnut.

"We've had some pretty places to work the past few days, Reggie. We spent yesterday on a porch overlook'n' a fall line of the Yadkin River. We spent the day with Jean's friend, now my friend, Willy 'the Fly' Choate. That's where I got this letter I gave you at lunch."

"Michael, I've done some serious thinking about how we ought to use this letter. At this point, we don't know whether the insurance company knows we have it or not. So my thought is we file a suit just against Henrietta. But the first deposition we take should be the deposition of Armand Chandler, the chief executive officer of the insurance company. If we can take him by surprise and first let him know we have this letter, we're more likely to get the truth out of him. It looks like this letter shows the cancellation of the million-dollar policy on Big Head's life about the same time the million-dollar policy on the life of Abner Stitt was canceled. If we can show a pattern that the life insurance company knew or should have known that Henrietta had a propensity to take out life-insurance policies on business partners and then kill the insured, we should be able to recover at least the money Henrietta's been paid for Linda and Harry."

We got down to business, and within a couple of hours, we had a wrongful death complaint drafted against Henrietta. We filed it the next morning, and Henrietta was served with a copy that same day. As soon as the return of service was back in the court file, we drafted a notice for deposition for Armand

Chandler, chief executive officer of the insurance company. We noticed Chandler to appear at my office. However, within an hour of the time Chandler was served with the subpoena to appear for the deposition, I received a call from Malcolm Saits with the Forbes-Grundy law firm. I had known Malcolm Saits for all three years I had practiced law. He had a reputation for being the most skillful and connected lawyer in Winston-Salem, if not the state. His law firm was the biggest and most respected in the state. They had offices in Charlotte, Greensboro, Winston-Salem, and Wilmington, North Carolina. They had hundreds of lawyers on their staff, some of whom were former judges. I knew that just this year they had hired away the chief district court judge from Greensboro who had practically written the new North Carolina divorce laws on the distribution of property so that they could assign him to represent one of the grandsons of the founder of the Chandler Tobacco Company. Everybody knew the tobacco heir to have an uncontrolled drinking problem and to be at risk to loose his share of the tobacco fortune to his Hollywood starlet wife, whom he had beaten so severely that her career in the movies had collapsed. She had been a trophy wife, but it appeared when she first filed suit for divorce that the tobacco fortune was going to end up being her trophy. The word was out among the lawyers in town that since her husband had hired the former judge at Forbes-Grundy that she had lost every motion her lawyer had offered in court. This was ironic in that her lawyer was himself a former judge specializing in divorce property law who had been hired by the second-largest firm in Winston-Salem. The firm hired him when she first left her husband, but the reason for the turnaround was clear. Her lawyer was a Republican, whereas her tobacco heir's husband's lawyer was a Democrat.

I immediately ran down to Scott's office on the second floor to ask for his advice. I caught him as he was leaving to go to court.

"I'm in a hurry now, Michael. Walk with me. We can talk as we walk."

"Reggie, I got a call from Malcolm Saits with Forbes-Grundy."

"Uh Huh, talk about hired guns. He's Paladin. My guess is Chandler Life and Indemnity Company has hired, or, let me rephrase that, they are the lawyers for Chandler, Chandler Tobacco Company, Chandler Life and Indemnity Company, and anybody who is anybody in Winston-Salem. I haven't looked at the file yet, but I would say Mr. Armand Chandler has been served with our subpoena and he has called on Malcolm Saits' direct line and asked Malcolm Saits to prevent him from being deposed. Call Saits back, and if all he wants is a change in schedule or location, agree to it and you and I can rearrange our schedules to meet Malcolm's. If he wants to cancel altogether, refuse to cooperate and tell him we'll see him in court. Come on to the courthouse with me and you can see if Mr. Armand Chandler has been served with our subpoena."

I checked the file. Chandler had been served with our subpoena. I returned Saits's phone call. He talked as nice as anyone could possibly have talked. He told me he looked forward to working with me and helping me with my case anyway he could.

"What could you possibly want Armand Chandler for, Michael?" Clearly he was probing, and I knew it.

"Malcolm, I don't know if you know enough about the case to know that Chandler paid a million dollars to Henrietta Handy on the life of my client's father."

"Well, yes, but I don't see how that could possibly justify you takin' up your time and pay'n' for the cost of a deposition. And Mr. Chandler is a very busy man. His company pays out hundreds, if not thousands of claims every day. I wanna help you out, but that's just not enough for Mr. Chandler to spend his time over."

"Well, Malcolm, I don't know. There is another matter. A year before the death of Harold Stennis Rains, Mrs. Handy had allegedly attempted to have another man murdered and Mr. Chandler had been made personally aware of that."

"You say he was made aware of that? I'll get him to give you a written statement of that if it's true."

"Well, Malcolm, it's more than that. You know U.S. Magistrate Tarleton Blevins out of Greensboro?"

"Yea, I know Tarleton. We're good friends. What about him?"

"He made contact with Mr. Chandler requesting that Mr. Chandler cancel the policy in the attempt to have the man murdered a year before Rains."

"Well, Michael, I guess we could make some compromises here. I would ask that the court seal the deposition if you take one, unless you would agree to that beforehand."

"What else do you want, Malcolm?"

"I want the deposition to be taken in the conference room here at Forbes-Grundy, and neither Mr. Chandler nor I can make it on the date you've requested."

"What date do you suggest?"

"Both Armand Chandler and I can make it exactly ten days later."

"Malcolm, I'll agree to your time and location, but I just can't agree to the sealing of the deposition at this point. If we see something come up during the deposition itself that might prejudice your client or his company, I'll reconsider. But for now all I can do is agree to the change of time and location. If that's agreeable with you, send me a letter by tomorrow, five o'clock at the latest, confirming time and location and I'll re-notice Charles Powers to the time and location you and I have agreed upon."

"I appreciate you returning my call. I'll let you know by tomorrow afternoon. I've already talked to Powers, and I believe everything would be okay with him."

"Good talking to you, Malcolm. Goodbye."

I was proud of myself. I felt I had held my own with the most powerful lawyer in the state. I thought to myself, the most powerful lawyer in the state, was it Malcolm Saits, or was it Charles Powers? Saits was clearly sending me a message by telling me he had already cleared everything with Powers.

The next day, I received the letter from Saits agreeing to my offer of no more than a change in time and location.

The secretary showed us into the conference room ten days later. There was a massive table we all could sit around. It made me think of something you would have seen diplomats at a UN meeting sitting on. Scott and I were the first to arrive. Later, Dustin, the court reporter, came in and began to set up. I had asked Dustin, who had sold me the brown-on-brown Coupe de Ville, to take the deposition. Malcolm Saits came in with an associate of his. He introduced his associate to Scott and me. The fellow was three years out of Duke law and had been first in his class. Forbes-Grundy hired nothing but the best, either the best ability or the best connections or the best connections and ability, which was rare though possible. Malcolm's associate was clearly a hired gun in training. Less than five minutes before the scheduled starting time, Malcolm went out of the room, and a minute or so later, he walked back in with Armand Chandler. Everyone in the room recognized Mr. Chandler. Not only was he the CEO and principle owner of a major insurance company, but he also owned controlling stock in the regional airline serving our area. I couldn't help but recall that as a second grader at Old Town Elementary school, my class had made a field trip to the local airport, which had been named after one of the tobacco company heirs. Our second-grade class was allowed to tour one of Mr. Chandler's airplanes, a DC 3 that was in use as a passenger aircraft up until about 1960, and either that one or one identical to it was still stationed at the airport and kept flying as a museum in the air.

"Michael, Reggie, this is Armand Chandler, who will be testifying today."

Armand Chandler was the younger brother of Charles C. Chandler. Everyone considered him to be meaner and more ruthless than Charles C., always trying to outdo his older brother and leave a greater legacy for himself in Winston-Salem. He was now almost ninety years old and still worked everyday. It was said that he was always the first to arrive at Chandler Insurance in the mornings and the last to leave. He watched his employees like a hawk. It was said he counted every paper clip and pencil to see that no one left Chandler Insurance with any of his property. He was skinny as a rail but stood six foot two. He had a full head of long gray hair that appeared to have never been combed. He had long fingernails, so long that they began to double under at the ends. He had black piercing eyes that caused you to have difficulty concentrating on your thoughts without yourself looking away. "It's an honor to meet you, Mr. Chandler." We shook hands. This day, however, he appeared to be scared, not the powerful presence I had expected. We sat back down and made small talk. Time came and passed for the deposition to begin. Charles Powers had not yet appeared.

"I talked to Powers just yesterday afternoon. Don't know what would be keeping him. I'll go call and see if I can get him on the phone," Malcolm said and then stepped out the door. He couldn't have taken more than two steps until I heard boom out,

"Malcolm Saits, you old dog. Is your golf game getting as good as mine now?"

I recognized that voice. I had heard it many times in court. Charles and Malcolm came back into the room. Everyone in the room knew Charles and said hello and shook his hand.

"Armand, I've seen you play golf before out at the country club. And if you and Malcolm don't get any better, I think they ought to ban both of ya from the course. After you fellows play through, there are so many divots, the greens look like my yard did the last time they dug up my septic tank to pump it out." We all laughed. It appeared Scott and me were the only two men in the room who didn't play golf.

"Charles, you caused us all to be twenty minutes late getting this thing started," said Reggie.

"Send me a bill, send me a bill. All of ya know where to find me."

Powers clearly was the center of attention. He didn't try to be; he just was. Dustin was anxious to get started, and he shoved a Bible over in front of Mr. Chandler.

"First, gentlemen, I need to know what stipulations you fellows are gonna make," said Dustin. "All objections are reserved except as to form, I assume?" We all agreed. "Mr. Chandler, place your left hand on the Bible, raise your right hand please, sir. No sir...I said your left hand on the Bible, and raise your right hand, Mr. Chandler."

"As many times as I've testified, I've never made that mistake before," Chandler said as he placed his left hand on the Bible and raised his right hand.

Dustin rapidly repeated, "Do you swear to tell the truth, the whole truth, and nothing but the truth, so help you God?"

"I do," Chandler said.

"Your witness, Reggie," Malcolm said.

"No, Michael is lead council. He's much more prepared for this deposition than I am."

"Mr. Chandler, state your name for the record, sir."

"Armand Charles Chandler, Sr."

"How old are you, Mr. Chandler?"

"Objection," Saits shouted out.

"What basis, Malcolm?" Reggie asked.

"Mr. Chandler's age cannot possibly be relevant to this matter, Mr. Scott."

Scott and I conferred whispering to each other. "Let it go, Michael," Reggie whispered.

"Would you give your address, Mr. Chandler?"

"Again, Malcolm raised a mundane objection.

"Where do you work, Mr. Chandler?"

"Objection," Malcolm boomed out again. "You know where he works. You served him there."

"Malcolm, we need to get these things on the record under oath, whether I know them or not. They can't be used as evidence."

"Evidence? What are you talking about evidence? Mr. Chandler is not a party to any suit."

Reggie whispered in my ear, "He's just trying to rattle you. There's no time limit on this deposition. We'll build a record of his abuse, and if we have to, we'll take it before a judge to make him answer."

This was a deposition. There was no judge present, and there rarely is a judge present for a deposition. Attorneys and parties and witnesses and the court reporter are usually the only people present at depositions. Depositions are, in lawyer talk, known as discovery tools and used to discover what evidence there may or may not be before a trial. I continued on with the deposition, hardly getting a thing out of the witness because of Malcolm's objections. Finally, I reached the Abner Stitt situation with my questioning.

"Mr. Chandler, do you know who Abner Stitt is?"

"Objection," once more Malcolm said.

"Now, Malcolm, you and I talked about this issue when we rescheduled this deposition and you know the Abner Stitt matter is one of the most important parts of this deposition."

"I will let Mr. Chandler answer that question, though I doubt he knows this Mr. Stitt. And if he does not know this Mr. Stitt, that will be his answer."

"I don't know a Abner Stitt," Chandler now answered after clearly being told through his lawyer's objection what to say.

"Don't you remember talking to Tarleton Blevins about Abner Stitt a little over a year ago?"

"Objection." Again, Malcolm was trying to interrupt my deposition.

"What basis for your objection, Mr. Saits?"

"I'm objecting to the form of the question, Mr. Spears. It's clearly a leading question. Mr. Chandler probably doesn't remember that conversation you are asking him about, and if he doesn't, he may say so."

"No, I don't recall that."

"Do you know who Tarleton Blevins is, Mr. Chandler?"

"I talk to a lot of people named Blevins every day, and I wouldn't want to say I know a Tarleton Blevins. I just don't recall," Chandler said, beating Malcolm's objection. Malcolm just smiled.

"Didn't you cancel a life insurance policy on the life of Abner Stitt a little over a year ago?"

Simultaneously, Malcolm said "Objection" and Chandler said "I don't." Malcolm grinned and said, "Go ahead, Mr. Chandler. You go ahead and answer."

"I don't have the authority to cancel any insurance policies myself."

"I'll re-phrase the question. Did you order someone else to cancel the life insurance policy of Abner Stitt a little over a year ago?"

Again, before Malcolm could object, Chandler said, "I don't recall that."

I whispered to Reggie, "I don't see any use in us continuing this deposition. Malcolm's not gonna let him tell the truth about anything."

"You're building a record, Michael," Reggie answered back.

"Mr. Chandler, I am going to show you a document I have here."

I started to hand Chandler a copy of the letter I had gotten from the Fly. Malcolm quickly grabbed the letter out of my hand.

"Objection," he said. "We're going to follow the basic rules of court. Before you show my client any document, you have to first show it to me. Now, I'll take a look at this and determine whether I'll let my client see it or not." He held the letter up in front of his face and Chandler leaned over and looked at it over Malcolm's shoulder with Malcolm knowing fully that Chandler was reading. Neither man was at all surprised at the letter or it's contents, nor did they appear to be surprised that I had it.

"Mr. Spears, this is the very reason I considered getting the protective order to prevent my client from being humiliated and embarrassed in a deposition like this. I'm going to move for a protective order that this deposition not be held and that the court seal this session at this point. You are trying to bring a copy of something of a letter in here that you clearly don't know whether it is authentic and take my client by surprise. I assume you don't have the original of this, otherwise I assume you wouldn't be passing a copy to my client. As you know, or should know, the best evidence rule requires you to bring in the original of any document you might present to the court. I'm adjourning this deposition this minute and will seek a protective order to protect my client from further harassment and embarrassment."

I felt like a ton of bricks had been dropped on me. I guess I had always played softball and was now learning what hardball was really like. Reggie and I left the room and headed back to his office. We didn't speak to each other until we got into his office.

"Michael, you now know what hardball really is, don't you?"

"I guess. I don't know what really happened."

"It should be obvious to you that they knew that letter was comin' and that the Abner Stitt matter, though it may be important, is a firecracker compared to the bomb that that letter is. I had thought that there was a possibility that Henrietta had somehow forged the letter. It's clear to me now that that letter is authentic and that the signature is the signature of Armand Chandler. We are going to have to prepare an order for sanctions under the rules of discovery. We are going to have to ask a judge to order sanctions against the most powerful law firm in North Carolina and his client, one of the most powerful men in North Carolina. Under normal circumstances and dealing with normal people, we would get it for the asking. But the reality is, any judge we ask in North Carolina owes his position to that law firm and that man. And what's worse, if it could get worse, is that it's in Winston-Salem. You see, we're finding every time we draw an ace of spades, they trump us with two aces of spades out of their sleeve."

We began preparing the motion.

Chapter 23

On the morning of the hearing on the deposition, I called Rick Stanton. I didn't know whether it was really appropriate or not, but I figured it couldn't hurt anything.

"Rick, we've got a hearing this morning before Judge Case. Let me fill you in quickly and briefly about what's happening on the Rains case."

"I don't have much time. Please be quick. They've arrested a suspect in the Charlotte Pendelton murder case. He's a black man and a street person. It's all I have right now, but go ahead, Michael."

"Rick, I've become myopic and haven't paid attention to anything but the Rains case for a good while now, but I'll be quick. I've got a letter canceling the million-dollar life policy on Rains nearly a year before he was killed."

Rick interrupted me. "That's incredible. How the hell did you ever get anything like that?"

"It's a long story. Jean Duncan helped me get it. If you have time, I'll go into the details."

"My God, let me see what I can do."

"Rick, the letter is signed by Armand Chandler."

"The same Armand Chandler who canceled the Abner Stitt policy and saved Stitt's life?"

"That's right."

"Look, Michael, they've got me on the Pendleton case with everybody else in the building. But this is important enough. I'll see if my editor won't let me cover your hearing this morning. I'm gonna put you on hold."

Rick was gone for a good ten minutes. Normally, I would have hung up, assuming that our connection had been broken. But this time I figured this was too important, and I waited. Rick came back to the phone.

"That son of a bitch. My editor says I've been assigned to the Pendleton case and I'm going to work the Pendleton case. And, listen to this, he says people have been calling who pay for our advertising complaining that I haven't been fair and for some reason I'm too close to you. He says I've got to do some writing that's critical of you. You and Scott are activists first and foremost, who just happen to be lawyers. I'm a reporter, not an activist, and I've got to do what my editor tells me. I can't make the hearing today, but I will wish you good luck. Let me know what happens."

"Rick, I understand, but I do want to say it was you reporters, not us lawyers, who got Richard Nixon a year ago. My profession as an attorney is thoroughly controlled by the people with the gold."

Rick interrupted again. "And that's right. The people with the gold control and us reporters don't get nearly as much of the gold as you lawyers. I've got to go."

"I'll keep you posted, Rick."

Damn, I thought. It was like Scott said: every time we trumped their hand with an ace of spades, they pulled two out of their sleeves and we were trumped. Their pressure had gotten to the press. I knew that Judge Case, being a political animal, would have considered his ruling more carefully under the scrutiny of the Fourth Estate. I wasn't wanting Rick to say or do anything unethical, but I knew for a certainty that his very presence in the courtroom would bring a decision that would have been closer to justice than we could possibly get without him.

I still had some time before I needed to be in court, so I decided to run a copy of the Chandler letter and leave it on Rick's desk if he wasn't there. His office was only two blocks away, so I hurried up the street, said hello to the lady at the front desk, and walked on back to the news room. Rick was still at his desk feverishly typing. He glanced up and saw me coming towards him with the letter in hand. I handed it to him. He rapidly read it.

"This is incredible, Michael," he said. "Good luck in court."

The clerk of court had assigned our motion and Saits's motion to Judge Anthony Case, a Democratic hack. As a lawyer, the man had lived off state contracts, condemnation proceedings, and other business funneled to him by the Democratic Party. He had been loyal to the party essentially all of his life, being a member of the young Democrats while he was in college and serving as his college young Democratic president his junior and senior years. He had been willing to put his name on the ballot to run as a candidate for district court judge during the Republican years, when the people of the county weren't about to elect a Democrat and he knew it. Then he had run for congress all pumped up by a bunch of his Democratic party cronies who had convinced him through his gullibility that he was the chosen one and could put the Republican Congressman out of office. He and his wife had spent everything they had on the campaign, even mortgaging their house and signing "IOUs" to their campaign workers that they could never pay unless he won the election and could hold post-election victory dinners to pay off those campaign debts. He came in third out of a field of three in the Democratic primary. His was one of those cases where a pig on the ballot would have stirred more interest and received more votes than this man, who was now a judge, received.

He was a dejected, defeated, and depressed man. All that money, time, and energy had produced less than nothing. His wife went to Paul Winfrey, the leader of the George Wallace faction of the Democratic Party. These were the days before the Democratic Party told the George Wallace people to go fuck themselves and thus created the North Carolina Republican party. These were the days before the Democratic Party began to suck up to the black ministers and civil-rights leaders.

"Paul, you've got to help Anthony. He can't work, he can't eat, he won't even leave the house. I'm so worried he's gonna do something to himself."

Paul Winfrey was a man who knew what it was to be slapped on the back one minute and praised for what you were doing for the Democratic Party and then the next minute to turn around and have the same Democratic hacks kick you in the balls and tell you how ashamed they were that you were a part of their party. Winfrey had already twice led the North Carolina George Wallace campaign to victory and fully believed if George Wallace could keep the health and energy that he had shown in his first two campaigns for president, he would surely be elected and win the nation in a third try.

Winfrey felt for Attorney Anthony Case and thought the least he could do was go talk to him. Winfrey couldn't believe the man he was seeing. He looked like a street person. Case kept babbling on about what he could've done and how he could have and should have won and what a great congressman he would have made. Paul was blunt with Case and pointed out how the Wallace people had been screwed over time and time again by the Democratic Party.

"They don't even want us to attend precinct meetings, Anthony, much less county, district, or state conventions. You know who the George Wallace supporters are. They're working people. They're mill hands. They're tobacco farmers. They're the men and women who stack cigarettes for ten hours a day and stink to high heaven when they go home to their husbands and wives at night. They're the people who fought in the wars. They're the people who support the troops who fight the wars. They're the people who don't expect to get anything out of a war other than to be able to keep their freedom. And sometimes, When I say that word freedom, I think that little commi hippie girl Janis Joplin just might be right when she sings 'freedom's just another word for nothing left to lose.' Anthony, this Democratic Party used to stand up for those people, and now it don't stand for nuthin other than bigger and better welfare checks."

Winfrey may as well had been talkin' to an empty chair. Anthony Case sat there like a zombie. His response to Winfrey's soliloquy was, "Paul, you and the Wallace people still have the governor's attention. I want to be a superior court judge. Paul, I ain't nobody. I want to be somebody," Case said with tears in his eyes. "I've worked hard for the party, and I deserve something. Please talk to your folks and get the governor to appoint me as a judge."

Case's response to Winfrey made Winfrey sick to his stomach. Case hadn't listened to a damn thing he had said. Case represented all of the bad things that Winfrey's precious Democratic Party had come to be. The Democratic Party was now the party of jobs as pay-offs, whereas the Democratic Party formally had been the party working to create jobs for the average working stiff. The Democratic Party now was the party that rewarded the individual who brought in the most votes with the government job and the promise of a good retirement, whether you worked or not.

Winfrey stood up to leave. "Anthony, I'll talk to the governor myself and get as many of my people behind ya as I can."

Winfrey's parting words to attorney Anthony Case turned out not to be empty, but for whatever reason, Winfrey and the Wallace people went to work on the governor, and within six months, Anthony Case was sworn in as a superior court judge.

"All rise. Here ye, here ye, here ye. All persons having business this day before the Superior Court of Forsyth County, come forward. The Honorable Anthony Case, superior court judge presiding," the bailiff chanted.

Judge Case strutted up to the bench and took his seat

"Be seated," Judge Case said, and then he made a dramatic pause and said, "Good morning, gentlemen. I understand from talking to Malcolm that we've got some serious business before this court today."

Oh shit, I thought. The son of a bitch already is telling us he talked to opposing council and decided what he's gonna do. We all know that these exparte conferences between judges and lawyers are expressly prohibited by the code of ethics for lawyers and the judicial code of ethics for judges, but we all know they happen all the time between the connected lawyers and the Democratic judges they've put into office. Just six months ago, I had a district court case down in Siler City. I had arrived about thirty minutes early and was just sitting in the jury box killing time waiting for court to begin when another lawyer walked in and sat down. We introduced ourselves. I had discovered he was from Chapel Hill. I told him I was from Winston-Salem. Just making small talk, I mentioned to him I was having a lot of problems in one case in particular in Abingdon, Virginia, where the lawyer on the other side would walk into the judge's office and discuss the motion or whatever that would be coming before the court, and these conversations they were having, of course, were without me being there or having any chance to be there, and the lawyer and the judge would decide what they were going to do. So when the date of the hearing came, the two of them would nonchalantly notify me in open court and with a record being made of it that they had discussed the situation in an exparte conference and decided what they were going to do and then just notify me and draft an order accordingly, which the judge would sign and mail to me after the other lawyer had approved of it. The Chapel Hill lawyer told me not to feel like the Lone Ranger, that everybody he knew saw these unethical exparte conferences all the time.

He went on to tell me that the last time he was in that court in Siler City, he had arrived early as he had this day and was just sitting in the jury box waiting for the opposing attorney and the judge to come in. He said that he had never met either the judge or the opposing attorney, but he had seen them at various bar dinners. The Chapel Hill lawyer told me that the judge had walked in to the courtroom from the back and his opposing attorney had walked in from the front. When the judge and the opposing attorney saw each other, they greeted each other on a first name basis and the judge asked the opposing attorney to come on up and tell him about the case he was there for that day. The opposing attorney told the judge his side of the issue, and the judge asked him what he wanted to do about it. The attorney told the judge what he wanted to do, and the judge agreed to do it.

I said to the attorney, "And you saw all of this unethical conduct take place right here in this courtroom?"

He answered, "Yes."

"Did you report them to the ethics committee?" I asked.

"No," he answered.

"Why not?"

"I knew it wouldn't do any good."

"Why?"

"Because he's chairman of the ethics committee."

Judge Case interrupted my musing about the Siler City incident. "We have cross motions here. We have plaintiff's discovery motion to compel and for sanctions and then we have, we won't call it defense motion, lets call it the deponent's motion for a protective order. Now, I've read all the pleadings. Does my description sound correct, gentlemen?"

We all answered yes.

"Well, I got the deponent's motion first, and Malcolm brought it over to my office and I know right much about it. So, ah, I'm going to let Mr. Scott and Mr. Spears go first with their motions. Now, I understand from talking to Mr. Saits that there is a very serious document which may be a forgery." He emphasized forgery as he looked down at Scott and me. "Now, I want this record to be as clean and honest as the driven snow, and I don't want anybody in here to discuss the contents of the document, and I want you all to refer to it as 'the document.' With that said, I will now hear the motions of the plaintiff. Which one of you is going to speak for the plaintiff?"

"For the record, I will, your honor. Michael Spears appearing for the plaintiff. Your honor, I feel constrained if I can't talk about the contents of 'the document.' It handicaps my argument about 'the document.'"

"Mr. Spears, you have a wrongful death suit. Someone has clearly died and the implications of 'the document' could be very serious."

"Your honor, the deponent questions the authenticity of 'the document' and the major objection that we have at this time to the presentation of 'the document,' in a deposition or otherwise, is that we have never been presented with the original of 'the document,' Malcolm said.

"Your honor," I said, attempting a response. "The document is signed b...."

The judge speaking again cut me off. "Mr. Spears, I thought I told you no one was to discuss the content of that document. Now you're trying my patience. You're trying to get into the record the contents of 'the document.'"

"Your honor, as I've tried to say, how can we determine the presentation of 'the document' for discovery purposes without going into its contents to at least some extent?"

"Your honor I might suggest and make this request of the plaintiff," Saits said in his condescending and slicing manner. "If the court would ask the plaintiff to produce the original of 'the document,' I believe that might help advance and move this hearing along. I would be willing for the court to postpone this hearing for a reasonable period of time to allow for Mr. Spears to produce the original."

"Mr. Spears, you know we're all here right now and Mr. Saits has every right to have a final determination of this issue, but he is indulging you with the opportunity to help yourself, and thus your client, in this case. So how much time do you need? Would an hour be good enough?"

"No, your honor, but I believe I could get it here by tomorrow morning."

"Well, let me see. If I set this hearing until two o'clock tomorrow afternoon, can you be here, Malcolm?"

"Yes, I can," Malcolm responded.

"Gentleman, I'm going to set this hearing to reconvene at 2 o'clock tomorrow afternoon. Mr. Spears, I expect you to have the original of the document for me to examine at that time."

"Thank you, your honor."

As we left the courtroom, Scott emphasized, "This is a discovery deposition. The best-evidence rule does not apply in a discovery deposition. If Chandler wrote that letter and signed it, he knows he did, and he has a copy of it in his own file. But we're clearly in trouble in Forsyth County if we can't produce it. Get on the stick, Michael. Go get that thing."

Chapter 24

"Jean, what are you doing?"

"Just help'n' momma around the house. What's up?"

"The court insists upon the original of that letter."

"Well, Willy's still got it. I thought it was best for you and me to bring it with us regardless of any kind of law that you said Willy needed to keep it. The boy ain't right, and he ain't long for this world."

"I told you I had to as a precautionary measure not to break the chain-of-evidence rule. But, anyway, can you ride up with me?"

"I can if I hang up now. I'll jump in the shower. Be here in twenty minutes."

I was really worried at this point. Lawyers like Saits will use anything to win. Winning is everything to them. They see kindness and accommodation as signs of weakness in their opponents. If Saits hadn't objected using the best-evidence rule to the copy at the deposition, he would have used the chain-of-evidence rule if we'd produced the original copy of the letter. Saits would now be arguing to Judge Case that because the chain of evidence had been broken, the letter had probably been altered, and therefore Judge Case should deny any use whatsoever of the "altered letter" and therefore seal the letter and the deposition forever more from the eyes of man. I felt confident that Judge Case would not now ban the letter as violating the chain-of-evidence rule, even if Saits now had the audacity to raise that objection to the letter. However, I couldn't help but be concerned that somehow the original of the letter could not be found when Jean and I reached the Fly.

Jean's house was on the way to Elkin, so I felt good that I was going in the right direction, and I really wanted to pick her up for her to go with me. I was at a point that I was drawing strength from her, and I needed her. She was watching for me and came running out to the car. I didn't even shut the motor down. We went the back roads cross-country to where highway 67 crossed the Yadkin River into Yadkin County. We would cross the Yadkin again going into Elkin and actually end up at the Fly's little shack on the same side of the river as before we crossed into Yadkin County.

"Don't worry, Michael. Willy's a tough old goat. Let's just take our time and enjoy the ride up there."

"Jean, I can't get out of my mind that car I nearly backed into and then I saw as we were leaving the Fly's."

"Take it easy, Michael. We'll be up there in thirty minutes and you'll see everything's okay."

I remembered the way. Jean didn't have to give me any directions. We pulled up in front of the Fly's shack. His front door was standing wide open. It was now fall and the air was a little chilly and that door should have not been standing open. A pane of the living room window was missing, so anyone could have reached right in, unlocked the window, and pushed it right open. Our thoughts were the same. Before I even stopped the car, Jean was out the door, up the porch, and into Willy's house. As I entered the house, I saw Jean staring at the little cedar chest. It was open and the papers were scattered all around it. We looked every place for Willy. We yelled for him. Our thoughts again were the same. We ran down to the edge of the river on a path that really would have been difficult for a disabled man like Willy to use everyday.

There he was, fishing with a string of about six middle-sized catfish.

"Son of a bitch, Fly. You had us scared shitless. How'd you get down here?"

"I walked," he said. "And I reckon it'll be the day the Lord takes me away when I don't walk down here no more. I been fish'n for catfish down here ever since I was a youngun."

"Willy, how do you get up that hill back to your house?" I asked.

"Oh, it ain't easy," Willy said. "I just throw my catfish over my shoulder and pull my oxygen bottle with this little cart and take it one step at a time. It takes me over thirty minutes to get back up to my house, but look around you at the mountain laurel, the white water, the ferns. Ain't it worth it?"

"It sure is," I said. "But it's so pretty sittin' up on your porch looking down here that I'm not sure I'd bother to come all this way."

"Michael, I couldn't a caught these catfish from my porch and I don't know what kinda plans y'all got, but if y'all was to help me fry up these catfish, y'all 'd make me really happy if y'all 'd stay and have supper."

Jean carried the catfish, I pulled Willy's oxygen cart, and the three of us made what Willy said was record time of twenty minutes getting back to his porch. It was getting late in the evening, and we just sat out there until dark until it was too chilly to be out there anymore. Willy might've had electricity, but he still preferred his wood stove, which also served as his primary heating source. I had enjoyed food prepared on my grandmother's wood stove up in Allegheny County when I was a child. I skinned and cleaned the catfish at Willy's direction while Jean prepared an egg batter and then cornmeal to fry them up. One thing about the wood stove: you have to really go out of your way to burn anything you fry on the top of one. The catfish cooked slowly, and Jean kept them warm on top of the stove with the plastic plates we were going to eat from. When we finally sat down to eat, I began explaining to Willy what the court had said. I told him we needed to take the original back with us this night because the judge had demanded to see the original. Willy said it was no problem; we could have taken the original with us when we were first up there. He said he trusted Jean. He said he trusted me and that I was going to do my best for Linda and Harry. Jean asked what had happened to his window. He said that shortly after Jean and I had left his house the last time, a man had stopped by. The man had said that he was a detective from Winston-Salem and had even shown Willy a badge. Willy said he believed the man had been lying about being a detective and that he had had enough experience with the police that he thought the badge was phony. Willy said the man had asked him if he had any documents that Harold Stennis Rains had asked him to keep. Willy said he told the man no, Big Head Rains never asked him to keep anything, which was the truth because when Big Head gave him the letter, he just told Willy that was how he could trust Henrietta and why he felt it was safe to go back with her. Willy said he was really suspicious of the man and had never locked his door before, but he started locking it after the man left. Willy said he locked himself out when he went fishing and had to break his own window to get back in his own house. And after that, he said he took the letter out of the cedar chest and hid it under his mattress.

"Jean, you go look under my mattress and find that letter and you and Michael take it down to Winston and y'all help them younguns."

Jean and I thanked Willy and headed back to Winston-Salem. As we headed back down 67, Jean said to me, "Is there anything I can do for you, kind sir?"

"Oh, Jean, you know I'd like to, but we'd be up all night. I've got to be fresh and perked for court tomorrow afternoon. But let me say this: I've wanted to take you up to the mountains ever since I met you. This weekend's forecast is for an Indian summer with highs around 90. There are two places I've just got to show you. One is called Pot Rock, and the other is called Bear Hole. How about we leave Friday night, take my little travel trailer, and stay until Sunday night or Monday morning? Bring your swim suit, or, better still, don't bring your swim suit and we'll go swimming and rafting in a cold mountain stream."

Jean said she couldn't wait for us to celebrate over the weekend as we kissed goodnight at her mom and dad's door.

Chapter 25

"Are you gentlemen ready to reconvene?" Judge Case asked. We all answered in the affirmative.

"This court is in session, reconvening in the matter of Rains vs. Handy. Michael, you seem to have a smile on your face. I assume you are ready to present me with the document in question. Have you shown that document to Mr. Saits?"

"I have not yet, your honor," I said as I handed Mr. Saits the original of the Chandler letter. I started to take it back from Malcolm after he had had several moments to look it over and confirm that it was indeed the original of the letter copy I had previously furnished him with.

"Hold on, Mr. Spears. I want to take some time to look this over. This may or may not be an original, and I am not prepared to concede that it's not a forgery and thus I'm holding the original of a forgery."

I was really beginning to get angry this time. There was no doubt in my mind that if I had taken the attitude that Malcolm Saits was showing at this time, at the very least Judge Case would have threatened me with contempt.

"Your honor, I'm concerned about the chain of evidence with this document. I'm concerned that should this document be authentic, there is still the possibility, if not the probability, that it has been tampered with and altered to reflect poorly on my client, who is perhaps Winston-Salem's greatest living benefactor."

I grimaced and shook my head in disgust.

"Now, Mr. Spears, I saw that. You best show this court the respect it deserves. Any other actions like that and I just might have to find you in contempt."

My God, I thought. Are we in the courts of the middle ages? I tried to control my temper. I wanted to respond, "Judge, I'll show you the respect you deserve, which is absolutely none, you Democratic Party hack." Reggie grabbed my arm and whispered that he'd better take it from here.

"If it please the court, may I argue our client's position, your honor?"

"Well, it's not just up to me," said Judge Case. "What do you think, Malcolm? Mr. Saits, don't you want to make a motion to suppress this evidence on the grounds that it's been tainted under the chain-of-evidence rule?"

Good God, did I just hear that right? It sound like the Judge just made the motion. As a lawyer, I was never taught what to say in law school when the judge makes a motion against me on behalf of the other side. What do you say? "Sustained"?

"Judge, that is exactly the motion I was thinking about. However, I would add to it that the court seize this purported original copy and seal it and that my client be discharged from any future depositions in this matter in view of the harassing tactics used by the plaintiffs in the case. Furthermore, I ask the court to award attorney fees to the deponent's attorney and law firm under the rules of discovery."

"Mr. Saits, what are your attorney fees up to this point?"

"Your honor, up to this point the attorney fees, including the time of both myself and my associate, are in the amount of two-thousand dollars, and I've taken the liberty to prepare an affidavit of those attorney fees."

"Would you show that affidavit to plaintiff's attorneys?"

As angry and disgusted as I was, I was able to carefully examine the affidavit of attorney fees. Even at three hundred dollars per hour, it should have been clear to anyone that Malcolm and his associate didn't spend that much time on this case.

"Now pass that affidavit up here, Mr. Saits."

The judge took a recess and went back to his office. He told us to remain in the courtroom. The old hack clearly wanted to draw out the suspense against Reggie and me. He returned in about fifteen minutes.

"Mr. Saits, I'm going to grant your motion in its entirety."

Damn, I thought. I hadn't even heard Malcolm make a motion. The only way you could put together a motion was to repeat what the judge had said the motion ought to be and add the part where Malcolm wanted the letter seized and sealed and was asking for attorney fees. The only thing I felt good about was the fact that I knew that anybody who looked at Malcolm's affidavit of attorney fees would know that Malcolm was lying about the amount of time spent.

Judge Case went on: "Except that, Malcolm, due to the fact that I know these two lawyers here to be good and honest men, I don't believe that they would do anything like this again. Therefore, I'm gonna deny your attorney fees. Malcolm, Armand's got all the money in the world, and it won't hurt him that bad to pay you that two-thousand dollars." Judge Case chortled, and Malcolm and his associate joined in.

"I'll prepare the order, your honor," Malcolm said, "and submit it to Mr. Scott before 5, and if I don't hear from him by 10 tomorrow morning, I'll bring it over for your signature." Malcolm and his associate closed their briefcases and walked past us as if we weren't there. As a matter of fact, they were riding so high, I'm not sure they didn't walk through us. Powers had been sitting at the back all along and was standing at the door when Saits reached him. Powers slapped Saits on the back, and they both walked out of the courtroom laughing.

Even dumb Judge Case had recognized the danger of including the attorney fees in that order based upon that inflated affidavit Malcolm had signed. And all that bullshit about me and Scott being a bunch of good old boys he was gonna let off the hook was merely done so some slick reporter wouldn't publish it and outrage the public in a way that clearly showed what shysters lawyers really were.

Chapter 26

I called Jean and told her the bad news.

"How can they do that?"

"They had it all worked out before Scott and I even got to the court room. I don't think it will stand on appeal, but in this state, who knows?"

Scott and I were both so defeated that neither of us wanted to deal with the situation just now. Remarkably enough, I was able to put this out of my mind and get a good night's sleep. I was in my office early the next day and received a call at 10:30 from Scott.

"Saits never brought me a copy of the order before Judge Case signed it, and I see why," Scott said. "He's got it in the order that 'the document' is to be sealed, the court having heard the facts and the arguments of plaintiffs and deponents. And then listen to this, Michael: in the next paragraph it is hereby ordered that neither the parties nor the council are to disclose any of the material contained in the document to anyone or any source, and such disclosure by plaintiffs or their council shall be grounds for an order finding them in contempt of court."

"So he's got a gag order in there too, Reggie. The issue wasn't even raised of a gag order at the hearing. I had wondered why they hadn't said anything about a gag order."

"They simply forgot to, and this is why this order wasn't submitted to me before Judge Case signed it."

"Reggie, we should be able to get the ruling reversed by the Court of Appeals. The record will clearly show that no such motion for a gag order was made and there are no facts to support it in the order or in the record. Don't you think the Court of Appeals will overturn it based on that?"

"It depends in part upon which three-judge panel we get."

"Before the hearing began yesterday, I took a copy of the letter over to Rick Stanton with the paper. As I left his desk, a crowd was gathering around him with several folks looking over his shoulder to read it."

"You took that letter to a reporter? You took that letter to a reporter! A reporter has that letter in his hands! You're a genius!"

"I didn't really expect the audacity of Saits to raise the chain-of-evidence rule on top of the best-evidence rule and for Judge Case to seal the original. I was just proud of the fact that my leg work, with Jean's help, had discovered the piece of evidence."

"Let me read over this gag order again. I don't see that it could be applied as written in any way to Rick Stanton. It just says you and our clients are not allowed to discuss the contents. Maybe the paper can bring some daylight into this case. I'm going to prepare a notice of appeal of this order. You come on down and sign it."

I walked down to Scott's office.

"Reggie, lets file a motion to remove Henrietta from the administration of the estate. Blaine indicated that if the money can be taken out of her hands, that might loosen up some of the people he knows can help us. Here, sign this notice of appeal while I prepare the motion to remove Henrietta from control of the estate."

We took the notice of appeal straight down to the courthouse, as well as our motion to remove Henrietta from control of the estate, and filed them both. The court gave us a hearing date set for two weeks later.

Chapter 27

It was Friday evening, and although it hadn't been a good week, we were having a beautiful Indian summer. I drove back home and, without calling Jean, drove my Jeep pick-up and little camper trailer out to her folks.

"I've had a bad week, Jean. Make me feel better."

She jumped in the truck and we headed north toward Galax, Virginia. At times like this, I felt like giving up the practice of law and going up to my farm on the banks of the Crooked Creek in Blue Ridge country and becoming a hermit. The way I felt right then, if Jean would have said she would have stayed with me, I might've camped out on the banks of the Crooked Creek and never returned to the city.

I remembered as a five-year-old child my father taking me up to visit a man who I remembered as Santa Claus. As an adult, I knew the man's name was really Monroe. My dad had told me Monroe, and that is "Munn-row," was a hermit, although Monroe was always the center of attention, as opposed to some fellow living alone way back in the woods and never seeing other folks. And talk about way back in the woods. To get to Monroe's, you would go way down a dirt road, then way up a dirt path, then park your car, then walk up the side of a mountain to a little hollow with a pretty little cascading branch running down the center of the hollow. You would step on a few stones to cross the branch, walk up the branch past Monroe's liquor still, and see Monroe's little shack clinging to a hill just below a forty foot granite cliff that, to me, as a little fellow, made his house look like the manger stable below the alter of a mighty cathedral at Christmas. And there sat Monroe in the center of a group of fellas who looked like they all were kin-folk to the two bad guys in the movie *Deliverance*.

I remember the first time my dad and I walked up to Monroe's. My dad said to me, "You see that man sittin right there? The one who looks like Santa Claus? That man is free."

There was that definite envy in my dad's eyes and voice when he said Monroe was free. My dad always longed to return to the mountains of Allegheny County, but knew he never would, and he never did, other than for the one week each summer when the mills would close down and we would go stay with my grandmother. My dad would always say, "Even the air is free in the mountains." I knew for certain the air was different in the mountains. After sitting for a day in downtown Winston-Salem, a car would be covered with soot. After a week in the mountains, your car tires would be muddy, but there wouldn't be any soot on the car.

There sat Monroe, long white beard, long white hair, and a big old banjo on his big old belly. "Who's that youngun, Floyd?"

For a moment there, Monroe had made me the center of attention

"That's my boy, Michael. I wanted him to hear some banjo pick'n."

For the next thirty minutes, Monroe would sing and pick and sing and pick, and some of the fellas would be flat-foot'n, and all the fellas would be drink'n' what daddy said was water (it looked like it to me) out of mason jars. The more they drank of that water, the happier all those fellas got.

In time, my dad and I would have to walk down the hill before it got too dark to follow the path. With envy and a longing in his voice, my dad again would say, "That man is free."

My first year of law practice, I'd gotten lucky with a Ford Pinto case where a drunk had rear-ended a Ford Pinto and turned it into a ball of fire, injuring the husband and wife in the Pinto. When the movie *Chariots of Fire* came along, all my lawyer buddies told me I ought to go see it, telling me it was about a Ford Pinto. Anyway, I had gotten enough money out of the case that I'd been able to buy a hundred and thirteen acres on the banks of the Crooked Creek in Carroll County, Virginia. There were two really nice swimming holes on my property. One was at an old church camp meeting site, which two hundred years earlier had been the site of an Indian village and Indian burial ground. It had a gorgeous waterfall that stretched all the way across the narrow stream as the water fell shortly for about four feet until it hit its end. Below the falls, the water stood about five feet deep and made it perfect for swimming and the obvious spot of countless parties from the locals. A boulder, of sorts, stood adjacent to the waterfall where one could see as far down stream as the creek stayed straight. After floods that came across the boulder, a sandy beach was created that stretched out from the stream to where the boulder ended.

The spot had been dubbed "Pot Rock," not for the excessive use of marijuana by the locals, but by these mysterious perfect circles, or potholes, in the boulder.

"Where in the world did this come from?" Jean asked, looking at the potholes.

"No one really knows, Jean. Some say it came naturally from the water digging its way to the top of the boulder. Others say it was an old-day aquarium crafted by the Indians."

As I stepped from the boulder onto the top of the waterfall, I grabbed Jean's hand and told her I would lead her across it. At first she seemed scared of the strong current that could throw a man off this ledge onto the water below, but I gave her a look to show her it was okay. We walked across slowly until we got to the edge of the actual falls itself.

"Will you jump off with me?" I asked, looking at her with a grin. I saw hesitation on her face and volunteered to jump myself and then catch her afterward. She agreed. I kissed her forehead and took a jump into the icy cold creek. For her confidence, I caught my balance as fast as possible and held my hands out for her to come to me.

"I don't know, Michael. This seems crazy."

"You can trust me. I promise I will catch you, okay? On three. One. Two. Three."

She jumped into my arms and kissed me as I caught her. I told her that the waterfall cupped over the rock to make a pocket where one can breathe through, while a wall of rushing water came over you. Together, we went through the waterfall into a place that's indescribable. I held my hand over her eyes so the water wouldn't drip onto them and we held each other close. I asked if she wanted to go to the sand, and she agreed. We broke the plane of the falls and drifted down until we landed at the sandy beach.

"This sand is as fine as the sand at Myrtle Beach."

"Isn't it incredible to come up here in the mountains and find a sandy beach beside a waterfall?"

It was getting dark, so we started gathering wood to start a campfire. We rolled a log over beside our campfire and held each other as we looked at the dancing flames. I'd brought a couple of steaks and a case of beer. We suspended the steaks over the fire with a makeshift wooden rotisserie. We cooled our beer in the edge of the stream. When our steaks were ready, we took them out and sat Indian style while we ate our steaks and drank more beer.

"The Indian graveyard is on the opposite side of the creek from us. I've never been to it. The locals say it's bad luck to go there. Can you imagine what it must have been two or three hundred years ago when there was an Indian village here?"

"I guess they had to make everything they had, their pots, their pans."

"Yes, they were made out of baked clay, and you can still find pieces of their pottery here. It gets down to below zero here in February. I don't see how the Indians possibly could have stood that."

"They were a lot tougher than we are. I'm part Cherokee, did you know that?"

"I had guessed you might be, with your straight black hair and olive skin. My best friends from North Carolina Central University Law School were Lumbi Indians. They've all returned to Robeson County and are deeply involved in Democratic politics, helping their people down there. One of my friends even became the first Indian judge in North Carolina."

It was a clear night. It had been a long week and a hard day. As the chill crept over us, we crawled in the trailer and slept like logs, listening to the roar of the waterfall. The next morning, we unhitched the trailer and drove around so we could get to the other side of the creek.

"Jean, I'm going to show you my second-most favorite swimming hole." We drove across the ridge, then down the winding road to the edge of the creek, then walked up the creek for about three hundred feet to Bear Hole. The stream narrows at Bear Hole from its normal 100 ft. width to about 20 ft., where all of the current of the stream is forced between two giant boulders. As you look up stream, you see the boulder that Bear Hole gets it's name from. It's a large rock about 40 ft. long by 20 ft. wide. Just below this boulder is another boulder about the size of a Volkswagen. These two boulders resemble a mother bear and her cub crawling out of the water. This gives bear hole its name.

"Jean, can you swim? When we went to Myrtle, we didn't go out far enough to really swim, and I'd never thought to ask you."

"Can I swim? Hell yes, I can swim. I was the first girl to be a lifeguard at the Lewisville pool, but I ain't getting my clothes wet like we did yesterday at Pot Rock."

Jean and I began to strip our clothes off.

"Jean, I didn't mean to insult you, but the current here is not for the faint of heart. As you can see, the entire stream is forced into a narrow slip one-fifth the width of the normal stream. I'm a good swimmer too, but when that water comes through that shoot and falls that 7 ft. into that pool, it can catch you in an eddy and hold you under water that's 7 ft. deep. It will tumble you over and over under water like you're a rag doll. It's done it to me before. I'm a good swimmer, but it scared me. If that waterfall catches you like that, the only thing you can do is plant your feet on something solid and either kick to the surface or at least kick out of the eddy.

Jean had her clothes off before I did and was about five feet into the water, headed for the momma bear.

"Goddamn, this water's cold."

"Yea, this water never gets warm, and this time of the year, it's really chilly."

"I can't keep my balance," Jean said.

"Hold on a minute." I hurried on into the water after her and took her by the hand. We were both about waist deep.

"Okay, Jean. It's gonna be over our head in a couple of steps."

We let go of each other and began swimming across the stream. Just below the waterfall, the water is over seven feet deep and very treacherous. But it begins to widen and get shallower until about three hundred feet down stream from the falls the water is only knee-deep. On the side of the creek where momma bear and baby bear were crawling out is a large gentle eddy that's about fifty feet wide that churns clockwise and makes a complete revolution about every two minutes. This was perfect for Jean and me to ride the four-man raft I had brought. When we got to momma bear, Jean crawled on top and stretched out in the noon-day sun in all her beauty. I told her I was about to get the raft and bring it so we could lounge in that while getting our sun.

"Jean, help me with the raft," I said as I reached momma bear.

She reached down, her breasts swaying, and grabbed the rope at the front of the boat. She pulled and I pushed until we had the big raft atop momma bear.

"Be prepared for the ride of your life," I said. "Follow me up stream."

I drug the raft up above the falls about a hundred fifty feet.

"Okay, get in, Jean."

I held the raft steady and watched her cute little butt as she crawled onto the raft.

"Sit in the bottom, Jean, or you'll fall out."

We both sat in the bottom of the raft as it began to drift downstream toward the falls.

"Okay, if you fall out, remember what I said. Plant your feet on something solid and kick yourself out of the falls."

The roar of the falls became louder and louder. Jean's end of the boat went over first, and she disappeared from sight as the boat bent in half. In a split second, my end of the raft followed her over the falls. As usual, the force of the falls took the raft, and us with it, completely under the surface. But it didn't trap us, and we shot to the surface ten feet downstream from the falls. I started paddling like a madman to get us into the eddy beside momma bear. We made it, although our raft was completely full of water, making the level of water in the raft actually higher than the surface of the water the raft was sitting on.

"Whoa," Jean screamed out loud. "What a rush."

Jean and I emptied the boat and took two more rides down the shoot. I really enjoyed the fact that she enjoyed nature as much as I did. I even thought maybe the two of us could come on up here, build us a shack like Monroe's or the Fly's, and grow old together. I could see Jean and me in our 60s or 70s scoot'n' down that shoot in a rubber raft, then popp'n up. It was burned in my mind forever, her scream, "Whoa, what a rush," when we first popped up after going over the falls. By our third trip over the falls, it was nearing 2 o'clock and we were becoming exhausted from the lifting and pulling of the boat, so we emptied the water from the boat once more and just drifted around the eddy, enjoying each time the eddy would near the falls. It would suddenly spin the boat around like one of those saucer rides at the fair. I had once heard someone say riding on the back of an elephant is like riding on the finger of God. Riding a raft over a waterfall or being caught in a swirling eddy is no less like riding on the finger of God. Before we left Bear Hole, we once more climbed on the back of momma bear, and Jean sat between my legs facing the fall as I held her with both arms, clutching her around her waist with both arms. The cold mountain stream had taken most of the heat from our bodies, and we warmed each other so intimately entwined.

"Didn't you and Scott have a rock concert up here?"

"That's what everybody thinks and everybody says. No, it was New River Jam, a fiddler's convention. Every year, the best talent in bluegrass music assembles at Galax, Virginia. It's the oldest bluegrass festival in the world. My daddy used to bring me to it when I was a little boy. They have banjos, country gospel, fiddles, and, my favorite, clogging. Everybody just cuts loose and has a good time. The artists, and I think they deserve to be called artists, range from little five-year-old kids clogging to eighty-year-old men and women out there flat-foot'n' and clogging. The best part to me is to walk through the crowd and stop at the camper trailers late at night. The folks will have little campfires built, and groups of artists from two or three to ten or so will just get together and jam. The fiddle, I guess you would say, is what fancy people would call a violin. When the British banned my Scottish ancestors from playing the bagpipes because they incited them to go to war against the English, the Scottish people found out that they could make the same whaling and whining sounds with a fiddle as they could with a bagpipe. Anyway, when you go to those little circles late at night, you can get up close and personal with the artists themselves. I've never seen one of them who didn't enjoy having an audience formed in front of his tent in the campfire light. They definitely play better when somebody's watching. And they'll talk to you just like you're family. I'll bring you to the festival next summer."

"What was your festival like?"

"Our festival was the same week as the Galax festival, and a lot of the artists from the Galax festival came on over and performed on our stage. Our crowd wasn't very big, but I had a great time. It was like a three-day party. About the worst thing that ever happens is somebody gets drunk and picks a fight. The local law has told me it's almost always the same local boys every year who they hafta take in for cause'n trouble.

"In the past few years, a lot of hippies have started coming to the Galax festival and the pretty young girls will bathe and swim without any clothes on in the Chestnut Creek that runs through Galax. With these pretty spots that you've seen here, Pot Rock and Bear Hole, we had alotta naked people comin' down here, too. Unless you're bothering somebody, the local law lets you do pretty much anything you want to, and they don't consider pretty girls play'n in the water naked to be the sort of thing that bothers anybody. It seems to me that a festival like the Galax fiddler's convention gives ordinary people a chance to let off steam for a while and sort of go wild and do stuff they wouldn't ordinarily do, but stuff that doesn't hurt anybody. It sort of seems to me it's like the medieval fairs that used to be held every year in medieval Europe five hundred years ago. Everybody would work hard for fifty one weeks a year, they wouldn't take any time to rest, they wouldn't have any time to rest, but then for one week everybody would just sort of go berserk, and the freedom that that one week gave them would be good enough to last most all of them 'til the next year. Somehow, the freedom people have with these festivals will not last forever. For one thing, people seem to me to be getting meaner, and the free love of the '60s is becoming a thing of the past. Also, you got too many people who call themselves fundamentalists of one kind of religion or another. And fundamentalists, whether they're Christians, Muslims, Jews, or whatever, seem to believe that at any given time somewhere, someplace, somebody's having a good time and they, the fundamentalists, want to put a stop to that. Jean, this place right here, Bear Hole, was just full of naked people just a few months ago. I was sittin right there on the bank by that big poplar and got to see three beautiful girls come walking out of the water naked and walk past me. Now, I don't figure that that hurt a thing, and Jean, you know how weak I am. I will admit, I looked at those girls and I enjoyed it, but I know there're a whole lot of people who, for some strange reason, would want to put a stop to that sort of thing. What do you think?" I said as I gently raised my arms between her breasts and drew her even closer to me.

She was asleep. I shook her. "Jean, damn it, I just solved all the problems of humanity talkin' here for ten minutes and nobody listened to me but these trees and God, and I think I've already forgotten what I've said."

She laughed and looked at me and said, "Sure you did."

"I don't get no respect," I said.

"What did you say?"

"Nuthin."

Chapter 28

I had had another incredible weekend with Jean, this time all pleasure, no business at all. She had known how badly I felt, and I don't recall more than a dozen words being spoken about the case.

Two weeks later.

Here we were again before Judge Case. We'd asked the clerk, Scott and I had actually pleaded with the clerk, begged if you will, for our motion to remove Henrietta from administering Big Head's estate to be held before another judge, any judge other than Case. However, Case had insisted upon hearing the motion, claiming that since he had heard the prior motion that he was familiar with the case and any other judge would need to take time to make himself ready. So there we were before the honorable Anthony Case, as chief superior court judge, for a second time in three weeks.

Since our case was one of the newer cases on the court calendar, we were listed next to last. At Monday morning calendar call, it's customary for the opposing attorneys to appear and announce when they can be ready or, if need be, to ask that the case be held open. Judge Case himself said he was going to hold our case open and for the attorneys to wait until the end of the calendar call. We all waited. After the courtroom had cleared and there was no one else there to hear what Judge Case was saying, he announced to us that he would hear the case in chambers that afternoon at 2 o'clock.

When 2 o'clock came, Reggie and I appeared at Judge Case's office door. No one was in his office. In a few minutes, from around the corner came Charles Powers and Judge Case. Judge Case unlocked his door, and we went into his chambers. He asked us all to be seated and then took his seat. He leaned back in his chair and recounted how his father had once told him, "After you've chased a rabbit half a day and haven't caught him, son, it's time for you to start chas'n' another rabbit."

"Michael, you and Reggie ain't never gonna catch this rabbit. Now, why don't y'all go ahead and look for another rabbit to chase? Charles Powers and I just happened to have lunch over at the Big City Club, and we talked about this case. Now, he pointed out something to me that I hadn't even thought of. Y'all got this case on appeal to the North Carolina Court of Appeals, and I don't even have any jurisdiction to make a ruling one way or another about that estate and whether Mrs. Handy, Mr. Power's client, should have the control of the estate taken away from her."

"Your honor, it will be six months before the court of appeals rules, and all of the assets will be gone by then," I said, trying to keep calm.

Judge Case responded, "Michael, I'd like to help y'all. You know I'd like to help y'all, but it's just out of my hands. Motion denied. Now, Charles, I think you told me you'd already prepared an order denying their motion. Is that right?"

"Here it is, your honor." Powers started to hand it to Judge Case.

"Oh no, Charles, we gotta do things right," Judge Case said, pushing the paper toward Reggie and me. "You let Michael and Reggie see that before you hand it over to me in case they have a problem with it and wanna add anything to it."

Again, everything had been decided by a conversation between the judge and the opposing attorney, and no matter what Scott and I had said, everything had been decided, including the wording of the order denying our motion, even before we were able to say word one. Again, Scott and I walked away from the courthouse defeated and dejected.

"How many body slams can we take, Reggie?"

"Michael, you've practiced law for three years. I've practiced for eleven. What we're seeing is what used to be common practice in the South. Consider what black people used to face here in Winston-Salem. Consider what that fellow who's been charged in the Charlotte Pendleton case is gonna hafta face. You've heard the interviews the TV people are giving about how all of the white women are scared to death now. That young man is gonna be convicted. He might be guilty, I don't know, but he's gonna be convicted. At least if we never get anything for our clients, they just lose what they never had and we as lawyers just don't get paid for a few hours we worked. That young man in that Charlotte Pendleton case is facing hard time for a crime he probably didn't even do.

I reflected upon what Reggie had said. I recalled what my black criminal law professor, Mr. Henderson, at North Carolina Central had said. In that time when black teachers and professors had been paid half what their white counterparts were paid, the whole faculty at the black law school that was North Carolina Central University in Durham, North Carolina, had worked full-time practicing law to support their families.

Professor Henderson had his demons. These demons drove him to drink and there would be nights his demons would not let him sleep. At those times, Professor Henderson would come into class smelling of alcohol and as unkempt as a street person. It was those times he gave his best lessons, history lessons.

He told us of those times when the black man and the black lawyer were considered by the North Carolina courts to be less than men and less than lawyers. He told us of that time when he would represent "well to do" black executives from the black bank in Durham founded by the Micheaux family. He told us of the times he had represented the well-educated black professors from Central and prominent black insurance executives.

Every time I advised a client to look their best for traffic court, I remembered how Professor Henderson had told us law students how he had felt it necessary to tell these proud black men he represented to buy a pair of bib overalls and dirty them up before they wore them to traffic court so the white judge wouldn't punish them for being "uppity Niggers."

The ultimate demon Professor Henderson lived with was the "Brothers Case." Two Durham brothers were charged with raping and killing a white woman. The mother of the two young men had retained Professor Henderson.

It was that time in North Carolina when black men charged with killing white women were going to be convicted. In fact, they were lucky to be tried and not lynched. There was no such thing as a black person on a jury.

The "Brothers" were convicted despite a spirited defense. They were sentenced to die together on the same day.

Professor Henderson prepared an appeal that would certainly have, at the least, brought a new trial. He hand-carried his appeal brief to the North Carolina Supreme Court on the day it was due. He had allowed plenty of time for his drive from Durham to Raleigh, but an accident delayed him. It was 5:10 p.m. when he arrived at the door of the clerk of the Supreme Court. A clerk had locked the door and was leaving. With tears in his eyes, Professor Henderson begged the clerk to open the door and clock in the appeal. He refused. Professor Henderson got the janitor to lift him so he could throw the appeal papers into the office over the transom.

The Supreme Court refused to consider the appeal and reset the date of execution of the "two brothers."

It is customary that the attorney representing the condemned attends the execution. Professor Henderson sat with the mother of the "Two Brothers."

"Their mamma and I looked at the boys as they brought them in. Their momma was crying. When the boys saw her, they began to cry. The boys were tied in their seats. Two large tablets were dropped into a pan of acid."

Our classroom was totally silent with reverence for the two innocent men Professor Henderson was describing.

Tears began to flow down Professor Henderson's face. He lowered his head and slowly walked out of the classroom.

I didn't even go back to my office. I went walking back toward my car. It was time to talk to the Sage. I guess I could say the Sage had become my best friend. He was at the back of the store when I walked in. His mother was at the cash register.

"Michael, you look like you're having a bad day. With that letter you got on Chandler, you ought to be on top of the world."

I had forgotten I'd left a copy of the Chandler letter with Simon. Jean and I had been so exited, we'd made ten copies of it when we first got it, and I really couldn't remember if I'd given copies to anyone other than Reggie, Jean, Rick Stanton, and Simon. I certainly wasn't upset at myself for having distributed the copies. It certainly hadn't been in violation of the gag order that now existed. That order was in effect, at least until the court of appeals reversed it, but it only prohibited me from disclosing the contents of the letter. I suppose you could say it had been a fortuitous circumstance that I had previously distributed so many copies, and thus the contents, to so many people. Since I was coming from the courthouse, I had my file, and without saying anything, I pulled out a copy of the order sealing "the document" and handed the order to Simon. I knew I didn't need to explain the order to Simon. He was a genius, although I didn't really believe that you had to be very smart to understand the order and it's implications.

Simon read the order with shock and amazement. As he finished reading the order concerning "the document," I handed him the motion concerning the removal of Henrietta from administration of the estate and the order Judge Case had just signed denying that one.

Simon held up the order denying the removal of Henrietta and shouted, "Catch Twenty-Two! If you don't appeal, you lose; if you do appeal, you lose. In this first order, Michael, Judge Case thinks he's Judge Sirica, only Judge Case when he plays the role of Judge Sirica, he reads the incriminating evidence and says it doesn't say what it says it says. This is frightening, Michael. Judge Sirica, like Judge Case, could have read the transcripts from the Watergate tapes and said his conclusion was that they never showed any criminal intent on the part of Richard Nixon, then sealed those transcripts, ordered the tapes destroyed, and Richard Nixon would have remained president."

"Simon, you're a real genius. So few people in America, including lawyers, would have drawn that analogy. In the Watergate case against Richard Nixon, the federal District Court Judge Sirica ordered that the tapes be turned over to him for judicial review of whether they showed criminal activity by President Richard Nixon. If he'd been as corrupt as our judges, all he would have had to have done is written an order saying that he had reviewed the evidence and there was no criminal activity by Richard Nixon and he was sealing the transcript and ordering the tapes to be destroyed. That's what Judge Case has done in this case. One thing about it, Simon, before Forbes-Grundy's actions and Judge Case's rulings, I had tended to believe that Henrietta had forged the Chandler letter. But at this point, I don't doubt for one moment that that is in fact Armand Chandler's signature on his insurance company's letterhead. But I'm in a quandary, Simon. As you see, that order will find me in contempt if I discuss the contents. Fortuitously, I had distributed I don't know how many copies of the letter, having no idea that this order would follow. I don't want to be found in contempt. As one of my law professors once told me, If a superior court judge finds you in contempt of court, you're not getting out of jail any time soon, unless you have a real good friend on the North Carolina Supreme Court. So what's happening in that Charlotte Pendleton case? Reggie says they've got a black fellow they've already arrested."

"They got Jason Mackie. The word I have is he had a young white girlfriend and they had a fight. She was picked up with drugs, and as usual, they offered her a deal on the drug charge if she would say Jason killed the Pendleton girl. I've known Jason since he was fourteen. He's no model citizen, but he's not a murderer. The black community is upset. They know he's being railroaded. It might've been a black man killed that Pendleton girl, but it wasn't Jason. The black ministers are holding a rally tonight to back Jason. It's gonna be at 8 o'clock at Shilo up the street from here. I'm going to the meeting. Why don't you go with me?"

"Let me get to your house about 7:45 and we can ride over together."

"7:45 will give us plenty of time. The meeting probably won't really start 'til 8:30, so we can talk to a lot of our old friends before the meeting starts."

I left Simon's store with a good feeling. It would be good to get back into the civil rights movement on this grass roots level. My three years organizing for the NAACP in the late '60s had been the best years of my life. I knew that period of time had been a real turning point for America, and I'd really been a part of it. Since I was often the only white person at NAACP rallies, being asked to speak and was almost always made a panelist and given a place on the stage always honored me. Jesse Jackson had definitely touched a nerve, not only in the black community, but in the nation as a whole, when he had adopted his slogan, "I am somebody." I had met Jesse and most of the great civil rights leaders of the '60s. It was my greatest regret that I had never had the privilege of meeting Dr. King before he was murdered. I called Jean, hoping that she would go with Simon and me to the rally tonight.

"Jean, whatcha doin tonight?"

"Having sex with you, I hope."

Laughing, I said, "Before that, how 'bout we do something meaningful?"

"Meaningful? Hell, I mean to get laid. That has a whole lot of meaning."

"No, seriously. I really want that, but there'll be plenty of time. But I'm excited about getting together with a bunch of old friends and doing something."

"Whatcha got in mind?"

I had told Jean about how much my years organizing for the NAACP had meant to me, so I jumped right in, hoping I could get her interest, too. I told her, and she had agreed, how the interest of the poor black man and the poor white man were common, but the kind of people like the ones she and I were fighting in the Rains case had played the poor black man and the poor white man against each other, keeping them from coming together to work for their common good, as with the tobacco company union attempt of the '40s. Jean was no dummy by any means. She wasn't well educated, but she was really smart, and that's what I really liked about her, in addition to that beautiful body.

"Jean, have you been following that case of that newspaper girl who was raped and murdered?"

"I sure have. Everybody has. Even if you didn't want to follow it, if you read the newspaper, listen to the radio, or watch TV, you can't help but follow it. It's all that's on. They've already got that fellow convicted who they caught by the TV coverage. Did you see them show him walk'n' over to the jail?"

"No, I didn't. All my time and energy has gone into two things, first and most importantly, you."

Jean interrupted, "Aww, Michael, you just know how to sweet talk a lady."

"And the Rains case. What did they show on TV, Jean?"

"As he was comin' out of the jail house, they showed him chained to a whole bunch of other prisoners, and then they moved in to his face. The way they showed his face, channel 12 has a guilty verdict for that man already. Those eyes, those eyes. Nobody will forget seeing those eyes. Have you seen it, Michael?"

"No, I haven't."

"Just turn on your TV. They're showing it every hour. You'd think the Martians had landed, the way they're playing this. Just wait, tomorrow morning's paper will have that same picture. What was he going to do? I've been in jail and I've been led up to the courthouse. It's pretty hard to look pretty in jailhouse clothes and after two days without a shower."

I was delighted with Jean's reaction. Activism meant as much to me as a relationship, and to get both in one package was like getting gravy with my steak.

"A group of black ministers are holding a meeting in support of that fellow who's been picked up at 8 o'clock tonight at Shilo church. My friend the Sage and I are going. He's my best friend. I'd like for you to meet him. Would you go too?"

"Sure."

"Jean, I'll pick you up in fifteen minutes. We'll catch a bite, and then we'll run over and pick up the Sage. He's the guy I wanted you to meet."

"See you in fifteen."

We reached the Sage's house on 1st Street by 7:45.

"Jean, this is Simon 'the Sage' Epstein."

"Now, I understand where you've been disappearing to."

Simon and Jean talked non-stop from his house to Shilo. When we walked in the front of the church, everybody knew Simon. It was like a family reunion. I knew most everybody, but the folks I didn't know knew Simon and welcomed me and Jean since we were with Simon. The main speaker was one of my old friends. He was a black lawyer from Charlotte. The only other white person in the church besides the three of us was a lawyer from Greensboro with an excellent criminal-law background. We all talked and chatted about old times for about thirty minutes, and then the meeting began. My old friend, James Leary, a former Black Panther and the most respected activist in the city, introduced Spencer Bragg of the NAACP from Charlotte. Bragg was careful in his rhetoric, using terms such as "allege" and "we believe." James then took the microphone from Bragg and stirred the crowd with his usual rousing speech about the need to stop the oppression of people without power by the rich and powerful. I became lost listening to him and couldn't help but think how unfortunate that there were only four white people here. James's speech was not racial, it was not about the oppression of black people, but rather it was about the oppression of people without power. I dreamed that someday, as Dr. King had said, we would look at each other and not see color, but see that the struggle we were in was a struggle between those who had the gold and those who didn't. How could we ever bring more white people to see that it was their common interest to unite with people like James and see that he was not the enemy, but was our natural ally? James got to that point I knew he inevitably would: "Now, a legal defense fund don't come cheap. Dig into your pockets. This is the beginning of the Jason Mackie legal defense fund." James chanted, being as much the preacher as any of the ministers in this crowd of over two hundred. Buckets were passed on both sides of the aisle, and people including Simon and me contributed to getting the Jason Mackie defense fund on its way. At the end of the meeting, we all stood and sang the anthem of the NAACP, "We shall overcome." We were all excited. It was like the old great civil rights rallies and marches of the '60s. It was such a good feeling that we had come together to accomplish something good and we were going to spit in the eye of the power structure through the power of the people. How would we have felt if we had known then that it would be more than twenty years before Jason Mackie would begin to receive justice?

Chapter 29

The next morning, I walked into Reggie's office. He was in. "You got a minute?"

"Just a minute. I'm on my way to court. I have a million things to do. Don't you practice law anymore?"

"Well, yes, but last night, Jean, the Sage, and I went to a meeting where we formed the Jason Mackie Defense Committee. Spencer Bragg out of Charlotte spoke. Spencer is going to be lead council in Jason's defense with the backing of the NAACP. I've seen few cases in Winston-Salem where the community came together on a man's side to the extent I'm seeing it in this case."

"You mean the black community? What did you have, two hundred black people? And how many white people were there last night, Michael?"

"You're right, Reggie. There were only four white people: me, the Sage, Jean, and Spencer's co-council out of Greensboro are white. I'm gonna call some of my white minister friends, some ACLU people, and some of the anti-war activists to see if we can't make this defense look more bi-racial."

"Call, umm, some of the women's groups. I know they're on this anti-violence against women crusade, which both of us know is long overdue, but it will give them a lot more credibility if they stand up for the rights of an innocent man, even if it is a rape case. But have you thought about the possibility that this fellow's guilty? And all of you could end up with egg all over your faces if he is."

"Reggie, whether he's guilty or not, he's being railroaded. And I feel good about demanding that basic civil rights be upheld, even for the guilty. Can you imagine how fast the killer of Rains would be put away if the same powers pushing to put Jason Mackie away were pushing to put the killer of Rains away?"

"If that were so, there would already be a trial date for Rains's killer. But instead of working to put Rains's killer away, those same forces are working to prevent that prosecution. I've got to get to court," Reggie said as he stood up and started walking quickly toward his office door, leaving me in my seat. "You and Jean come on out to the millhouse at 7 tomorrow night. We'll talk about the Rains case and the music festival. Bye."

I went on over to the courthouse. I had some papers I needed to put in a file on the second floor. I saw my old friend, Racy Goins, a black female deputy who had been at the Jason Mackie meeting.

"Hey, Racy, how you doing?"

"I'm doing good, and I saw you were doing good the other night. How'd an ugly old fellow like you get a pretty little lady like that on his arm?"

"It's a long story, Racy. I met her through a cop."

"You reckon that might go any place, Michael?"

"I hope so. We've only known each other a couple of months. It's like we've known each other forever. She likes all my friends, and all my friends like her, especially Reggie Scott."

"Uh-Huh, you keep that pretty lady away from that little runt. He's a dog. First thing you know, he'll have her over at that millhouse, and they won't be mak'n' cornmeal."

"Aww, Racy, you know better than that. He's my friend."

"Yea, a friend. Pretty little things like her' are kinda rare. First thing you know, you'd be looking for a new friend and a new girlfriend."

Just then, a portly black lady about sixty years old tapped Racy on her shoulder.

Racy turned around. "Can I help you, ma'am?"

"My grandson is here on a child support, and that baby ain't even his. I need to find Mister Linstrom and help me get this straightened out."

"Mr. Linstrom, he the district attorney. He ain't gonna help you out in this."

"Yes he will, miss lady. I'm his maid, been his maid for ten years."

I couldn't help it. Opportunities like this don't come along every day.

"You're Mr. Linstrom's maid?"

"Yes sir, I be his maid for ten years now. You a lawyer?"

"Yes, ma'am."

"Then you know Mr. Linstrom too?"

"Yes, ma'am. Do you know Mrs. Handy?"

"You mean Miss Henrietta? Sure, I know her. She over in Mr. Linstrom's all the time. They like family."

"And you used to know Mrs. Henrietta's old boyfriend drove that big brown-on-brown 74 Coupe de Ville?"

"I didn't know him, but I saw his car over at Miss Henrietta's."

"Could I get your name and telephone number, ma'am?"

"You need some clean'n' done or sumthin like that?"

"Something like that."

She wrote her name and telephone number down.

Racy then said, "You go up to the fourth floor. His office is on the left after you get off the elevator."

After the woman left, I looked at Racy. "Racy, did you hear what she said?"

"I sure did."

"Racy, I guess…." She interrupted me.

"Yea, that woman used Linstrom's name to get somebody to kill her boyfriend."

"Racy, you busy tonight?"

"No, lets go talk to that lady."

Racy and I went to the maid's house that same night. We got there about 8. We were shown into her bedroom.

"I don't know nuthin 'bout no murder case."

"Nobody said you did," Racy said. "Won't you just talk to us for a minute?"

"I'm took sick to talk to anybody. I took sick right after I saw y'all up at that courthouse. My blood pressures just giv'n me a headache. They told me not to talk to you. Now, I got to have me some rest."

Racy whispered to me, "Lets go on."

After we stepped outside, I looked at Racy. "What do you think?"

"Linstrom's got himself in some deep shit."

Chapter 30

After Racy and I parted, I drove straight to Jean's. It was 11 o'clock, but she wasn't in bed yet.

"What're you doin' here this late?"

"I've become dependent upon you. Let's go get a beer and let me tell you what happened."

We drove a mile up the road to the Blue View Bar. Jean knew everybody in the bar and was given a happy welcome by everybody.

"Haven't seen you in a while, Jean," the barkeep said. "I thought you'd quit drink'n'."

"The day the earth quits turning is the day I'll quit drink'n'. This is my friend, Michael."

I said a polite hello but was anxious to get to a booth so Jean and I could talk. I couldn't believe how much I needed her support. I told her about the episode with the maid. I told her what Racy had said.

"You got more lady friends."

"Racy is engaged. Her and the chief deputy are supposed to get married in the next couple months. Come'on, what'd ya think about what happened?"

"I think you doubt yourself. Isn't everything pointing in one direction? Have you seen anything yet that hasn't pointed to a major cover-up, including the DA himself? Follow your instincts and follow the money, and I'll be with you every step of the way."

She had put me at ease as she always did. We talked and enjoyed each other's company until last call, and then I remembered to ask her if she was going to be able to go with me to Reggie's the next night.

Jean and I got to Reggie's about 7 the next evening. I brought a bottle of wine so we could mix business with pleasure. I felt guilty about the drinking problem Jean had told me she had, but I had learned that if we only had wine rather than beer, the little lady didn't drink as much. Reggie grabbed Jean, picking her up and hugging her.

"You ready to leave Michael for this old miller yet, Jean?"

Jean looked over toward me and said, "Not quite yet; he's still getting better. I've cleaned him up, and he takes really well to training."

We went into the kitchen and all three pulled up chairs so we could talk and look out the window at the waterwheel and waterfall.

"Michael, I've come to a conclusion. I've lost so much money, I can't really stand to lose anymore, and I just don't have the time to spend in the music festival business anymore."

This hit me like a ton of bricks. We'd been like Mickey Rooney and the "Our Gang Group" when we had been doing our music festival. The bonding as friends that we had done had been priceless, and I was extremely disappointed that Reggie wasn't going to be a part of the project for the bicentennial year. I didn't know if I could do it alone. Although it was a tremendous amount of fun, there had been decisions that Reggie had made that had made everything possible, such as sitting down with the sheriff to let him know just what we were up to with our festival so the natural suspicions he would have had had been allayed. It had also been Reggie's idea that we make contact with the local civic groups and help make possible their participation in our festival if they so chose. Reggie had also taken care of the insurance and permits for health and so on. I knew these things had all been done successfully before, and all I should have to do was to follow Reggie's example, but I still felt two heads were better than one.

"I'll understand, Reggie, if that's what you feel you have to do, but isn't there some way you'll reconsider?"

"No, that's my final decision. It's down to this: either drop out of the Rains case or get out of the music festival business, and I'd prefer we work on the Rains case together."

Jean could tell how devastated I was.

"I think y'all have something great started up there, and I'd hate to see it not continue."

"Michael told me the two of you went up there. It's one of the most beautiful places I've ever seen, and I've been all over the world. Now, let's get down to the Rains case. We have been notified by the court of appeals of our briefing schedule. I just got this in this afternoon. The court is going to give us oral argument two months from Monday. That's rare. It's usually an indication that the court considers the issue more important when they agree to oral argument. I think the real outcome in the court of appeals depends upon which three judge panel of judges we get. I do believe there are enough honest judges in the court of appeals that we could get a panel that would not be controlled out of Winston-Salem."

Reggie showed me an outline of the points he felt we should stress in our brief.

Reggie continued, "I think we should consider putting some pressure on for a criminal prosecution. The district attorney, for whatever reason, has asked me to ask you to come in and talk to him. Why don't you give him a call tomorrow morning and set up an appointment?"

"Michael, didn't you tell him?"

"Oh, crap, no. Reggie, Racy Goins and I ran into Linstrom's maid at the courthouse yesterday after you and I met in your office. The maid indicated Henrietta Handy is 'All the time over at Linstrom's house.' That, in itself, may not be all that much. Racy and I went to the maid's house last night. The maid was scared to death. She said they had told her not to talk to us. Racy's conclusion was the same as mine, that Linstrom's got himself in deep shit."

"He wants to see you for some reason. Go ahead and talk to him. It can't hurt."

Chapter 31

The next morning, I called and reached the district attorney's secretary. She was pleasant enough. She knew who I was and said that the district attorney had told her I might be calling and for her to set up an appointment as soon as possible for the DA and me to talk. As a matter of fact, she made it for that day at 2 o'clock.

The DA's secretary showed me back to his office. That he was very red-faced and angry was clear to me.

"Who the hell do you think you are?"

"Just a Forsyth County lawyer working on a murder case."

"I'll tell you what you're doing: you're interfering in the prosecution of a criminal case. And where do you get off using my name in the case?"

"Tod, I, Ahh, ran into your maid in the courthouse the other day, and she volunteered to tell me that Henrietta Handy was over at your house all the time."

"Henrietta Handy is a neighbor of mine. My campaign manager represents Henrietta Handy. And that's all there is to it. I'm telling you, I'm hearing from every corner in the county that you're asking about my connection to a murder case. You wouldn't believe how many people' told me that."

"Well, have you given an interview to the police?"

"That's none of your business. I'm gonna tell you one thing, I'm gonna tell you one time, I'm gonna tell it to you straight: you bring my name up one more time in connection with a murder case and I will see that you don't make another cent practicing law in Forsyth county. I am the District Attorney of Forsyth County. No one is prosecuted in Forsyth County unless I want'em prosecuted in Forsyth County. Got it? Anyone who is prosecuted in Forsyth County is prosecuted in Forsyth County because I want them prosecuted in Forsyth County. Now get out of my office."

Chapter 32

I left Linstrom's office shaken. Where do you go to get a murder case prosecuted when the DA won't prosecute? There was the Abner Stitt case that Linstrom had known about for nearly two years. No action had been taken in that one. Now there was the Rains murder and no prosecution. The DA's response was to threaten the lawyer in the civil case that if he continued with his investigation, he would be run out of town. I stopped by Reggie's office.

"How'd your meeting with Linstrom go?"

"Short and simple, Reggie. He said if I kept asking questions about him, he's gonna run me out of town. He vaguely threatened to prosecute me, I think. He threatened criminal prosecution against me for interference with an ongoing criminal investigation. It seems we need a special prosecutor here."

"We've needed a special prosecutor in this case since the day the Winston-Salem police department began it's investigation, and I don't know why we haven't had one appointed already. It's standard procedure when a local law enforcement officer, or a local lawyer, or member of the DA's staff becomes the subject of a criminal investigation, that a special prosecutor out of Raleigh is appointed. The purpose of this is to avoid obvious conflicts of interest in the prosecution of the criminal case. The evidence in this case has been, from the beginning, at the very least that the names of the sitting district attorney and his campaign manager were used to solicit for murder. Now, if that's not enough to get a special prosecutor in, I can't imagine what it would take."

"How do you usually get a special prosecutor in?"

"In any case I've ever heard of, the district attorney requests either the governor or the attorney general send a special prosecutor from the attorney general's office in Raleigh. Michael, you know people who work for the AG in Raleigh. Why don't you drive down there and have lunch with one of them and ask them how we can get a special prosecutor in this case?"

The next day, I called Bill Taylor, an assistant to the attorney general. We'd been in law school for three years together and I knew and trusted him. I told Bill about the special circumstances about the case and how there was a question concerning the Forsyth DA. I also told him how the Forsyth DA had threatened me. Bill told me to put together an affidavit of the evidence, as I believed it to be to this point and to include the conversation where the DA had threatened to destroy my law practice. I sent the affidavit down, and within a week, Bill and I were sitting in the office of the Attorney General of the state of North Carolina.

"You and Bill went to law school together, Bill tells me."

"Yes, sir, that's correct. Three hard years together. Three years in central prison would have been easier, right Bill?

"Much easier," Bill said.

We all laughed.

"Oh, by the way, Michael, I'm Leon," the attorney general said. "No need of any of that sir and stuff like that; we're just all regular folks sittin' in this office here. I've read this affidavit you've put together. I think it's incredible a special prosecutor has not been appointed to this point in this case. I can assure you, by the time you get back to Winston-Salem, there will be a special prosecutor out of Raleigh, not Forsyth County, handling the murder case of Harold Stennis Rains."

"Thank you, sir."

"I told you, it's Leon, not sir, and I ain't gonna shake your hand until you make it clear to me."

"Thank you, Leon." We shook hands. "Thank you, Bill." Bill and I shook hands.

I was ecstatic as I headed back to Winston-Salem. My work had finally produced something positive in the case, and although there may never be a conviction anyway, at least now it appeared something was going to be done about the murder of Big Head Rains. After fighting all of the Raleigh traffic, it was well after 11 o'clock before I got home. I had a call from Jean. Of course, I had planned to call her to tell her the good news. I also had a call from Reggie. He said to look in my mailbox; he had gotten a copy of the evening paper and knew I'd want to see it before I wanted to talk to anybody. His message said he'd left a copy of the evening paper there. I couldn't imagine what he could be talking about. I ran out my door to the mailbox, grabbed the newspaper, and ran back inside. There it was on the front page. The Rains case was on the front page again. "Governor David Cox appoints special prosecutor in murder of Harold Stennis Rains at request of District Attorney Tod Linstrom."

Chapter 33

I called Reggie and Jean before I went to bed about the trip to Raleigh. Of course, both of them knew the truth and saw that we were just being screwed again. It was so late, I told Jean I was tired and asked if we could spend the next evening together.

The next morning, I parked my car as usual. As I walked by the Sage's store he came out smiling that big toothy grin-that was the Sage when he had something on somebody.

"They trumped you again, Michael."

"Yea, they did it again," I said, not even trying to hide the dejection in my voice.

"You've got no reason to hurry. Come on in here and let me tell you about how the Democratic Party works. Do you know who the special prosecutor is?"

"No, Simon, I don't."

He held up the paper. "He's Larry Franklin. He's listed right here on the front page. He's a Democratic hack. During the '50s when they were having all those investigations in Washington of the Klan activity, it was Larry who helped the Democratic Party Klansmen. You see, Michael, at the end of Reconstruction in the 1870s, the Democrats seized power again in the South from the Republican carpetbaggers, scalawags, and blacks. The experience that the wealthy Southern genteel population had experienced with blacks in elected positions had left the Democrats determined that no blacks would ever hold public office again in North Carolina. The Democratic Party used the Klan as its primary instrument to hold the blacks in check, and this was true up to and including the administration of Franklin Roosevelt. However, the leadership of the Democratic Party always kept their distance by using lackeys like Larry as their go-between, between the official party and the Klansmen who would knock heads."

"Simon, I detect an anti-Klan bias in the way you talk of the Klan."

"Michael, you don't seem to understand, and really I guess most Southerners are the same way. The Klan was as anti-Semitic as it was anti-black, and my personal memories of that are vivid. My own dad was run out of Mount Airy, North Carolina, by the Klan up there, and that had nothing to do with politics: it was pure anti-Semitism. Believe me, I've known what it is to be called a 'Christ killing Jew' by a Klansman. Anyway, by the 1950s, the Democratic Party had to totally divest itself of its Klan connections. They saw the writing on the wall that they couldn't continue to exist as the racist party they had been, and that left Larry Franklin out in the cold. But Larry had been a loyal Democrat and had served the party well, so they came to his rescue. They gave him a new job with a real title. His title was special prosecutor, and his job was to fix it when a Democratic sheriff, district attorney, or other high up got in trouble. Larry would ride into town on his white horse. He would proclaim that he was going to clean everything up and then proceed to fix it up so the party wouldn't suffer. The newspaper, and nowadays radio and TV, report to the people that a clean up is being done out of Raleigh, when the fact is it is a whitewash coming from Raleigh. Also, Larry always works with a fix-it judge. That would be Superior Court Judge Horrace C. Linney. They say Mr. Fix-it, Horrace C. Linney, has never seen a plea bargain, or, as the folks call it, a 'flea bargain' that he didn't like. Michael, you got screwed again. You can't beat these people."

"Simon, you talk in such a negative way about the Klan and yet you are friends with and have so much respect for Paul Winfrey, the leader of the Wallace group."

"That's a different situation, Michael. George Wallace was certainly no saint, but in many ways, he was all working-class America had left until he got shot. Do you know how George Wallace came to be known and first came to power?"

"I do remember my administrative law professor from North Carolina Central talking about an administrative law case where the civil rights commission was issuing its own subpoenas to government officials and former government officials in Alabama during the '60s under Lyndon Johnson. My professor said those subpoenas were so broad that they were no less than fishing expeditions by the civil rights commission to dig up anything and everything to show violations of people's rights, in particular those of blacks, by government officials in Alabama. As I recall, George Wallace was a superior court judge in Alabama and issued an injunction blocking these fishing expeditions by the civil rights commission as being unlawful search and seizure protected under the American Constitution."

"That's right, and when the case was appealed by the Civil Rights Commission to the U.S. Supreme Court, the majority of the U.S. Supreme Court ruled to overturn George Wallace's injunction. They thus legitimized these administrative fishing expeditions. Their reasoning was these were administrative actions, not punitive in nature, and any disclosures by these searches were not intended to deprive anyone of life or liberty."

"That's right, Simon, and Justice Hugo Black wrote a strong dissenting opinion in the case calling it a pyrrhic victory for the left. In other words, Hugo Black was saying another victory for civil rights such as this, and civil rights are undone. Justice Black pointed out that although all of the majority, and he himself, felt the intent of the Civil Rights Commission in issuing these subpoenas for these blanket searches of records was good, they should consider what could happen if an administrative agency not so benevolent as the civil rights commission should have the same power to issue administrative subpoenas."

"As a Jew, this sort of thing is especially frightening to me. It's the sort of thing that creeps in and takes your freedom away. Suppose the United States should someday be attacked on it's own soil and the president created a huge bureaucracy to ferret out internal terrorists. That decision would justify their actions to search and seize at will just about anybody or anything, as long as they claimed it was in the interest of national security. And that was Judge Hugo Black, whom you and I both consider to be the greatest protector of the American constitution who ever lived. And Justice Black was affirming a ruling of George Wallace."

Simon went on to say George Wallace and the Wallace people were different. The working man in America no longer had a friend in the Democratic Party. It was like the Democratic Party was now treating the working man in America the way they used to treat the black man. The Democratic Party treated the working man in America as though they could take his vote for granted because he had no place to go. After all, what did the Republican Party offer the working man? Jessie Helms, with the help of the old Wallace coalition had surprised everyone and won a senate seat in 72. But what could Jessie Helms do, or better still, what would Jessie Helms do for the mill hand and tobacco workers of North Carolina other than promise them he wouldn't take their tax money and pay welfare checks out of it? On the other hand, Wallace had promised trade barriers to protect the jobs of the working man. People had wondered how George Wallace had won in the steel-belt state of Michigan. Of course, racism had played a role in it, but those autoworkers in Detroit believed that Wallace would protect them from the Japanese and German imports, and he would have.

Chapter 34

I knew that the Adam McGee probable cause hearing had to be coming up soon, so I called the clerk of court to see if she had placed it on the district court calendar. She had, and it was only three days away.

I called Jean.

"Jean, do you know if Angie Snow is out of the hospital yet?"

"I'll make a few calls and call you right back."

Jean called back in a few minutes.

"Angie and Adam are living in an old trailer close to me out here in Lewisville."

"Can you…."

Jean interrupted me. "I've already taken care of it. Pick me up and we'll ride on out there."

As Jean and I rode out to Adam's, I tried to stress to her that I needed to talk to Angie without Adam around if possible.

"That will be impossible, Michael. That's why you got me. You want to ask Angie without Adam there who was driving that car. Just you and Adam step out into the yard to check your oil or whatever and I'll talk to Angie. What would you do without me?"

"I don't know, Jean. Sometimes I think I just ought to let you do everything and get out of your way."

"Now, you do alotta things right," Jean said as we pulled up into the dirt driveway of the old shack of a trailer.

Adam was doing something with the gas bottles on the front of the trailer when we drove up. He was already letting his hair grow and apparently intended for it to grow long. I had heard he normally wore it in a ponytail before the accident. Jean ran up and hugged Adam, and he picked her up off the ground and swung her around.

"Angie inside? We need to talk to her."

"What's this 'we' shit?" Adam asked.

"I'm becoming his legal assistant. He can't do nuthin without me."

It wasn't noon yet, and Adam already had a Budweiser in his hand. We went into the trailer and I met Angie for the first time. I guess you could say she was a larger version of Jean. Angie was probably 5' 8" or so, which made her about a half a foot shorter than Adam.

"Hey, girl, I heard you had you a man. Is this him?"

"Yea, this is him. He's a project. I try to keep him cleaned up so I can take him places. It ain't easy, but you know I try."

We sat down. As usual, I listened to Adam, Angie, and Jean talk about old times and the fun they'd had. After an hour or so, we got down to business.

"Adam, it looks like Hairston's trying to frame you."

Adam stood up. "That nigger don't know who he's fuckin' with. I've been shot five times, and it didn't even hurt me. Had my Goddamned neck broke, and you can see right here I ain't got no mother fuckin' problem with my neck," Adam said as he twisted his neck back and forth. "That motherfucker don't know who he's fuckin' with."

"Your probable-cause hearing will be in three days."

"I know that. I got the Goddamned subpoena right here," Adam said as he reached over and picked up a yellow paper and handed it to me. "That nigger cop brought a subpoena for Angie, too. Here it is."

Angie interrupted. "I don't know what they want me for. All I can say is Cindy was drivin' the car when we came to the stop sign and I was yellin' at her to stop but she was goin so fast, ain't know way she could stop. That's all I remember, and they told me I was unconscious for nearly three weeks."

"Angie, you…."

Angie interrupted again. "Yea, I know, everybody's told me that that nigger cop says I told him two times Adam was drivin the car. How could I've said that? I couldn't even say nuthin."

"Adam, you know anything about tires? That Coupe de Ville I've got is making a roaring sound. I hope it's not the transmission and it's just the way the tires sound when they start to wear down. Would you mind help'n' me take a look?"

Adam got up from his seat. We started out the door.

"I've replaced transmissions in Buicks and Chevy's before, and I guess a Cadillac would be about the same." As Adam bent down to look at my rear tires, he said, "Jerry told me you had this car. He said he thought it was strange you had one like this."

Adam and I were playing cat and mouse now.

"Jerry said Jean and one of them strippers put on a show at that titty bar down at Myrtle where he works."

I considered whether to go ahead and ask Adam about the murder and what his brother, Jerry McGee, had told him about the murder of Big Head Rains, but I held myself back, knowing that Jean could and would do a much better job of digging out this information than I would. Adam didn't say anything else about Jerry, and he didn't mention the murder of Big Head. He told me the tires looked like they probably would be making a roar, and unless it got real loud, I shouldn't bother to do anything.

Jean and I excused ourselves, telling Adam and Angie we were hungry and since we hadn't had breakfast, we needed to go have lunch.

"Angie said a lot," Jean began as we sat at the greasy spoon where we had first talked. "She wouldn't quit talking. She said Cindy was driving the car, but I'm like you, I think the three of them might've been so drunk that I'm not sure either of the three could've told you who was driving the car, even if Cindy had lived. Angie will testify for Adam at the hearing. She's really looking forward to it. And, best of all, Michael, she told me that Jerry had been up last week and woke up in the middle of the night with a nightmare, and they all three got up at three in the morning and Jerry sat there crying as he described how him and Joe had killed Big Head Rains. Jerry said that Henrietta had shown a copy of that insurance policy to James Crow and had also shown James something from the DA's office. Here's the kicker, Michael: James is waitin' to go to prison and he's out on appeal right now. Henrietta told

James that Linstrom would keep him from going to prison if James would help her. She said that James, or whoever helped kill Big Head, would never be prosecuted for the murder, that Linstrom would see to that. Henrietta said that she would give James fifty thousand dollars out of that life insurance policy if he would help get Big Head killed. Angie said that Jerry was crying so hard, he couldn't even talk. Jerry said that him and Joe walked into James Crow's bedroom and there was Big Head sittin on the edge of the bed wearing his under shorts and a pair of socks, and Darlene was laying naked on her back. He said Darlene jumped up and ran right in front of Joe's 38, the same kind that I've got. Angie said Jerry said that Big Head got on his knees and put his hands together praying, 'Please, God, help me. Joe, I'll do anything. Please don't kill me.' Jerry said that Big Head was crying like a baby when Joe raised that gun and shot him. Jerry said that Big Head had held his hand right over the barrel of the gun as it went off with the first shot. Jerry said that Big Head fell over with his eyes open after that first shot, and he figured that first shot killed him. Jerry said Joe shot him two more times to make sure he was dead. Angie said Jerry's been having nightmares and can't sleep since he and Joe killed Big Head. She also said it scared the shit outta Jerry when me and you talked to him down at that titty bar and that he come close to going ahead and spilling his guts to you and me the way he did to her and Adam the other night. Angie said Jerry needs to tell somebody what he's done, and if he could work out a plea bargain, he'd turn on Joe. Joe's already threatened to kill him if he turns on him."

"Jean, you never cease to amaze me. I think you could've talked to Adolph Hitler and gotten him to admit he'd been a bad boy. But you know what? If we can't get anybody to prosecute the case, no matter how much evidence you and me get together, nobody's gonna be convicted."

"Michael, why don't you and Reggie prosecute the case?"

"Linstrom made it clear in that meeting we had he specifically told me he wasn't about to let me and Reggie prosecute the case. And he emphasized anybody who is prosecuted in Forsyth County is prosecuted because he wants them prosecuted and anybody who is not prosecuted is not prosecuted because he does not want them prosecuted, and that's the law."

The probable-cause hearing was called in district court three days later. I looked over and Tod Linstrom, the district attorney himself, had taken the seat of the assistant DA who had been there just a few moments before. This was unheard of in district court in Forsyth County. As a matter of fact, Linstrom motioned for the assistant prosecutor to go ahead and leave the room. This, in itself, was a slight to the assistant prosecutor. Our procedure was for one or two assistant prosecutors to become familiar with probable-cause hearings in felony cases and for the more experienced district attorneys to work exclusively in the higher court, which was superior court. The sole purpose of a probable-cause hearing is to determine if there probably is enough evidence to bind the defendant over for jury trial in superior court. Democratic District Court Judge Redd Hill began.

"This is the case of the State of North Carolina vs. Adam McGee."

Linstrom took it from there. Linstrom didn't look my way. He and Judge Hill looked intently at each other.

"Mr. Adam McGee, you are charged with two counts of death by motor vehicle resulting in the manslaughter of two separate human beings. How do you plead?"

"My client enters a plea of not guilty to both charges, your honor," I said on behalf of Adam.

"Mr. Spears, I want to hear your client enter a plea," Linstrom said.

"Your honor, I...."

Judge Hill interrupted me. "Mr. Spears, Mr. Linstrom and I have discussed this case. I agree with Mr. Linstrom. Have your client enter a plea."

Oh shit. The judge tells me in open court, as usual, everything has already been decided without me or my client being able to say a thing. I looked at Adam and whispered to him, "Go ahead, Adam, say not guilty."

"Not guilty."

Clearly Judge Hill and Linstrom were doing everything they could to humiliate and degrade me in front of my client and thus destroy whatever confidence my client might have in me.

"The State of North Carolina calls to the stand at this time Angie Snow."

Again, I thought, what do these two have up their sleeve this time? At a probable cause hearing, normally the cop can simply testify, and if there's enough evidence he's gathered, even though it may be hearsay evidence, to show that the defendant probably committed the crime, then the defendant will be bound over to superior court. Again, I noticed Linstrom didn't so much as glance at me. He and Judge Hill had their eyes locked on each other.

Linstrom began, "State your name and address for the record, please, ma'am."

Angie gave the address of the trailer where she and Adam were living.

"Mrs. Snow, did you have occasion to be involved in an auto accident where in both you and the defendant were both injured?"

"Objection, your honor, the question pre-supposes so many things, and it is in fact a leading question," I objected.

"Overruled, Mr. Spears. This is a probable-cause hearing. Mrs. Snow, you go ahead and answer that question."

Angie began to answer. "Well, I don't know how to answer that question. Me and Adam was in a wreck."

"Mrs. Snow, you gave two separate statements to Officer Hairston here, didn't you?" Linstrom questioned.

"I didn't say anything to him."

Linstrom interrupted. "Officer Hairston, would you stand up, please?" he ordered. "Mrs. Snow, do you deny ever seeing this Winston-Salem police officer before this day?"

Angie answered, "No, sir, I don't deny ever seeing him before. I saw him last week when he brought me the subpoena."

"Mrs. Snow, I'm gonna remind you, although I shouldn't have to, that you are under oath."

"Objection, your honor, there is no need for the district attorney to intimidate and harass the witness."

"Mr. Spears, I'm gonna overrule that objection. Mrs. Snow, you are under oath, this is a court of law, you are under penalty of perjury, and you must tell the truth, the whole truth, and nothing but the truth."

Now the judge is clearly attempting to aid in the prosecution. Thankfully, I had called my friend, Dustin, the court reporter, and he was taking down every word that was being spoken in this kangaroo courtroom.

Angie began again. "Your honor, I am telling the truth. That wreck knocked me out cold. I was in a coma for three weeks. How could I have made a statement to Officer Hairston? Officer Hairston tried to get me to say Adam was drivin' the car when he came out and brought this subpoena, but I wouldn't talk to him, and I told him I wadn't gonna talk to him."

"Objection, your honor. The witness is not being responsive to the question. I ask that her last comment be stricken from the record."

"Your honor...."

"Mr. Spears, I don't need to hear from you. I'm going to sustain Mr. Linstrom's objection and instruct the court reporter to strike from the record the last comment by Mrs. Snow."

My friend, Dustin, the court reporter, looked over his glasses at me and curled his lip. Neither he nor I had experienced until we got into this Rains case anything to compare to what we were seeing now.

Linstrom began again. "Mrs. Snow, I'm going to ask you point blank, and I expect a truthful answer, was not Adam McGee driving the car at the time of the accident?"

"Your honor, I have to object. The state called this witness. She has not been declared a hostile witness, and the state may not use this intimidating means of questioning."

"Mr. Spears, from what I've heard so far, I'm going to make the motion to declare Mrs. Snow a hostile witness."

Again, I was faced with that strange question: when the judge himself makes a motion, what does the defense attorney say then? "Sustained"?

"Answer the question, Mrs. Snow."

"No, Adam was not driving the car. Cindy was driving the car when it wrecked."

"The State of North Carolina calls Officer Hairston."

Without having the common decency and respect to ask Angie to come down from the stand, or even to give me an opportunity to question her, Linstrom was now calling the police officer to the stand. I knew full well that I could object, but I didn't see that it would serve any useful purpose, so I acquiesced. As Angie was coming down from the stand, it being clear to her that she hadn't said what Linstrom wanted her to say, Judge Hill ordered, "Mrs. Snow, you stay in the courtroom right now."

Officer Hairston took the stand, and after stating his name and that he was a Winston-Salem police officer on the force for over ten years, Linstrom began the substantive questions.

"Officer Hairston, did you have occasion to investigate the automobile wreck in question here?"

"I suppose you're talking about the accident that you were questioning Mrs. Snow about?"

"That's correct, Officer Hairston. Officer Hairston, you were present and heard the testimony thus far in this case, did you not?"

"I was and I did hear the testimony."

"Officer Hairston, would you recount for his honor what occurred at that scene?"

"When I arrived on the scene, there were two victims who obviously were deceased. I found Adam McGee."

"Would you point out Mr. McGee to the Court?"

"He's that white male sitting beside Attorney Spears."

"Go on, Officer Hairston."

"I determined that Mr. McGee had run the stop sign and had broad sided the car of one of the deceased. I attempted to question Mr. McGee, who was clearly too drunk to talk to me, and then I began to question Angie Snow. She gave me a statement at the scene that Adam McGee was driving the white Ford that had caused the accident. Approximately 45 minutes later at Forsyth County Hospital, Angie Snow repeated her statement that Adam McGee was driving the car that ran the stop sign and thus resulted in the deaths of two women."

"Your witness, Mr. Spears."

I was satisfied that with this transcript that Dustin was producing for me and the statements of the Forsyth County medical examiner and my nurse friend from high school, I could discredit Hairston in the future. I saw no need to produce a record with any further perjury on Hairston's part. I thus spoke, "No questions, your honor."

Judge Hill let me argue first, and I argued, of course, that the state's witness, Angie Snow, had said my client was not driving. Linstrom didn't even bother to argue. He and Judge Hill had worked it out before we had got to Court anyway, so why take any more time? Judge Hill bound Adam over for trial in superior court and left him with the bond he was already on.

Adam and I stood up and started to leave, and Judge Hill sounded out, "Madam Bailiff [The bailiff had been my friend, Racy Goins], take Mrs. Snow into custody. I'm issuing three bench warrants on her: two counts of perjury, and there may be more when I look at the record, and a warrant for cohabitation with one Adam McGee, which, of course, is still a crime in this state."

I looked at Linstrom. He was grinning ear to ear. I looked at my friend, the court reporter, and he was shaking his head. I believed they'd gone too far this time and determined to continue my fight.

Chapter 35

Linstrom put the Angie Snow perjury case on fast track. He had the common sense to dismiss the cohabitation charge, which Judge Hill had so piously created against Angie. Any DA who would have used superior court jury time in a cohabitation case would have become the laughing stock of the county and state in 1975 or 1976, and Linstrom was smart enough to know that. For him to have tried the cohabitation charge would have drawn unwanted attention to the case from areas of the state that the tobacco company might not control and would have jeopardized the cover-up of the bigger and more important murder case. It was absolutely clear to me by now what was happening and why it was happening. The tobacco company heirs who had created and owned this locally based insurance company didn't want the fact that they had allowed Henrietta Handy to draw them into an actual contract murder to be made public. The contract murder of Big Head Rains had the potential, if not the probability, of destroying this nearly one-billion-dollar in asset Insurance Corporation. If Reggie and I were able to succeed in exposing the culpability by the insurance company publicly, it would surely destroy the company's reputation, whether Reggie and I were able to recover one dollar for Linda and Harry or ten million dollars for the two children. I couldn't remember who had said it or where I had heard it, but I could not get out of my mind that old saying, 'Oh, what tangled webs we weave when first we practice to deceive.' What had first started out as a refusal to cancel the life policy on Abner Stitt had grown in its web to the point where the insurance company had to win, no matter what.

Linstrom's strategy was clear here. He was going to pressure Angie with a perjury charge, which he would offer to dismiss if she would give the evidence Linstrom wanted to put Adam away. And once Linstrom had put Adam away, he would have discredited me in my opportunity to bargain with Adam for his brother's cooperation for evidence and the Rains case would be gone. On this one, I was not going to allow Linstrom and his backers to beat me.

I referred Angie to the man I considered to be the best criminal defense trial lawyer I had ever seen. This was Xeno Price.

"Michael, this is Xeno. Angie Snow has come to me with one of the most incredible stories I've ever heard as a lawyer. Now, you and I both have heard every defense in the book offered, and we both know that every drunk driver claims to have had two beers when it was more like two fifths of liquor. Angie says Redd Hill issued a bench warrant for her when she testified truthfully in behalf of your client who was charged with vehicular manslaughter."

"That's right in a sense, Xeno. She did testify for my client, but she was the state's witness at a probable-cause hearing in district court. I hadn't called her as a witness. Here's the situation, Xeno: two people were killed in this wreck. One was Adam McGee's sister. The other was a black nurse on her way home from a job at the nursing home after midnight. Officer Hairston was the first police officer to get to the scene of the accident. He recognized Adam McGee, who has a reputation among every cop as a real thug. Hairston determined that Adam's car caused the accident, which in my opinion is correct. Then Hairston went on to determine that Adam was driving it and went about proving the fact that Adam was driving the car that killed the two people. Now, Hairston wrote in his report and testified in district court that your client, Angie Snow, told Hairston at the scene of the accident that Adam was driving the car, and Hairston went on to say that Angie repeated the statement that Adam was driving the car approximately 45 minutes later at Forsyth County Hospital. Now, Xeno, you know Patrick Sparks, the medical examiner?"

"I sure do. He's a fine man. I've worked with him many times. He's an auxiliary officer with the police department."

"Xeno, Sparks tells me that he was the first on the scene with the rescue squad and he was the first person to see Angie Snow lying exactly where she was after she'd been thrown out of the car. Sparks says Angie's windpipe was blocked, Angie was comatose, and he performed a tracheotomy at the scene without anesthetics. He says he didn't need anesthetics because she was in a coma. Sparks says he then went to Forsyth County Hospital, where Angie was on life support and drugged so she could not come out of her coma. I've also got an old high-school friend who treated Angie at the hospital that night. She actually referred me to Dr. Sparks."

"What does Sparks say about Hairston's statement?"

"Both Sparks and my nurse friend say Hairston is lying, and I've talked to Sparks since Hairston's district court testimony and Stringer says it's perjury by Hairston. He doesn't equivocate. I've got a transcript of the district court hearing, and I've got the statements from Stringer and my nurse friend."

"Well, now, we all know that cops do lie, but this is a big one, and what's the possible motive?"

"I know it's gonna sound crazy, but you know I'm representing the children of Big Head Rains. This fellow Adam McGee has the potential of blowing this Rains case wide open for me, but for whatever reason, Linstrom and company are in the process of covering it up."

"I've heard much of the same circulating around town."

"If the DA's office can pressure your client into giving a false statement to convict Adam McGee in this vehicular homicide case, they can discredit me and stand a good chance of preventing me from getting anywhere in the Rains case."

"What can I do for you, Michael?"

"Don't let anybody in the DA's office, or detectives, or anybody, for that matter, talk to your client, and don't plea bargain this perjury charge away. She's not guilty."

"This is a wild one. I'll help you as much as I can. Good luck with the Rains case."

Although Angie's case was on fast track, Adam's case came up for trial on a Monday before Angie's case. I had no way of knowing whether the case would actually be tried that week or not, but I was prepared to make a fool out of the DA this time. The DA has full control over the trial-court calendar and makes it up and schedules cases to be tried as he sees fit. The criminal trial court clerk simply places the cases on a calendar and in the order the district attorney directs her to. Although there were older cases that chronologically should have had higher priority than Adam's case, we were number two on the calendar.

I had subpoenaed my old high-school friend, Stevie, to be present for the Monday afternoon session, but had put Dr. Sparks on standby. I was confident that no Forsyth County judge could, or would, manhandle Dr. Sparks, the Forsyth County medical examiner, the way they were manhandling me and Reggie. Both of these witnesses were willing and able to testify. My client, Adam McGee, was extremely nervous. Although he and I both knew that with a conviction for both women's deaths, he would never be out of prison again in his life, I somehow expected to see that raging bull of a man that I was coming to know as Adam.

My old friend, Stevie, was excited about the case. She had shown her boss her subpoena and managed to get the entire week off with pay for her court appearance. Stevie actually showed up in the antechamber outside the courtroom and was waiting for me in the morning well before I got to the courthouse.

"Hey, Stevie, you didn't have to be here 'til 2 o'clock."

"I was so excited, I couldn't sleep last night. I've never been a witness in a case, much less a murder case."

"Stevie, this isn't a murder case; it's a manslaughter case," I said, laughing.

"Who's that short little man over there?" Stevie asked, pointing out Tony Southern, Linstrom's chief assistant, as Southern crossed the antechamber, passing back into the district attorney's office. I told her that was Tony Southern, Linstrom's chief assistant.

"The last time he passed by me, he was holding a file and stopped to look at me before going back where he is now."

"I wonder if he didn't look at the subpoena that I had issued for you and get somebody to check you out before trial."

Southern had clearly seen Stevie and me talking. Just then, Southern came back out of the DA's office, walked straight up to Stevie, and, as if I wasn't even there, said in his Billygoat gruff sort of way, "Miss, who are you and what are you doing here?"

Stevie sort of stuttered and then answered, "Michael subpoenaed me to be in a case here."

"Mr. Spears subpoenaed you to be here in the Adam McGee manslaughter case?" he questioned.

"Yes, sir," Stevie answered.

"Come back here to my office," Southern ordered Stevie.

Stevie obeyed Southern's command. In about thirty minutes, she came back out.

"Mr. Southern said I was free to go, Michael."

"What the hell, Stevie? You're my witness. It was my subpoena. I need you for Adam's case."

"Mr. Southern said he's not gonna try the case today."

"I guess with that, you might as well go on. I really do appreciate you being here. Before you go, Stevie, what did you and Southern talk about?"

"I just told him what I'd told you about Angie and that I'd talked to Patrick Sparks about it too, and he told me to go home."

"Stevie, thanks again for coming. I'll go talk to Southern myself."

I was mad as hell and really pissed off how they were jerking me around. I barged into Southern's office.

"What the hell is going on here?" I shouted.

Southern walked up and got right in my face and said, "I've dismissed all charges against Adam McGee, now get the hell out of my office."

"Southern, what about Hairston's testimony?"

"What about Hairston's testimony?" Southern said.

"Have you read the transcript of the probable-cause hearing?"

"I've read it," Southern said.

"It's perjury. Hairston lied under oath, Southern."

"I don't see any perjury," Southern said, looking straight at me.

I couldn't wait to tell Jean. I left the courthouse absolutely elated. I had needed a victory, and finally I had one.

"Jean, they dismissed everything against Adam. Let's celebrate tonight."

"How 'bout you get some steaks and we celebrate at your house? Come and get me right now. I can't wait to see you."

When I got to Jean's house, she came running out of the house, jumping up and down. She had needed this win as much as I did. She had a little overnight bag with her. I asked her if she happened to have a little maid's outfit in there.

"I might," she said. "Hey, do me a favor. When we stop for those steaks, get some Budweiser to go with it. You know those are my taste, and I need the celebration too.

On the way to my house, I asked her, "Jean, you don't think Adam'll let us down now, do you?"

"Hell no, he won't let us down," she answered. "I'll see to that."

When we got to the house, I had one more important thing to ask her. "Jean, since Reggie is out of the music festival, would you be my partner in that?"

"I thought that was settled already," she said.

We enjoyed each other way into the early morning hours, and it was noon before I was able to get back into the office.

Chapter 36

Jean and I worked hard for the next two winter months preparing for our summer music festival. She had grown up a fan of bluegrass music and thoroughly enjoyed the job I assigned her of lining up the talent. She made calls to bluegrass artists all over the country, and actually as far away as Japan and Scotland. It was sort of like she had never really had a direction before, or maybe she had never cared to have a direction before, and I valued her help so much and told her so. We spent many weekends traveling to the mountains to the festival site located on my farm. We stayed in close contact with Adam and Angie. Both of us wondered why Angie put up with all the beatings that she took from Adam.

In early January, Reggie and I received notice of the schedule date for our hearing on the Chandler letter, or "the document" as the court had named it. We were scheduled for late February. The court was granting oral argument, which encouraged Reggie and me. The court of appeals only grants oral argument in about a third of the cases they hear, and when they grant oral argument, it usually means that at least one of the panel of judges is seriously concerned about doing justice in the case. Two out of three cases that are appealed to the North Carolina Court of Appeals are only considered by the court of appeals on written brief.

A few days after Tony Southern dismissed all the charges against Adam, Xeno Price had called me to thank me for my help in Angie Snow's case. Like Adam's case, Tony Southern dismissed all charges against Angie Snow without comment. When Xeno called, I had asked him if he didn't think Hairston should have been charged, and Xeno gave me an answer that really shouldn't have surprised me.

"Michael, I represented Angie Snow, and, with your help, all charges against her have been dismissed. I don't represent Officer Hairston. That's not my business, and it's not my problem."

I thought when Xeno gave me that answer that in a way it must be nice to simply dismiss injustice out of hand. Most lawyers do this without ever really giving it any thought. In a way, I envied them that they were not forced by their conscience to spend time and energy on every injustice they saw in society. Sometimes I wished I could be that way.

When our court of appeals hearing date came near, I asked Reggie if he minded if Jean went down with us.

"If we win, I want to celebrate with her, Reggie. If we lose, she'll be there to give me support."

Reggie laughed. "You really have it bad, don't you? Sure, it'll be all right for her to go with us."

The weather forecast was for possible snow and ice, so the three of us drove down to Raleigh the night before the hearing. On the way down, Reggie broke some bad news to me. The senior judge on our three-judge panel was Cletus Freedman from Winston-Salem. Judge Freedman had been a bagman for the Democratic Party, and the Sage had told me that at one point the tobacco company executives had gotten together fifty thousand dollars. The Sage said attorney, now judge, Cletus Freedman had carried that fifty thousand dollars to a black alderman as a bribe not to run for mayor of the city of Winston-Salem. The Sage said the alderman had refused the money and had run for mayor.

It was a three-hour drive from Winston-Salem to Raleigh, and we had plenty of time to talk. I was driving and for the most part wrapped up in my thoughts and listening to Reggie and Jean talking. When Reggie had described Judge Freedman as a bagman for the Democratic Party and an Uncle Tom to his own people, it had piqued Jean's curiosity.

"How does anybody get to be a judge?" she asked Reggie.

Reggie began by telling her all judges, other than magistrates who hear small claims cases and issue some search warrants, arrest warrants, and the like, must be elected by the voters in general elections.

"In theory, at least, the people elect the judges. But the reality is judges are hand picked by the people who control the Democratic Party. If you are a loyal Democrat and work hard for the party without question beginning in high school, and then as a young Democrat in college and law school, you earn points with the Democratic Party for qualifying as a judge some day."

"Sounds like the young pioneers in communist Russia and the Hitler youth of Nazi Germany," I said.

"There are definite similarities to the young pioneers of communist Russia and the Hitler youth of Nazi Germany in the way the Democratic Party runs this state. Although most people wouldn't begin to admit it, the biggest difference between the young pioneers of communist Russia or the Hitler youth of Nazi Germany is that the Democratic Party has controlled the judges of North Carolina longer than both of those other two groups combined controlled their countries. Anyway, if you have served the Democratic Party well, by the time you get out of law school, the connections you've made through that service will get you a job as an assistant district attorney.

"Now, when a sitting judge decides to retire, the Democratic Party expects him to notify his party chairman that he's going to retire. And it's also expected that he retire leaving around two years of his term so that a new Democrat can be appointed to replace the retiring judge and will have at least one year to spend as a judge before he has to face the voters in an election. Most of the time, the replacement judge is one of those loyal Democrats currently serving as an assistant district attorney. After this new district court judge has been in office a year or so, he runs for election with the endorsement of the Democratic Party executive committee. All of the powerful people in the Democratic Party will use their influence to get the local newspaper, and in this day and time television and radio stations, to give coverage to their man and to endorse him because he is the experienced judge. You see what I'm saying? He has served the party, the party has rewarded him by appointing him as a judge, and then he has the upper hand over any rogue lawyer who might want to challenge him because this sitting judge will have the endorsement of the newspapers and everybody who counts, which is mainly the lawyers who have the most to gain when they have a case in front of this judge whom they put into office. It goes on that when a superior court judge is ready to retire, he again contacts his party chairman and a replacement is chosen, primarily by the lawyers who seek to profit by the choice of the new judge who will become their judge and reward them with favorable rulings.

"When a sitting judge runs for re-election, he'll usually ask a group of lawyers to support him, and most of the time he's going to be doing this asking at the courthouse. And he's going to be asking lawyers to support him who have cases pending before him. These lawyers whom the judge is asking to support him know that the judge can make or break them by the decisions he makes. One of my best friends, himself a former Republican judge, was called into chambers during the break in a property settlement case, and the Democratic judge asked this lawyer for his support in the coming election. What could he possibly say under those circumstances? He wanted to win his case, so of course he agreed to support the Democratic judge, and he even agreed to write a letter to the editor endorsing the Democratic judge over a Republican lawyer who was challenging the Democratic judge because of just this kind of corrupt practice. Everybody knows if you have a judge in your pocket, you can get anything done you want. Jean, as you have seen with this Rains case, the judge can determine whether you win or lose. Of course, you have the right to a jury trial, but the judge determines what evidence the jury is allowed to hear.

"The court of appeals is supposed to allow you an appeal to correct the wrongs of the local judges, but there are several problems with that. The first problem is that most appeals cost many thousands of dollars, which the average person can't afford. The next problem is court of appeals and Supreme Court judges are brought up through the same corrupt system as the district court and superior court judges. Most court of appeals judges, like Cletus Freedman, who we're going to be before tomorrow, became district court or superior court judges as a reward for service to the Democratic Party, and then after they showed their loyalty to the party as a district court or superior court judge, the party rewarded them by making them a court of appeals or supreme court judge.

Few people even begin to understand the powers of a judge. I was once down in Raleigh for a hearing in the Supreme Court. During a break in one of the cases that was being heard before mine, one of the Supreme Court judges walked into the clerk's office. That Supreme Court judge was complaining about a lawyer who had long hair who was arguing the case before them. The judge said to the clerk that it ought to be against the law for a lawyer to come before the Court looking like that with long hair. The clerk of court said, 'Well, that's not really the law, is it judge?' The judge said, 'If I go upstairs and get four of my friends to agree with me, it will be the law.'

"If a judge does not want you to win your case and he's willing to do it, he can sabotage your case in subtle ways such as voice reflection and facial expressions that direct the jury the way he wants them to go. I wish it weren't so. I wish the people would wake up to the corruptness of the judicial system, but I don't believe I will see it changed in my lifetime."

We reached our motel. We grabbed a bite to eat. All three of us were pretty much silent as we ate. Even Jean didn't have much of anything to say. After Reggie's discussion on the corruptness of the judiciary, I was truly concerned about the outcome of our case. Jean slept well during the night. I tossed and turned, trying to tell myself it was just another case, but I couldn't convince myself. The case had come to mean too much to me. And, besides, I didn't want to let Linda and Harry down.

The next morning, we walked into the court of appeals. For all the power this building and courtroom controlled, neither the building nor the courtroom was impressive. They were actually no larger than what we had back in Winston-Salem.

Our three-judge panel entered the room. It was clear to me by Judge Freedman's demeanor that he was controlling this show. The case had come out of his town, and he expected the other two judges to defer to him. As he walked into the courtroom, I recalled a Playboy cartoon that I had seen. The cartoon showed a longhaired young man sitting on the witness stand and an old baldheaded judge leaning down from the bench admonishing the young man.

"You best show me some respect, young man. I had to kiss a lot of ass to get where I am."

Judge Cletus Freedman had kissed a lot of ass to get where he was, and now he was using that power as if he were a feudal king. He expected everyone to kiss his ass.

"Good morning, gentlemen," Judge Freedman said to Malcolm Saits and his Forbes-Grundy associate and Reggie and me. We all acknowledged Judge Freedman's pleasantry. "Gentlemen, I've read your briefs, and I want to get right into this matter. Let me say right up front that I've spent a lot of time over at the Chandler Life and Indemnity building. I've eaten in that cafeteria, and I have a lot of friends, who work there, one of whom is, of course, Mr. Armand Chandler. As a matter of fact, just last month I was Mr. Chandler's guest at the company's annual awards banquet where they honor the employees who have served the company best over the past year."

Yea, I thought, and you're probably on their pay roll and they were already honoring you for what you're gonna do for them today.

Judge Freedman went on. "Of course, this case was not mentioned at all since Armand and I both knew the case was pending before my court and I was already in the process of reviewing the written briefs."

Yea, right, by that time, both of you knew that this case was under review by you. And of course you didn't discuss it at the dinner; you'd already decided what to do while sitting in Armand's living room having cocktails, and you were thanking him for that color TV and sound system he'd sent you for a Christmas present.

"It's clear to me that plaintiff's attorneys are serving their client well by bringing this case before this court. This issue should have been appealed so that this independent panel of judges could look at it and give it the proper and honest review it deserves. Before I hear from either side, I am going to instruct both sides not to discuss the contents of 'the document.' It's good to see both of you gentlemen. I want to tell the other members of the court that I have personally known all of the attorneys involved who are appearing before us in this case for several years and have a great deal of respect for all of them. Mr. Scott, it appears you will be making the oral argument for the plaintiff's position. Is that correct?"

"That's correct, your honor," Scott responded.

Since Reggie had appeared many times over the years in both the North Carolina Supreme Court and Court of Appeals, we had both agreed it was best for him to make the oral argument this morning.

"May it please the court, we are before the court at this time appealing the ruling of the honorable Superior Court Judge Anthony Case from Forsyth County. Judge Case ruled that 'the document' that we had discovered and attempted to use to question Mr. Chandler of the defendant insurance company could not be used because we had violated the best-evidence rule. Prior to our attempt to make use of the original of the document, Judge Case had admonished us that we could not question Mr. Chandler with a copy of 'the document,' and he had demanded that we produce the original for his viewing."

Judge Freedman interrupted. "Mr. Scott, don't you agree that Judge Case's original objection to the introduction of a copy of the document was reasonable in view of the possibility, if not the probability, of forgery of that 'document'?"

"No, your honor, I don't. This was, after all, part of a discovery deposition."

Judge Freedman again interrupted. "Mr. Scott, you know, as they say, although it's certainly not a legal term, once the bell's been rung, you can't un-ring it, and, of course, what I'm saying here is, if you had been allowed to use that copy and it turned out to be a forgery, the good folks of Winston-Salem who woulda heard about the forged document believing it was authentic would not have paid attention to the newspaper's retraction buried deep in page five or six admitting that the paper had been misinformed."

"But, your honor, Mr. Saits, on behalf of his client, could have simply said and requested, and I would have agreed, to it being made part of a stipulation that nothing contained in the deposition or 'the document' would be disclosed to anyone unless and until the parties had reached an agreement concerning its disclosure."

"Did you make that proposal to Mr. Saits, Mr. Scott?"

"I didn't have a chance to. It wasn't…." Scott started to say it wasn't his responsibility to.

"Now, Mr. Scott, you had a couple days between the adjournment of the deposition and the beginning of Judge Case's hearing, and then more time before his final ruling. I just don't accept that you didn't have enough time, but the issue to the introduction of a copy is, after all, not what we are arguing today. What we're here today for is whether you broke the chain of evidence when Mr. Spears walked in with what the court will accept for argument purposes today to be the original of 'the document,' and laid it on Judge Case's desk."

Reggie, believing Judge Freedman had concluded his statement, began, "Under the circumstances, your honor…."

"Mr. Scott, I am not finished."

"I'm sorry, your honor."

"Mr. Scott, you have practiced law nearly as many years as I have and you know why it is so important that we follow the chain-of-evidence rule. If lawyers and the Court don't insist upon a clear adherence to the chain-of-evidence rule, they open up the opportunity for evidence to be tampered with by those who would perpetrate frauds upon the court." He clearly looked at me as if to encourage everyone in the courtroom to believe that somehow I had tampered with "the document." Now I was calling it "the document" rather than the letter! "You know that it's just too easy for an unscrupulous person, and these days with our profession falling to the lows it is coming to, and you know what I'm talking about, lawyers will even stoop to a point where they will lie and even alter documents."

There was a long pause as Judge Freedman stared at me. He wasn't even beginning to make an appearance of fairness. He was making the argument for his good friend, Armand Chandler, and his Billion-dollar insurance company. If he had been the lawyer for Chandler, he couldn't have done a better job than he was doing from the bench.

Judge Freedman continued. "Your time is up, Mr. Scott. Now I will hear from Mr. Saits and his associate, unless any of the other panel members have a question."

The two judges on either side of Judge Freedman both leaned and the three of them whispered to each other, and then all three men sat back in their seats.

"Mr. Saits, we will hear from you now."

"May it please the Court, the respondents in this appeal chose to rest upon their arguments made and submitted in their brief. I do want to say that with our motion, which Judge Case granted and which is on appeal to this Court at this time, we do not mean to suggest in any way that we believe the honorable lawyers for the plaintiffs, Mr. Scott or Mr. Spears, altered the document in any way. Our problem is that the chain of evidence was broken at some point and could not be expected to be re-established so as to authenticate the document."

"Thank you, Mr. Saits. Are there any questions of Mr. Saits from my colleagues? I see none, so I'm going to give Mr. Scott a moment of rebuttal as a courtesy."

"Your honor, as to the gag order that was made a part of Judge Case's order, at no time was a gag order either discussed or requested, as the transcript before this court clearly shows. I would ask, at the very least, that in view of that fact the court reverse the gag order Judge Case made a part of the order that is before this court."

"Mr. Scott, I've read the transcript, and you are right, a gag order wasn't requested. It wasn't even discussed at the hearing, but I would have done the same thing Judge Case did, so I see no need to reverse on that basis. Thank you, gentlemen. It's been good to see a group of my old colleagues from Winston-Salem down here in Raleigh. The court will be in recess for fifteen minutes before the next case is heard."

Chapter 37

On the ride home from Raleigh, Jean suggested we use the letter to take a deposition of Henrietta. Reggie and I discussed it, but the gag order that Judge Case had imposed would have prevented us, at least me and Reggie, from using the letter for any purpose, including questioning Henrietta in a deposition we might take of her. Reggie and I discussed different options we might take. We considered whether we might be able to do anything in the criminal case. The criminal case was on hold, at least for the moment, while the special prosecutor, Larry Franklin out of the attorney general's office, brought himself up to speed.

Reggie and I discussed the possibility of taking the case to the North Carolina Supreme Court. Reggie said that with nine judges on the supreme court, we would stand a better chance of finding at least one judge who would care about our clients and/or our case. If we could find just one judge who we could convince that our clients and/or our case had merit, there was the possibility that he would convince at least another four of his colleagues to side with him, or that he would write a dissenting opinion that the paper, and thus the public could be stirred up with. We didn't doubt for one minute that we had right on our side; it was just a matter of getting justice on our side as well. Reggie and I had challenged the rich and powerful before with our civil rights cases. When Reggie had fought for the street preachers to be allowed to continue preaching on the sidewalks of Winston-Salem, he had caught the wrath of every merchant in town except the Sage. Although not a Christian, the Sage had written letters to the editor as a Winston-Salem merchant backing up the first-amendment right of the street preachers to be on the sidewalks of Winston-Salem, even in front of his store if they wanted. The Sage had argued in his letters that although he didn't agree with what the street preachers were saying, he would fight for their right to say it. The Sage argued that if you didn't like what the street preachers were saying when they held out their Bibles and told you to prepare yourself, Christ was coming back, you could just keep on walking. But there was a difference in the case we were fighting now. The tobacco company had never become involved in the street preacher fight, but the fight we were in now was over their family, their money, and the insurance company they had created.

It was ironic that Reggie and I were now talking about finding a judge who would care about our clients and our case. Reggie and I had sat beside each other at a bar association luncheon a couple of months after Judge Freedman was elevated from the superior court and was made a North Carolina Court of Appeals Judge. Judge Freedman had been the speaker at that luncheon. He told us in his speech to make him care. He told us that one thing an appellate court judge wants to see in an argument in a brief or an oral argument is that you make him care about your clients and/or your case. With that inspiration of care, he said, he would go out of his way to find a way to rule in your favor, and I will never forget how he so vividly concluded a very moving speech: "A judge can always find a way to rule in your favor if he cares." I was moved by the speech at the time, but I should have known it was just rhetoric.

Within a couple of weeks, we received the court of appeals order. The court of appeals affirmed Superior Court Judge Case's order in total, as we had thought the probably would do by the way the hearing had gone. However, the one thing notable about the court of appeals order was that the court of appeals had declared their order to be an unpublished order. Unpublished orders are rare in cases other than cases such as prisoner appeals claiming prison toilet seats are cold and other clearly trivial matters that are intended by the person making the appeal to just waste the court's time. Unpublished opinions are sometimes, but rarely used when the appellate court is so ashamed of its decision that it wants to create limited viewing and limited access to anyone who might be interested in reading the opinion. Lawyers are discouraged from citing unpublished opinions, and the unpublished opinions are given little credibility. Clearly Judge Freedman was ashamed of what he did in his ruling and didn't want anybody citing it in the future.

Ironically, on the same day that we received the opinion from the court of appeals, beside the daily article on the Charlotte Pendleton case, there was a picture on the front page of the morning paper of Henrietta and Powers leaving the courthouse. The caption read, "Local woman charged with soliciting to murder." Reggie had already read the paper, so he handed it to me. The text began, "A local woman, Henrietta Handy, was charged with attempting to solicit the murder of her business partner, Abner Stitt. Special assistant Attorney General Larry Franklin brought the charge against the Lewisville woman. Franklin was called in at the request of District Attorney Tod Linstrom. Franklin alleged the Stitt case occurred sometime in '74.

"The supporting documents, which have been filed along with the clerk of Court of Forsyth County, allege that Handy attempted to have several individuals murder Stitt. The documents go on to allege that Stitt and Handy were business partners and that the motive for the intended murder was a one-million-dollar life-insurance policy on the life of Stitt. The documents also say Handy allegedly approached Pricey Meyers, then of Lewisville and now of Texas, and requested Meyers assistance in finding someone to kill Stitt. Meyers formerly ran a prostitution ring out of her home in Lewisville and was convicted two years ago in federal district court in Greensboro for tax evasion."

I went back to my office and called Rick.

"Rick, I saw the article you wrote about the Stitt case. Can you tell me anything about what's happening?"

"First, Michael, I wanna tell you I'm sorry about the Rains case. I just picked it up on the AP wire that the court of appeals has ruled against you. Our editor told Ron Goldstein

189

from our Raleigh bureau office to cover the hearing. I talked to Goldstein about it. He said it was clear from the hearing how Judge Freedman was gonna rule. Goldstein said he had never seen a more beautiful nor eloquent representation by a lawyer."

"You mean Cletus Freedman representing Armand Chandler?"

"How'd you guess, Michael? Goldstein joked about a bi-line 'Winston-Salem Judge Cletus Freedman prevails in argument for tobacco heir Armand Chandler.' Goldstein said he thought that anything Saits would have said would have taken away from the argument Judge Freedman was making on behalf of Saits's client. Goldstein wanted to write an article saying what he thought. Our editor pretty much agreed with Goldstein, but he said the pressure was just too great and he would catch too much hell. He wasn't about to stick his neck out, so the end result was we didn't say anything about your case. Michael, I'm so glad I was raised in Pennsylvania and don't have any ties to keep me here. Everybody knows how corrupt this judicial system is, but nobody does anything about it. The only time we ever cover a legal scandal is when some poor ambulance chaser takes a few thousand dollars out of a trust fund or when some judge like Judge Edward Angel from Claudville gets caught with his pants down in some kind of sex scandal. I've been talking to the *New York Times*, and there's a chance I'll be up there within the next year doing some real investigative reporting with an editor who'll back me up rather than hold me back."

"Okay, Rick, I hate to lose you, but I understand. I've got ties here, and I think about leaving a lot of the time. Can you tell me anything that's happening with Franklin and this Abner Stitt matter?"

"Franklin has taken Blaine Cromer and Donnie Drake off the Charlotte Pendleton case and has them working on the Abner Stitt case."

"Rick, I'll call Blaine and go see them. I'll let you know what I find out."

Blaine said to come on down. When I got to his office, he and Donnie were all smiles.

"Looks like we're back in business, Michael," Blaine said. "I've already talked to Abner Stitt. He's wanting a prosecution. I've talked to Pricey Roberts. She's willing to fly back into Winston, willing to testify. The preliminary hearing is set for tomorrow morning, and I don't see why we can't have a trial within a couple of months. Franklin has directed us to concentrate all of our time and energy on the Stitt case. I guess we'll deal with the Rains case later. Franklin has indicated there won't be any need to call anybody from the insurance company in. I feel good about the case against Henrietta, but I'm not sure about the case against that black boy."

"I guess you're talkin' about the Jason Mackie case, Blaine?"

"Yea, we were pushed too hard too fast on that case. Linstrom's determined to make a name for himself, make all the white people happy. The principle witness in the case is white and he wants that reward, and Linstrom has told him if he's asked by the defense whether he expects to get the reward to say he hasn't talked to anybody about the reward money, even though in his first contact with the department the first thing he asked was how could he get the reward money. That hundred thousand dollars the tobacco company put up has brought a lot of vultures down on us. Well, I guess we'll find out. The case is set to begin next Monday."

Chapter 38

The Jason Mackie case began the following Monday. Nearly two hundred jurors were called. Judge Case was determined to be the judge. Linstrom was determined to be the DA to try Jason Mackie. The defense had requested a change of venue because of the prejudicial atmosphere created by the newspaper, TV, and radio coverage of the case. Judge Case similarly dismissed the defense motion saying, "I'm sure you can find twelve fair and honest people in Forsyth County who can hear the evidence in this case and rule upon that evidence without the influence of this, what you call, biased reporting. After all, this was a brutal murder, and that's all the media has portrayed it to be."

Over half of the first one hundred jurors were dismissed for cause when they answered that they had in fact made up their minds that Jason Mackie was guilty from the TV and news paper coverage they had seen. Of course, all of the other jurors heard the jurors who were dismissed describe how they had been convinced that Jason Mackie was guilty. Finally, a jury of ten whites and two blacks was chosen. Linstrom had used peremptory challenges to dismiss all but these two black jurors. The two black jurors both had law-enforcement backgrounds. The black female juror worked in violence counseling for women.

The first witness was a black woman who testified she found the body of Charlotte Pendleton at the corner of North Trade Street and Northwest Boulevard. She testified in gruesome detail how the body had been nude with a lot of cuts, and she emphasized that Pendleton's eyes had been open.

The next witness called was the medical examiner, Dr. Patrick Sparks, who testified that he was called to the scene of the apparent murder on North Trade Street and examined the deceased and made a preliminary determination that she had died of multiple stab wounds. He further testified that he had sent the body on to Chapel Hill for an autopsy.

After Dr. Sparks' testimony, several police officers were called as witnesses, two of whom had arrived on the scene before Dr. Sparks and had called him to the site. After the police officers, the state medical examiner from Chapel Hill testified as to his medical examination. Linstrom insisted upon introducing large color photographs taken by the police officers at the scene and large color photographs of Charlotte Pendleton's body during the autopsy. The defense attorneys objected to the introduction of the photographs. Judge Case sent the jury out so the defense team's motion concerning the photographs could be made.

Bragg argued, "Your honor, these photographs are so gruesome they can't help but prejudice the minds of the jurors."

"You're not saying they're not relevant, are you?"

"Your honor, not at all. Of course, they're relevant to the case, but the defense is not defending that Charlotte Pendleton was not murdered. The defense is not defending that Charlotte Pendleton was not brutally murdered. As a matter of fact, your honor, the defense will offer to stipulate and speed this case along so we don't have to take up the jury's time with the introduction and viewing of these photographs that Charlotte Pendleton was in fact murdered, her body found on North Trade Street, and it was in fact a brutal murder. No, your honor, we are not contesting the murder, nor are we contesting the brutality of the murder. Our defense is that our client did not commit the murder, and we are asking that these photographs not be shown to the jury because they can not help but prejudice the minds of the jurors toward our client."

"Well, you know, Mr. Bragg, I'm going to instruct the jury that they are to put all prejudice out of their minds. I think that should be sufficient, don't you, Mr. Linstrom? What do you say? I haven't given you a chance to say anything yet."

"Your honor, the State of North Carolina has every right to show these pictures to the jury. As your honor says, you will be instructing the jurors to put all prejudice out of their minds. And as your honor says, this evidence is relevant."

"I'm gonna deny the defense's motion. Mr. Bailiff, call the jurors back in."

The first and second day of the trial were consumed totally with these gruesome photographs and the gruesome testimony that accompanied them.

Linstrom was ready to present his star witness on the third day of the trial. It was a white man wearing a sports coat, white shirt, and a tie.

"State your name please, sir. "

"Thomas Martin."

"And where do you live, sir?"

"14 Running Brooke Lane, Winston-Salem."

"What do you do and where are you employed, Mr. Martin? "

"I'm an automobile salesman at A and G Motors down on Peters Creek Parkway."

"Would you describe for the members of the jury what you were doing on the morning Charlotte Pendleton's body was found?"

"About 8 o'clock in the morning, I was driving east on 4th Street."

"Did you see anything unusual at that time?"

"Yes, I did. I saw a black male leading…."

"Could you sort of demonstrate what you mean by 'leading,' Mr. Martin?"

Thomas stood up and with his right arm sort of circled like you would grab someone's left arm.

"Go on, Mr. Martin."

"Well, like I say, this black male was leading this woman east on the sidewalk that borders 4th Street."

"Can you identify that man?"

"Yes, I can. The man I saw was the black male who is sitting at that table," Martin said, pointing with his right hand toward Jason Mackie.

"Is there any doubt in your mind whatsoever that Jason Mackie was the man you saw that day?"

"No, sir. When I looked into those eyes, I knew I would remember that man for the rest of my life."

Those eyes. There it was, the witness had taken his testimony straight from the TV and newspaper reporting. And as you looked at the jurors when Martin said "those eyes," all twelve jurors turned their heads toward Jason. All twelve of them programmed by the TV and newspaper coverage of "those eyes."

"That's all I have of this witness at this time, your honor," Linstrom concluded.

Bragg began his cross-examination. "Mr. Martin, I believe you testified you sold automobiles?"

"That's correct."

"Could that be new or used automobiles?"

"I sell used cars."

"And that would be down on Peters Creek Parkway?"

"Yes, sir."

"Now, are you a member of any clubs or organizations, Mr. Martin?"

"I'm a member of the Red Ridge Church of God, and I used to be a boy scout."

Everyone laughed.

"Are you a member of any other clubs or organizations of any kind, Mr. Martin?"

"No, sir, I am not."

Martin was failing to disclose that he was a member of the Ku Klux Klan. He had disclosed this to Linstrom, but Linstrom had intentionally failed to disclose it to the defense and had specifically told Martin not to disclose it during his testimony.

"Mr. Martin, you say you saw Mr. Mackie here on the morning in question while he was on the sidewalk and you were in your car. Is that correct?"

"Yes, sir, that's what I saw."

"Mr. Martin, isn't there a curve at the point where you said you saw my client?"

"Yes, sir, there is, but when I seen them eyes, I knew I would never forget that man."

"Mr. Martin, how fast were you going at that point?"

"That's a thirty-five-mile-per-hour zone and I always do the speed limit, not five miles over, not five miles under."

"So, Mr. Martin, you were doing thirty-five miles per hour in a curve months ago and you can now testify to this jury that this is the man you saw on that occasion?"

"Like I say, when I seen them eyes, I knew I would remember that man."

"Now, Mr. Martin, there is a one-hundred-thousand-dollar reward offered by the Chandler Tobacco Company and the Chandler Insurance Company jointly for information leading to the arrest and conviction of the person, or persons, responsible for the murder of Charlotte Pendleton. Are you aware of that reward offer?"

"I've heard about it."

"How did you hear about it?"

"Seems like it was on TV. Maybe it was in the paper."

"Have you ever discussed that reward with anyone, Mr. Martin?"

"No, sir, I'm here to help bring about justice."

"Do you expect to get any of that reward, Mr. Martin?"

"Like I say, I ain't talked to nobody about it."

Martin was doing exactly as Linstrom had told him. Linstrom was delighted with the way the case was progressing. Linstrom had felt the pressure of the Winston-Salem establishment, especially the tobacco company's newspaper, and he felt he had to have a conviction to have any hope of re-election. He had actually confided to the detectives who had produced this evidence he was using that he didn't believe Jason Mackie was guilty, but he knew the game. The practice of law is an adversary practice. You play to win, and winning is everything, especially as here where a loss would cost him this prestigious well-paying job he held.

Linstrom called his next witness. It was a morning clerk at the luxury hotel in the center of town. It had been built to replace the old Robert E. Lee Hotel that had been built in 1940 at what could have been considered the peak of the political power of Chandler Tobacco, the year that Charley Chandler, the son of the founder of the tobacco company, had saved the national Democratic Party and Franklin Roosevelt from defeat at the hands of Republicans who had pledged to keep us out of World War II. At Franklin Roosevelt's personal request and at a time that everyone else was deserting FDR, believing he was going to be defeated in his third try for the presidency, Charley Chandler sent one-hundred-thousand dollars in cash to Roosevelt in Washington. Roosevelt used this tobacco money on radio and newspaper ads and to buy party bosses in Chicago, Philly, and other places to give him the slight edge that kept him in office for a third term. As usual in Democratic politics, Charley Chandler's hundred-thousand-dollar investment in Franklin Roosevelt paid off handsomely. Roosevelt saw to it that Chandler brand cigarettes were included in C-Rations packages. By the end of the war upwards of eighty percent of GI's would be addicted to them.

The hotel clerk took the stand and testified that Jason Mackie had come into the hotel on the morning of the murder. He testified that Mackie had been covered in blood and had asked if he could use the men's room. The clerk testified that Mackie washed the blood off in the men's room and then left. No matter how illogical this testimony seems as you consider it now, in the context of the times, the jury believed it.

Again, as with the used-car salesman, the hotel clerk had called the Winston-Salem police department offering his information for the reward money. Again in cross examination, the clerk did as Linstrom had instructed him, proclaiming his civic duty and denying that he had any interest whatsoever in a reward that he had heard about.

The next witness was the white girlfriend of Jason Mackie. The police had taken her into custody, and as with just about every black person or white person who associated with black people who they took into custody after the Pendleton body was found and after the pressure was put on the police to charge somebody with the murder, the police used both the carrot and the stick approach with the young girl. The stick they used was they told her that they knew that she knew who had killed Charlotte Pendleton. They told her if she did not tell them who had actually committed the murder, they were going to charge her with the murder itself. The girl was a runaway. She was a drug addict. She had no one to call, and knowing they weren't going to really charge her with anything, the police didn't bother to tell her she had the right to see a lawyer or to talk to one. The cops played good guy/bad guy. One cop would come in and tell her since she knew who had committed the murder; he wanted her to have the hundred-thousand-dollar reward but that the other cop wanted to charge her with the murder itself. Then the bad cop would come in and question her for up to an hour. He would make her stand handcuffed the entire time he was talking to her and call her names when she would start crying. When she said she needed to pee, he told her go ahead and piss on herself, he didn't have time for her. She stood there and pissed in her jeans. It could be fairly said that she was being tortured. The cops weren't worried about torturing her. They had no intention of charging her with anything, so they weren't worried about evidence that they might get from her that they couldn't use against her. The cops weren't worried about a civil rights suit by this girl against them. Who in Charles C. Chandler's Winston-Salem would take the word of this "nigger fuckin" white "dope whore" against one of Winston-Salem's finest? After nearly six hours of this kind of questioning, the girl was willing to tell the cops anything they wanted to hear, so they wrote out a statement saying that Jason Mackie had told her that he killed Charlotte Pendleton to fit their hotel clerk's testimony. The statement they prepared for the girl also said that Jason had come in with his clothes all bloody.

However, as soon as the girl was free, and the police had no basis to hold her, the girl began telling how she had been treated and why she had signed a statement full of lies about Jason. So this was the situation when the girl took the stand. Linstrom knew she was going to tell the truth and would deny under oath that the statement she had signed before was true.

Linstrom and Judge Case had it all worked out. When the girl took the stand, Linstrom got her to identify herself and then presented her with the statement she had previously signed. Linstrom and Judge Case had planned for the girl to read her untrue statement to the jury so it would come in out of her mouth, but she refused. Instead, she attempted to tell the jury how the cops had tortured her and tried to bribe her with the reward until they forced her to sign the statement. Linstrom and Judge Case would have no part of that. Each time she tried to do anything other than read the statement, Judge Case would threaten her with contempt of Court and called the female bailiff to restrain the girl. Even this didn't get the girl to read the statement. So, in frustration, Linstrom over objection and in clear violation of North Carolina law, called the officer who had written the statement to the stand and had the officer read the statement the girl had signed. The officer went on to tell the jury that no force, promises, threats, or intimidation of any kind had been used against the girl at any time, but rather she had voluntarily come in to their office, sat down, and given them the statement. The jury, being like most folks, had little or no experience with the judicial system, and when instructed by Judge Case after closing arguments that the police officers have no reason to lie because they have no interest in the case, the jury inevitably found Jason Mackie, an innocent man, guilty of first-degree murder, and the next day, Judge Case sentenced Jason Mackie to die for the murder of Charlotte Pendleton.

Chapter 39

Linstrom was on a roll. The next week, Blaine called me to tell me that he had been ordered to be at court. Governor Cox had by now intervened in the case. Larry Franklin and Charles Powers had worked out a plea bargain. Tony Southern was now assisting Franklin with the prosecution of Henrietta.

Governor Cox had sent Judge Horrace C. Linney from down east to take the plea. The plea was set for 2 o'clock Friday afternoon, when normally you couldn't find a judge anyplace in the courthouse. Friday afternoon was also chosen because most all reporters would be off after noon on Friday for whatever weekend plans they may have had, and by Monday morning, the plea would have become old news. Judge Linney was given Judge Case's office for the day. It was the biggest and most secluded office, and you had to go past the secretary to get there. Judge Linney called Powers and Bernard Parson, who was assisting Powers into his office, as well as Larry Franklin and Tony Southern.

"Gentlemen, it's good to see you all today. I don't get up here much, and I always enjoy being here when I get to come. Of course, Larry and me work closely together a lot of the time. Governor Cox seems to like the work Larry and me do together, and he keeps us busy. Ain't that right, Larry?"

"That's right, judge. Six weeks ago, we did that case down east."

Powers spoke up. "You must be talkin' about Judge George Randall. The papers just blew that thing all out of proportion. I do hope Governor Cox has had the chief of the highway patrol dress down that highway patrol officer who gave Judge Randall that drunk-driving ticket. Judge Randall had just come from a fundraiser for Senator Smith's campaign against Jesse Helms, and, of course, there was drink'n there."

"Judge Randall only blew a ten on the Breathalyzer, and he was as sober as any of us sittin' right here in this room.

Blaine, you wouldn't have charged a superior court judge with drunk driving based on a ten, would you?"

Other than the lawyers in the room (the judge, Franklin, Southern, Powers, and Parson), Blaine was the only other person left in the room in the judge's chambers. Blaine knew that sometimes the investigating officer would be present in the judge's chambers for this rehearsal before the full play would be presented for public display in an open courtroom.

Blaine responded to Franklin's question truthfully and bluntly. "No, here in Forsyth County, I sure wouldn't have given a judge any ticket for nuthin, cause I know it woulda meant my job."

The lawyers all laughed at Blaine's answer knowing full well that it was the absolute truth.

Franklin went on to say, "Before Judge Randall's case, Governor Cox had sent us down east on that case over that bale of marijuana."

Tony Southern then spoke up. "We had a case similar to that right here. Two boys were charged with killing a drug dealer over a bale of marijuana. Both of the boys gave written statements that the other did the murder so they wouldn't have to pay two thousand dollars for the bale. Both denied they had anything to do with the murder, and each one blamed his partner for the murder itself. In our case, we just charged 'em both and the jury convicted them both of murder. But I believe in that case y'all tried, Larry, one of the boys was the son of the County party chairman and y'all chose to believe the Party Chairman's son as having more credibility."

Judge Linney spoke up now. "That's the way it worked out. One boy walked as a cooperating witness with a suspended sentence and the other is serving twenty years in central prison. I just hope that boy we let walk is gonna straighten his life out. His daddy's sent him to military school, maybe they can do something with him."

Blaine just sat and listened. He was now close to retirement. In his now nearly thirty years with the force, he had been in on many sessions like this. These were just a bunch of good old boys taking care of each other. These people didn't give a second thought to the fact that only a privileged few could get the kind of breaks that political connections made possible for the rich and powerful. Blaine even recalled how even in the 1920s when Herbert Hoover and the Republicans had controlled the national government, the local Democrats had been willing to lower their standards to call upon Republican lawyer Floyd Harding to help them out. It seems Charley Chandler, the heir to the tobacco fortune, was spending some time in London, England. Chandler had gotten drunk at a party. When Chandler left the party driving his Roles Royce, he was so drunk that he forgot he was still in England.

Chandler was driving down the right side of the street just like he would in Winston-Salem. He kept blowing his horn for the stupid people to get on their side of the road until he ran head-on into an elderly doctor who was on his way home from caring for a sick patient. The English, then as now, take drunk driving much more seriously than we do in America. They intended to hold young Charley Chandler and try him for manslaughter and give him about twenty years for killing the doctor. Charley Chandler's father, who had founded the tobacco company, looked for and found a Republican lawyer who had connections with the Republican administration of Herbert Hoover. This turned out to be the only Republican lawyer in town, Floyd Harding.

Floyd went to Washington and met with President Hoover and in fact carried monetary enticements that helped President Hoover decide to get the American State Department and Ambassador to England to intervene on behalf of young Charley Chandler. Floyd went on to London, and with the unlimited money available to Floyd from the tobacco company coiffeurs, Floyd was able to hire the best legal assistance and grease the palms of Englishmen who could, and did, help young Charley Chandler get off with a slap on the wrist. Charley Chandler would never leave the soil of the United

States again. This episode had, in fact, played a major role in encouraging the Chandler family to use their money to buy Allegheny County, North Carolina.

"Well, gentlemen, we better get down to business. I told my wife I'd be home for supper."

Powers interrupted. "Judge, I was hoping you and Larry would stay and you and Larry would have dinner on me over at the country club."

"That sounds tempting, Charles, but my wife is expecting me back for supper tonight. Let's get this thing done. Tony, you hand me them papers. Has your client signed, Charles?"

"She has, your honor," Powers said. "She didn't want to, she wanted to go on and have a trial, but I told her this was the best way for us to end everything."

"Blaine, you tell me a little bit about this case while I look over these papers. Governor Cox called me just last night, asked me if I could come on up here this afternoon and take this plea. Blaine, you tell me a little bit about it while I read over this plea-bargain agreement."

Blaine began summarizing the facts as he knew them. "Well, judge, this woman had a business partner, this Abner Stitt, and she got a million-dollar life-insurance policy on him. And then she tried to get him killed so she could collect that million dollars. Umm, my investigation has indicated that the woman had another million-dollar policy and she tried to get that man killed, and his body was found at Myrtle Beach, and she did collect that million dollars. Of course, this we're working with here today is only on the Stitt case."

Blaine had never heard of a judge turning down a plea bargain when it had been worked out between the prosecutor and the defense team. Blaine knew that Judge Linney was the "fix-it judge" for the governor and the party and always did what he was told. So Blaine assumed everything would be signed and sealed this afternoon and by six o'clock or so Judge Linney would be sitting down for supper with his wife.

The plea forms were short and sweet and to the point. They were signed by Larry Franklin and Tony Southern of the prosecution and by Charles Powers and Bernard Parson for the defense and by the defendant, Henrietta Handy. However, Judge Linney was taking his time. Judge Linney was taking a lot of time. Judge Linney sat back in his chair. He looked up at the ceiling. He swept the room with his eyes and looked into the eyes of each man there. He swiveled his large chair around and stared out the window, certainly in deep thought. Without turning around, Judge Linney began to speak as if to an audience.

"I've signed a lot of plea bargains in my life, gentlemen. In fact, I've never refused to sign a plea bargain." He paused. Everyone in the room who was listening stopped breathing; just waiting to see what Judge Linney was going to say. The pause lasted perhaps two, perhaps five minutes. Judge Linney swiveled his chair back around, facing Blaine and the lawyers. He looked into Larry Franklin's eyes. "I can't sign this," he said in a whisper. "It's outrageous."

Powers spoke up. "It's that Michael Spears and Reggie Scott have got to you, judge. We'll take care of them."

"No, Charles," Judge Linney said. "No one's gotten to me. It's my conscience, Charles. This is outrageous. This would end any prosecution of this woman. I can't sign this. Now, fellas, I've got to get back to my bride." Judge Linney stood and began removing his robe as Blaine and the lawyers slowly left the room.

Chapter 40

Bernard Parson and Charles Powers left the judge's chambers together. Blaine Cromer had been impressed that Judge Linney had refused the plea bargain. Blaine wasn't privy to the contents of the document, but he had been present when so many sweetheart deals had been made that he naturally assumed this one was no different. Judge Linney appeared to not want to talk to anyone.

Blaine stopped Judge Linney and said to him, "You did the right thing, your honor."

"I know I did, Captain Cromer," Judge Linney said, firmly grasping Blaine's outstretched hand. They stood looking at each other for an awkward moment, and then Judge Linney left by the back steps on his way to his car and his trip back east. Blaine felt Judge Linney would sleep better tonight knowing he had done the right thing. Blaine started through the superior courtroom on his way to the elevators, and he saw Henrietta, Powers, and Parson in an animated conversation at the back of the courtroom.

"You told me you had it taken care of, you lying son of a bitch," Henrietta screamed at Powers. "With all the money I've paid you, you haven't done a Goddamned thing for me. I'd just like to know where all that money went. The way you're charging me, I'm gonna end up paying you everything I got out of Big Head's death."

Parson saw Blaine and grabbed Henrietta by the shoulder. "Shut your mouth. That's the detective after your ass, lady."

Henrietta was out of control. "No, I know who's after my ass," she said. "It's that Goddamned Reggie Scott and Michael Spears, and as soon as you get me out of this, Charles, I want you to slap a suit on them that'll take everything they have. Charles, you told me the governor was sending a judge up here who would do whatever he told him to. Now, I wanna know what happened."

"Let's go back to my office and maybe I can explain everything to you, Henrietta."

Blaine hadn't hurried across the courtroom, but by this point he had reached the door and didn't want to make it too obvious how much he was learning from this attorney/client conference, so he went on through the door and on home for supper with his wife.

Of course, Powers and Parson didn't take Henrietta back to their office. They didn't care to hear any more abuse from this ungracious self-centered woman. They took her straight to her car and told her to go home and break out a bottle of Scotch. By the time Powers and Parson did get to Powers' office, Tony Southern and Larry Franklin were waiting there for them as previously planned.

"What do you have up your sleeve, Charles?" asked Tony Southern.

"Tony, you know me. I'm an old gambler, and it's not time to throw the cards in yet. First thing we're gonna do is call Leon. Myra, get Leon on the phone," Powers shouted to his secretary.

"Gentlemen, I'm gonna put us all on speaker phone," Charles said as he flipped the switch to speakerphone.

"Attorney General's Office, how can I help you?"

"Get Leon on the line, tell him Charles Powers is calling."

"Hello," the Attorney General answered.

"Leon, this is Charles Powers. I've got you on speakerphone in my office. Larry Franklin, Tony Southern, and Bernard Parson are here."

"Hey fellas, how are things up there in the tobacco city? Horrace C. take care of everything for y'all?"

Franklin said, "As a matter of fact, he didn't, Leon. Horrace C's gone soft. You'd think he'd got to be a judge on his own the way he was talkin today. Wouldn't have been nearly as bad except this detective Cromer was in the room there to hear everything he said, too. Horrace C. actually called the plea bargain we had worked out 'outrageous.' You know as well as

I do he's taken pleas that were a whole lot more outrageous than this one when the party needed him. Where do we go from here, Leon?"

"I don't know, fellas. The governor is running this show now. I'll give him a call. I'm just doing what he wants me to do at this point. I'll give y'all a call back after I talk to the governor no later than Friday of next week. Y'all keep your schedules open in case the governor wants to meet with all of us."

Leon had Larry call from Raleigh on Wednesday. The governor had set a meeting for Friday morning at 11.

"Gentlemen, I understand y'all got a little problem up there in Winston-Salem. I'm always willing to help my friends in Winston-Salem anyway I can. The good folks of Winston-Salem have supported me every time I've run for office. My good friend Armand Chandler called me Monday and asked me to have a meeting with you fellas on this matter of this dead body found at Myrtle Beach that just won't seem to go away for some reason."

Everyone in the room laughed. It was the same group who had called Leon Edwards the previous Friday, minus Tony Southern, who wasn't considered important enough to bring down for this meeting. In addition to Powers, Parson, and Franklin, the Attorney General Leon Edwards was present.

The governor went on. "I can see the seriousness of this matter, and I don't see the need to destroy a billion-dollar insurance company over one dead redneck. Larry, tell me what happened last Friday."

"Governor, you sent Horrace C. up there to take a plea and he refused to do it."

"What reason did he give, Larry?"

"Said it was 'outrageous,' governor."

"Outrageous? Did Horrace C. have a come-to-Jesus meeting with somebody?" The governor laughed, which in turn prompted all these subordinates to acknowledge the governor's comic ability by joining in with uncontrolled laughter.

"Governor, Horrace C. and I have worked as a team for over eighteen years, and I'm concerned if we can't get him to take this plea, we can't find anybody."

"Larry, hold on, it's not panic time yet. I know this Republican who's a judge down here in Raleigh who was appointed by my Republican predecessor in the governor's mansion. The man likes being a judge, and I know for a fact he wouldn't turn it down if I were to offer him another six-year term as a special superior court judge."

When there is a judicial vacancy, the governor appoints a successor to the retiring or deceased judge. With the surprise elections of 1966 and Winston-Salem, where the people had swept out all of the Democratic crooks in black robes in favor of a whole group of Republican incompetents, the Democratic party leaders became worried and began searching for ways to retain their power against the rising Republican sentiment of the people. One of the things the Democrats had done was to get the unsophisticated Republican legislators to agree to a compromise. By this compromise, any time a judicial vacancy occurred, the governor was to fill the vacancy with a judge of the same political party as the judge who had left creating the vacancy. In other words, the governor was supposed to replace a Republican with a Republican and a Democrat with a Democrat. However, this rule did not apply to what were called "special judges," and the governor was talking about re-appointing a special Republican judge, as a reward for doing what this group wanted in the Myrtle Beach murder case. To the Democrats, most of the time it wasn't a problem for a Democratic governor to appoint a Republican to replace a Republican because usually when a vacancy occurred when a Republican judge died or resigned, the Democrats would simply chose one of their own and have him re-register his party affiliation and, a week or so later, the governor would appoint a newly created Republican to replace a Republican judge.

"Larry, you know who I'm talking about. You give him a call and tell him what we're offering and see if he won't just roll up there to Winston-Salem and help those folks out."

Chapter 41

A few days and our festival would start. I could not believe how excited Jean was. I don't know how it happened, and I'm not complaining, but she had taken over and was running every aspect of the festival. She was running advanced sales, and she had moved in with me, finally, and I guess it was about time, into my Winston-Salem house. She was answering the phone. We had established an 800 number so anybody could call us. She was spending as much as twenty hours a day working on the festival. She had no time for me, and that was okay. I had to pinch myself in the mornings. I would thank God for her coming into my life in morning prayers and in my nightly prayers and time and time again throughout the day. It didn't really matter that she didn't have time for me or that we didn't have time for each other. I had experienced the festival of a year earlier and knew that everything would be over but the clean up within a week. I knew that the clean up would be massive, but I had told Jean as best I could what to expect about the mountains of garbage and the need to dispose of it as rapidly as possible to get the health people off our backs.

On Monday before the festival, Jean told me that we had sold five thousand tickets in advance.

"Jean, do you realize what that means? Five thousand tickets at twenty bucks a piece; that's a hundred thousand dollars. After ten thousand dollars prize money for the performers, ten-thousand dollars in advertisement, and ten to twenty-thousand dollars to pay the folks who are gonna help us, we've already made a profit of sixty thousand dollars!"

I had agreed to give her half of the profit, although she had said that a third was more than she deserved. I had pointed out to her that in the music business, you can go for years and never make a profit, and even the half of the profit I was offering her would probably mean that she would make nothing for this year. But she had had faith in me and faith in the project, and I couldn't believe her people skills. She was a natural at advertising. She had written all of the ads and placed them in trade magazines, newspapers, and radio stations. The festival of a year before had been an artistic success and Jean had already turned that artistic success into an economic success, this year.

"Jean, go ahead and put your half into a bank account of your own."

"I'm not going to spend any time worrying about money at this point. All my time and energy is needed on the festival itself. And besides, I know where to find you if you try to get away with my money."

Campers started coming in droves on Monday before the Thursday the festival was supposed to start.

"Jean, I'm worried."

"What about now?" she asked.

"What if we have too many people and they flood the whole area so that people can't get their milk to the dairy or sick people can't get out to get their medicine?"

"You're a natural-born worrier, Michael. You've been worrying for the past twelve months whether there would be enough people for us to show a profit, and now you're sick with worry because there may be too many people to get in and they may end up camping out in some of your neighbor's front yards. I'm telling you, these are good people up here. They know festivals, they are used to the festival over at Galax, and they will be more than willing to help people if we have an overflow crowd, so just stop worrying and let me take care of things."

By Thursday, the start of the festival, we had sold over fifteen thousand of the twenty thousand tickets we had had printed, and so many people were coming from so many directions that Jean told security to forget about collecting money and let everybody in who we could fit. My farm is adjacent to the Jefferson National Forest, and under these emergency conditions, Jean directed security to send people onto the national forest land. As part of our security force, Jean had hired Adam McGee, Angie Snow, and Jerry McGee. I guess you could say Jerry McGee was experienced in security. How else would you describe the job of a bouncer at a titty-bar? Angie and Adam were having a ball.

Jerry McGee didn't really seem to be a hundred percent into his job. I learned for the first time that James Crow's girlfriend, Darlene, and Jerry were sneaking around seeing each other. I knew for a fact that this, among other things, could get those two killed. Darlene came up on Friday for an indefinite stay with Jerry.

Jean had put Adam and Angie in charge of our money. When I asked Adam if they needed help guarding the money, Adam said, "Ain't no Goddamn mother fucker gonna fuck with me or your money. Michael, after what you and Jean done for me, I'll blow his mother fuckin' ass away in a Goddamn minute. Mother fucker don't know who he's fuckin' with when he's fuckin' with me." Adam had a way with words. He convinced me.

By Friday of the festival, all Adam was doing was drinking and going from campsite to campsite getting free beer, liquor, and pot. He was just as potty-mouth as ever, but there seems to be something about the atmosphere created by one of these open-air festivals that tames even the wildest heart. A lot of people had discarded their clothes as soon as they got to the festival and never bothered to put them on again. At the foot of the stage at night could be seen young longhaired men and women flat footing and clogging as naked as the day they were born, it was freedom, just total freedom and nobody cared. I had asked Jean whom she was going to hire as the announcer for the stage.

"Hire, hell," she said. "You're speaking to the announcer." And she did a marvelous job.

Over the past few months when she had been putting the talent together, Jean had personally come to know all of the artists who appeared. She was such a warm, vivacious person, they all liked her right up front, even when some of the more egotistical artists would complain about being placed too close to or too far behind someone they thought was not so good as they were. Jean would have them laughing and joking with her by the time they came out of the old school bus that Jean had bought for two-hundred dollars to serve as our office. Jean had asked that every artist personally autograph our bus with a paint spray-can she would hand them. There was even a John Hancock who had signed his name on the side of the bus, although nobody could really remember hearing him sing or play. I'm sure a lot of pot was sold and smoked at the festival, but we looked the other way when this was being done. Jean and I kept our heads clear so that we would be capable of handling any emergency. Neither of us had any alcohol for the entire three days of the festival. I was especially proud of Jean for that. This was a woman who I had been told had an alcohol problem. I think it was more that Jean had not had any reason not to drink in the past. The festival ended on Sunday afternoon, and Jean gave out money, ribbons, and trophies from the stage until about six, and then we all sat down for a temporary rest, knowing that we had to get up on Monday morning and begin the clean up.

From my experience a year before, I had told Jean the best thing to do with the garbage was to have a bulldozer come in, dig a hole, and bury it. And sure enough, at 6 o'clock on Monday morning, I was awakened by an eighteen-wheeler outside my door with the dozer and that was trailed by a dump truck. About twenty of our people were still there to help with the clean up. I just don't think anybody who has never held a music festival can appreciate how much garbage twenty thousand people partying for a week can generate. However, by Wednesday of the following week, we had cleared the roads for ten miles, all two hundred acres of my land, and the national forest land of the garbage left from the festival. With my blessing, Jean had given a bonus of a thousand dollars apiece to all of the people who had stayed with us throughout the festival and clean up. Finally, with everyone gone except for Adam and Angie, Jean and I could really rest and consider the success the festival had been. For one thing, it appeared we had cleared over two hundred thousand dollars profit, even after bonuses Jean had given out.

The only thing, and it really hurt all of us that happened concurrent with that festival was that on the morning after the cleanup, Jerry McGee and Darlene were found in Jerry's pickup truck in Bylsby Lake. The medical examiner ruled the deaths an accident. In his report he said that the couple were parked on the boat ramp and somehow the gearshift on the floor had become disengaged and the pickup had rolled into the lake, trapping the couple inside and drowning them. We all knew Darlene to be promiscuous and Jerry to have been hot for her. Also, Jerry's fly had been unzipped and Darlene's head was in his lap when they were found and her body was against the gearshift.

Chapter 42

Jean and I returned home to our home in Winston-Salem. We had both decided we were going to take a week off and think about our future. That evening so neither one of us would have to cook, I brought home Chinese take-out and Budweiser. I had to admit it, I really wasn't a wine or Champaign drinker. A good Bud after a hard day's work was all a man or a woman needed. However, we did treat ourselves to Champaign glasses and candlelight for our feast.

"Jean, you were so happy up there," I said.

"So were you, Michael. You're so much more at peace with yourself and with the world when you're sitting at the waterfall at Pot Rock or Bear Hole, and when you and I slip our clothes off and slide into that ice-cold water, you become a totally different person. Oh, I don't mean that you're not a good person down here, and you're a loving person, that's for sure, but there's something about the cold water of that waterfall, how it takes all of your tension away. When I touch you your body, is not near as tense when you're in that water, and even your voice is softer and sounds like it's more under control when you're in Crooked Creek and when you come out. I know that your battles for civil rights mean so much to you. I think they mean too much to you. After a judge stabs you in the back, and I think that's the best way to describe what they have been doing to you in the Rains case, you're so tense that I'm sometimes even afraid to speak to you for fear that you will explode and say something that you don't mean to say but can't help but say that will leave a scar on our relationship forever. You and I both know that you've wanted to live up there in those mountains since you spent your summers as a little boy at your grandmother's over at Sparta. Just think about this, just think about it. Maybe it's time."

She was so warm and comforting. Somehow, she had begun to read my soul. She was saying to me what I should have been saying to myself. I was so lucky.

Our week of rest was exactly what we both needed. I felt it had prepared me for the next phase of the Rains case. Rick Stanton had called me. Somehow, he had gotten wind of what had happened when Horrace C. Linney had come to town to take the plea bargain.

"Blaine told me about it, Rick, and how Linney had refused to take the plea. How did you find out?"

"It was a confidential source, Michael. That's all I can say. I hope you will respect me as one professional to another."

"Of course, I'll respect your right to your confidential source, Rick, but why didn't you write anything about it?"

"We're still under tremendous pressure here at the paper. We are to write something favorable to Powers and company or write nothing at all, so I write nothing at all. But that's not what I called you for. Governor Cox is sending another judge up here this Friday to take the plea. It's Judge Hiram Fisher from Wake County. Do you know anything about him?"

"No, I don't. Do you, Rick?"

"I know that he's one of fewer than five Republican superior court judges out of a hundred superior court judges in the entire state. I know that he is very ambitious and would like to be a court of appeals or Supreme Court judge. I know he's from Wake County and his term is about to expire, and that's all I know. I'm going to put everything aside so I can be there Friday afternoon. What about you?"

"I'll be there Rick, thanks for the information."

The setting was much the same as when Horrace C. Liney had come to town to take Henrietta's plea. Everything began in Judge Case's office.

"Gentlemen, I've already seen the plea transcript in this case, and it's beyond me why Judge Linney wouldn't accept it. Mr. Franklin, you and I have sat down and discussed this plea, and you tell me that you believe it's fair for the people of North Carolina. Mr. Southern, it's good to meet you. I know that you think this plea is good for the people of North Carolina. Is there anything you would want to add to it?"

Southern responded, "No, your honor, I've discussed it with Mr. Linstrom, and I'm here on his behalf. I don't see that he should have had any problem being here, but as you know, he requested the governor appoint Mr. Franklin as a special prosecutor to prosecute this case so that there would be no question whatsoever about any influence of Mr. Linstrom over the outcome."

Again, Blaine Cromer was sitting in the room. He knew that Tony Southern was lying, that Southern knew full well the special prosecutor had come in at my request. This was just another charade like Blaine had seen many times before.

"Yes, Mr. Southern, Governor Cox said as much to me. Governor Cox said that he didn't see any reason whatsoever why Mr. Linstrom couldn't have continued in this case. Governor Cox told me that Mr. Linstrom absolutely insisted, and I can't put that strongly enough, that Mr. Linstrom insisted that a special prosecutor be appointed and that all control over the prosecution of this fine lady, Henrietta Handy, be placed in the hands of the special prosecutor and taken totally out of the office of the district attorney here in Winston-Salem."

Blaine thought to himself, what a crock. Here's Tony Southern, Linstrom's chief lackey, front and center in this case, and yet the Winston-Salem DA's office, as this judge says, plays no role whatsoever.

"Mr. Powers, do you or Mr. Parson have anything to say about this plea? Has your client fully read this plea, and is she fully aware of the stain upon her record this case will cause?"

Powers began, "Your honor, if I may say, prior to just a few days ago, our client would have insisted upon a trial before a jury of her peers to determine whether or not she was guilty of this horrible offense with which she is charged. But, your honor, we gave her every option and we were willing, ready, and able to try this case, but she said to us, 'I want this over. You work out whatever you can.'"

Blaine didn't know whether to laugh or shout out "liar." After all the years he had been on the force, he still couldn't understand how lawyers could lie with such impunity. "I guess that's what they teach them in law school," he thought to himself.

"Well, lets go on out there and do this in open court."

Judge Fisher took his seat and began his performance.

"Gentlemen, I believe we are here for a plea, is that correct?"

Everyone nodded agreement and verbally expressed agreement for the record.

"Now, Mrs. Handy, can you understand what I'm saying?"

Powers had instructed Handy not to say a word without first consulting with him. He whispered to her to say yes.

"Yes, your honor."

"In this plea, Mrs. Handy, you plead nolo contendere, or no contest, to a charge of attempting to solicit the murder of Abner Stitt. Is that correct?"

Again, Powers whispered to Handy to say yes, your honor.

"Yes, your honor."

All of the lawyers up there, including Judge Fisher, knew full well that there was a civil suit pending relating to the death of Harold Stennis Rains. Judge Fisher had been told that suit was over an identical action by Handy in attempting to have another business partner murdered for an identical one-million-dollar insurance policy as in the Stitt case. Judge Fisher had also been made aware it was the same insurance company owned by the tobacco heir friend of Governor Cox that had issued both life insurance policies. Judge Fisher had also been told how important it was that this plea bargain not be made usable in the parallel case involving Rains. So here he was deliberately and intentionally fixing it to where this plea bargain would never be admissible in any civil or criminal case because under North Carolina law of evidence, a no-contest plea may not be used against the person making that plea in another criminal or civil case. In other words, Handy could not now be questioned concerning the Stitt case in a deposition or otherwise by being found guilty under a plea of no contest to soliciting to kill Stitt. Handy's lawyers had eliminated this evidence as use against her from this day forward. It was again a Catch Twenty-Two for the prosecution of the Rains case. If she had never been charged with soliciting to have Abner Stitt murdered, they could have questioned her about it. But now with this plea, a North Carolina court would not allow, over her objection, evidence to come in concerning the Abner Stitt case.

I was sitting on the opposite side of the courtroom from Rick Stanton. He was vigorously taking notes. I made myself a note to explain to him the legal implication of the no-contest plea after this hearing was over. I doubted that even Blaine Cromer understood that implication.

Judge Fisher went on. "Now, Mrs. Handy, by this plea of no contest, you do not admit the actions you are accused of. Your position is simply that you have chosen not to contest the state's evidence. Is that correct?"

Powers whispered to Handy, "Say, yes, your honor."

"Yes, your honor."

Fisher went on. "Now, Mrs. Handy, by the terms of this agreement, you are sentenced to unsupervised probation for a period of six months. Do you understand that, Mrs. Handy?"

"Say, yes, your honor," Powers whispered to her.

"Yes, your honor."

"And finally, Mrs. Handy, you are ordered to pay into the office of the clerk of court a one-hundred-dollar fine. Do you agree to that, Mrs. Handy?"

"Say yes, your honor," Powers whispered again.

"Yes, your honor."

I couldn't help but recall the words of the Bob Dylan song "William Zan Zinger a six-month sentence." Hell, I thought. William Zan Zinger got six months for murder. Henrietta was only paying a hundred-dollar fine.

"Mr. Bailiff, I believe that's all the business we have today. Adjourn court."

The next week, Democratic Governor Cox appointed Republican Judge Fisher to an additional six-year term. This would be the only Republican judge so blessed by Democratic Governor Cox in his twenty years as governor.

After the bailiff closed court, I noticed a woman sitting in front of Rick Stanton begin to stand, shaking her head in disgust. I believed she was Pricey Meyers.

Rick Stanton quickly ran up to Pricey to talk to her.

Blaine Westmoreland came walking toward the back doors to leave the courtroom.

"Can I walk with you, Blaine?" I asked.

"Sure."

We caught the elevator. We were the only two in it.

"I've never seen anything that disgusting in all my years on the force," Blaine said, red-faced with anger. "I used to have respect for Tony Southern, but I wondered in there whose side he was on. Larry Franklin and that judge there did a better job of representing Henrietta than Powers did. You notice they didn't ask me anything. I don't know a whole lot of law, but I didn't hear the judge ask anybody even so much as any evidence to justify that plea he had accepted."

"Blaine, I'll catch you later," I said as we reached the first floor.

I stayed on the elevator and hit the fifth floor button again. I wanted to catch Rick Stanton if I could.

"Rick, do you know what this does?"

"It kills your case, I guess, Michael. I've seen some deals made as a reporter in my day. Michael, I don't see how you're gonna be able to do anything with your case after this. Powers has clearly demonstrated he controls these courts, and I don't see how you're going to get any witnesses to say anything bad about Mrs. Henrietta Handy after that show. What're you gonna do, Michael?"

"Scott and I have appealed the court of appeals decision to the Supreme Court."

"Yea, my sources have told me that already, and they've also told me that after your appeal was filed in the Supreme Court,

Forbes-Grundy hired the chief justice to represent Armand Chandler and Chandler against you and Scott."

"Rick, are you telling me that Forbes-Grundy has hired the chief justice of the Supreme Court, a sitting judge, to argue against me and Scott before that same court?"

"That's exactly what I'm saying, Michael. But he won't be sitting on the court at the time he's representing the insurance company against you. He's going to resign after lobbying the other eight judges on the North Carolina Supreme Court, and then, as a former judge, he will argue against you and Scott."

"Are you sure about that, Rick?"

"I'm as sure about it as we're standing here."

"How do you know?"

"Michael, I can't give you my sources. You know as well as I do, I give up my sources and in no time I don't have any."

"That's wrong, Rick."

"Well, it may be wrong, Michael, but it's apparently legal. Who do you know that's gonna tell Chief Justice Smith that he's got to give all that money the insurance company's paid him back and he can't do that?"

I figured that was a rhetorical question, so I didn't even bother to try and answer.

Chapter 43

I know it showed all over my body and my face when I got home. Jean saw how distressed I was.

"Went like you thought, didn't it, Michael?"

"Yea, sure did, Jean. I keep praying for a miracle, but it just didn't come. These people got it wrapped up so tight. You know I went to law school to fight for people who couldn't fight for themselves, but in this case, the people we're fighting are so powerful they buy judges like some people buy puppies. You find an honest judge, or at least one who's decided to be honest like Horrace C. Linney, and in a couple months, they've bought 'em a new judge. I just don't know how you win."

"Do you feel like that fellow Don Quixote we learned about in high school who went around fighting windmills?"

"I sure do, Jean. And you know my buddy Rick Stanton with the newspaper? He says Forbes-Grundy and the insurance company have already bought the chief justice of the North Carolina Supreme Court and put him on their payroll. Rick said he couldn't tell me how he knew, but within a few days or a week or so the paper will be printing that the chief justice of the North Carolina Supreme Court has resigned to join the law firm of Forbes-Grundy and then he will appear before the supreme court against me and Reggie. I just wanna give up and you and me go on up to the mountains. This summer showed us we can make a hell of a good living up there."

"Michael, I know you're down and you don't need this, but I've got a letter here from our bank up in Galax. It's from the president of the bank himself. He says he's sorry to tell us, but Judge Leo Demarkus has seized our bank account and ordered it paid into the office of the clerk of court and intends to distribute it to some farmer who claims beer tabs from people who were part of the overflow crowd who camped on his dairy farm have destroyed his dairy herd and his whole dairy business. I would like to have kept this from you, I wish to God it had never happened and this had never come, but I didn't see any way I could avoid showing it to you as soon as you got here."

"Jean, you're right, you had to show it to me. I had to see this. I've got to say that is the damnedest legal theory I've ever heard in my life for liability. I don't see how they could possibly win, but we've got to defend against their suit. We're looking at a couple of months before we'll be in the North Carolina Supreme Court in the Rains case, so I've got some time to work on this thing up in Virginia. I guess it's fair to say all courts are crooked to some extent, but from what I've heard about Virginia, you have a lot better shot up there than you do in North Carolina. Let's try to get some sleep, then we'll drive up to the courthouse in Hillsville tomorrow."

Jean and I stopped for a breakfast of ham and eggs at a nice little restaurant on 52 just off the Blue Ridge Parkway. When we got to the courthouse, of course everybody recognized me. Just a few weeks before, I had been the king of the hill in Carroll County, Virginia, bringing jobs and prosperity to people all over the county who were selling goods and services to the crowd that had come to our festival. As I started in the courthouse, I saw Winston Peeler, a Hillsville lawyer whom I had come to know and like.

Winston said, "Michael, you better get in there. Your case is being tried right now."

Having no idea what on earth was going on, I rushed into the courtroom and there sat Judge Demarkus, and on the right was Francis Wyclif, the one-man Forbes-Grundy of Carroll County, Virginia, with a man beside him whom I thought I might have met at some time but couldn't really remember.

"Mr. Spears, you are charged in this civil action," Judge Demarkus began, "with letting one of your people sell ham biscuits at your festival after giving Mr. Porter here exclusive right to sell ham biscuits at your festival. How do you plead, Mr. Spears?"

"Well, for one thing, your honor, this is the very first time I've heard about this matter. I haven't been served with anything, and I deny liability of any kind, but I need a continuance to prepare a defense."

"Mr. Spears, I've got right here in the file that you were served by notice of publication in the Hillsville Tribune as Virginia law requires because you were not a citizen or resident of the state of Virginia."

"But, your honor," I protested, "although I'm not a citizen or resident up here, I do pay taxes up here, and anybody who wanted to send me a letter to serve me down in North Carolina could've walked right over to the tax office, gotten my address, and sent me a letter. What I'm saying, your honor, is I am denied due process for lack of service, and I'm sure the Virginia Court of Appeals up in Richmond would agree with me on that point."

Oh shit, I thought to myself. I had just insulted this hillbilly by telling him he didn't know the law in front of all his people sitting in his courtroom. And, furthermore, by implication, I had just threatened him that if he didn't rule my way, I'd see that the Virginia Court of Appeals gave me the justice I deserved.

"Mr. Spears, I don't know how y'all do things down in Winston-Salem, North Carolina, but we got our own set of rules here in Hillsville, Virginia. And I'm telling you, I'm gonna try this case whether you like it or not. And you sit down there and offer a defense, if you have one, to Mr. Wyclif's client, or you may leave if you want to, but I'm telling you, I'm gonna try this case right now. Your motion for a continuance is denied, and I think you might've made a motion to dismiss, it weren't clear to me, but if you did, that motion is denied. Now, it's up to you"

I sat down at the other council's table, and Jean sat beside me.

"Who's that lady there, Mr. Spears?"

"This is my," I paused, "my ah, my friend, your honor."

"Well, does she have a name?"

"My name's Jean Duncan, your honor."

"Well, y'all be seated, and lets get this thing started."

Attorney Wyclif began. "Mr. Porter, would you tell his honor what happened during that wild festival out there at Pot Rock?"

"Well, judge, it is like this. I come up to Michael there."

The judge interrupted. "Mr. Porter, would you identify who you're talking about?"

"I'm talkin' 'bout Michael. Everybody knows Michael. The feller sittin' right there beside that purdy girl. And I says to Michael, my wife makes awful good ham biscuits. I would like to sell some of them at that there festival you was hav'n', and Michael says to me, 'I is heard your ham biscuits is the best they is in Carroll County, Virginia, and I would be proud for you to sell them ham biscuits at my festival.' So I come up there each day of the festival and I sold nigh onto a hundred of them biscuits at a dollar a piece to them hippies that was at that there festival. But, judge, I tell ya I coulda sold a thousand more of them ham biscuits, 'cept Michael let one of them hippies he had work'n' for him sell ham biscuits, too."

Wyclif interrupted Porter's testimony. "Mr. Porter, how much money do you reckon you lost as a result of Mr. Spears hav'n' his worker up there competing against you selling ham biscuits?"

"Objection, your honor. This is a leading question. Mr. Wyclif is clearly telling his client what to say with his question. He's telling him to tell you he lost money, and, furthermore, he hasn't established any basis for any exclusive contract to sell ham biscuits, anyway."

"I'm gonna overrule that objection. I just don't see it that way. You go ahead and finish your answer, Mr. Porter."

"Judge, as I said before, I reckon I coulda sold another thousand ham biscuits at a dollar apiece, so I reckon I lost a thousand dollars."

I began to call to mind that I'd met this fellow in the community and he was always hounding me about some way he could make money doing this or that for me, and I vaguely recall him saying something about his wife made good ham biscuits. But, as a lawyer, I knew damn well I'd never given him any exclusive contract to sell ham biscuits. I couldn't help but think what a funny episode of the Andy Griffith Show this would make, but damned if it didn't make me mad that lawyer Wyclif and Porter and the judge were conniving to extort a few hundred dollars out of me. Hell, these people could nickel and dime me to death like this and tie me up in the courts for eternity. As funny as the episode might seem upon a retelling in Winston-Salem, I had to put a stop to this or these people were gonna take everything I had.

Attorney Wyclif asked his next question: "Mr. Porter, Mr. Spears gave you an exclusive contract to sell them ham biscuits, didn't he?"

"Objection, your honor. This is the very essence of what a leading question is."

"I'm gonna deny your objection, and I don't know how y'all practice law down in Winston-Salem, but up here, we let people give their testimony."

Porter answered the question. "Yea, he give me an exclusive contract."

"Your witness, Mr. Spears," Wyclif concluded.

"Mr. Porter, where did this discussion you're saying you and I had take place?"

"Oh, it was up at the gas station up in Hebron. You ought to remember, you was pump'n' gas and I come up to you and started tell'n' you 'bout my wife's ham biscuits."

"Well, while I was standing there pumping gas, I didn't tell you that nobody else would be selling ham biscuits at the festival, did I?"

"Objection, Mr. Spears." Suddenly from the bench, the judge was issuing his own objection. "You're doing exactly what you were objecting to Mr. Wyclif doing. That's a leading question."

Well, damn, I thought. When the judge objects, do I say sustained or do I make an argument? I chose the latter.

"If your honor please, this is cross-examination, and always for purposes of cross-examination of a witness not your own, you are allowed leading questions. Your honor is correct in that my question was, in fact, a leading question. But if your honor please, I would point out, with all due respect, that on cross-examination, leading questions are entirely proper and I do have the right to use them."

The judge took a moment to think...then looked over at Wyclif, who nodded in the affirmative, and Judge Demarkus said, "Well, Mr. Spears, I'm going to allow it this time, but you be careful. Mr. Porter, you go ahead and answer."

"You didn't exactly tell me that nobody else was selling ham biscuits, but that's the way I took it, the way you told me how good you figured my wife's ham biscuits was."

"Do you have any more questions, Mr. Spears?"

"No, your honor."

"Mr. Wyclif?"

"No, your honor."

Judge Demarkus leaned back in his chair and said, "I'm gonna make my ruling. Let me think just a minute."

"Your honor, you're not gonna allow oral argument?"

"I don't see no need to, Mr. Spears."

Suddenly, Judge Demarkus perked up and looked out into the audience. Jean punched me and told me to turn around.

"Who's that man?" she asked.

"That's the tax supervisor, Jean," I said as I looked out into the courtroom and saw Mr. Lowe, the tax supervisor, raising his right hand, opening and closing it, indicating five with his right hand and mouthing five thousand to Judge Demarkus. Judge Demarkus just grinned in response to the tax supervisor's coaching from the audience. This was surreal. I was sitting here in a courtroom with one of the county officials sitting in the audience giving extra assistance to the judge to come up with a figure as if we were on "The Price is Right" and the audience was yelling to bid five thousand on that new Plymouth.

Judge Demarkus began to speak. "I'm gonna find for the plaintiff, Mr. Porter, but I do think that a thousand dollars is too much. Them ham biscuits woulda cost you something to make, so I'm gonna give you seven hundred fifty dollars. Next case is called."

"Your honor," I spoke up, "I want to give notice of appeal."

"Well, now, Mr. Spears, you do have the right of appeal, but I am going to have to set an appeal bond. Now, let me see." He leaned back in his chair again and looked at Lowe, who was again mouthing five thousand dollars and holding up five fingers clasping and re-clasping his hand. "I'm gonna make that appeal bond five-thousand dollars cash. Now, I want the parties to the next case come up here. We've got to move along."

Jean and I walked out of the courtroom and out to the front of the courthouse. There was a newsstand out there with a copy of the Hillsville paper. The headline said, "Ministers outraged at conduct at local music festival."

"Oh, shit," Jean said. "Preachers didn't get nuthin out of the festival, so they gotta stir somebody up and make 'em hate me and you, Michael."

I put fifty cents in and got a copy of the paper. I began reading: "Local minister Jason Fellers leads group of concerned citizens before board of supervisors demanding that sheriff and board of supervisors clean up festivals in Carroll County, Virginia."

At least I wasn't all alone. The ministers felt the need to impose the morality upon the forty-year-old Galax fiddlers' convention in addition to mine. I was familiar with this sort of thing, having grown up in a fundamentalist Baptist church. I knew how a preacher could make a career out of attacking dirty bookstores; couchie shows at fairs, or abortion clinics. It was not uncommon here in the South for an evangelist to stir young men and women to violent acts, such as the bombing of abortion clinics and the tarring and feathering of the couchie dancers who used to come with the fairs to the rural counties.

It did look like the worst they were doing to me was stirring a bunch of fruit cakes up just to file suits against me, and no matter how unpleasant and time consuming it might be, I could handle that. Jean and I started to go back to our car to return to Winston-Salem, but suddenly both of us recalled why we had come up here in the first place, to see what had been filed against me in the courthouse. Jean and I both walked back into the courthouse and over to the office of the clerk of court. We started to walk around the counter of the clerk of court, as I had done at least a hundred times and as anybody is entitled to do in America, to take a look at the public records to see what had been filed against me. As I started to round the counter, suddenly Denice Morley jumped from her desk and ran up, blocking my way.

"We have been instructed not to allow you to see any of them files," Denice said. "Mr. White, come here please," Denice shouted out.

Mr. White, the clerk of court, came running from the back. At the same time, Nannie Edwards, the other assistant clerk, ran up to block my way.

Mr. White repeated, "We have been instructed not to let you see these files."

"By whom?" I demanded.

"Judge Demarkus come down here several days ago and told us we was to keep you out of here."

I thought to myself, this can't be happening. Even an ax murderer is entitled to see what he's accused of doing. And here we are, in the two-hundredth year of our freedom as Americans and these yokels are telling me I'm not entitled to see the civil files where I've been sued. I looked at Jean. She was fighting mad. I was afraid she was gonna jump one of these two women who was blocking our way. It was clear that nothing positive could come out of anything we could say and do in Hillsville, Virginia, this day, so I turned around and whispered to Jean, "Let's go."

I was able to calm Jean down by the time we got to the car. I knew that my experience as a civil rights lawyer was going to get me out of this situation. I truly felt for the first time in my life what it must have been like to have lived in the old South and been black. You can read about the cases, you can read about the lynchings, you can read about how our basic human rights were denied to people for hundreds of years, but until you actually experience that denial of basic human rights, it's hard to truly relate. On the way back to Winston-Salem, I told Jean that we would have to remove all of the cases to federal court in Abingdon, Virginia.

Chapter 44

I got out my copies of the United States code, the volume covering removal of cases from state court to federal court. Although I had done removals of cases from state court to federal court before, that area of law was so complex that no lawyer should ever attempt a removal without simultaneously consulting the federal statutes. One problem that I certainly was gonna have with the renewal was going to be that the federal court requires a copy of all of the pleadings from the state court to accompany the petition to remove. Here, my main reason for removing to federal court was the fact that the Virginia state clerk, Mr. White up there in Hillsville, refused to allow me to see the state court files.

To be entitled to remove from state court to federal court, there must also be either a federal question or total diversity of citizenship. I certainly had total diversity of citizenship because I was a citizen of North Carolina and anyone who was going to be suing me would have been a citizen of the state of Virginia. I knew I did have a federal question, at least in part. The federal question was the violation of my civil rights, specifically the denial by the clerk of court in Virginia to allow me to see the files. I was certain that any federal judge who looked at my removal petition would see this as a denial of due process of law, a fundamental right under the Bill of Rights of the American Constitution. I alleged in my petition that the refusal by the clerk to let me see the files was a denial of due process of law. Jean was with me and acting as a sounding board for my ideas in the removal petition.

"Michael, why do you think the federal courts are gonna be any better up there in the mountains of Virginia than that judge we saw yesterday?"

"Jean, the process by which federal judges are chosen is much more public than the process that Reggie described to you, the way North Carolina judges and judges like that yokel up in Virginia yesterday are chosen."

"You have more faith in the system then I do. I always thought judges were all crooks, and since I've been with you, I haven't had any reason to change my mind."

"Federal judges are scrutinized by the Judiciary Committee of the United States Senate and are appointed by the President of the United States. The Senators in the state where they will be a Federal Judge nominate them, but there is usually an FBI investigation of them and this report is given to the president and to the judiciary committee of the U.S. Senate before they can be confirmed as judges. The Senate Judiciary Committee is made up of both Republicans and Democrats. For instance, at the present time here in 1976, Republican Senator Orin Hatch, a Mormon from Utah, and Democratic Senator Ted Kennedy, a Massachusetts Catholic, are both on the Senate Judiciary Committee. Crooked federal judges have gotten through the process and been appointed before, but with people like Hatch and Kennedy and their staffs looking at the nominees, it is harder for a crook or a complete hack to be confirmed as a federal judge at any level from district court to the U.S. Supreme Court."

"Since you knew this already, why didn't you and Reggie file the Rains case in the federal court?"

"Believe me, Jean, we would've liked to, but we didn't have diversity of citizenship or a federal question to justify being in federal court."

"You mean murder's not a federal question?"

"No, generally murder is not. Now, if it were a lynching it would be because that would be a civil rights violation, but your old run-of-the-mill murder case just won't get you into federal court."

Jean and I finished the petition for removal to federal court and drove the original up to the federal courthouse in Abingdon, Virginia, the next day. On the way back, we dropped off a copy that we hand delivered to the clerk, Mr. White, at the Hillsville courthouse. You should've seen his face when he saw we had requested the federal judge issue an order to the clerk of court in Hillsville to provide me with the state court files and all cases wherein I was a defendant.

Within a few days, the federal judge issued an order directing State Clerk White to make the files available. Jean and I drove up to the courthouse at Hillsville with the order in hand. I don't know who White had talked to, but he was a changed man and couldn't do enough to please me and Jean. As a matter of fact, he already had a stack of nine files with various suits that had been filed against me and a certificate notarized by Judge Demarkus himself that these were all of the files from the office of the clerk of court of Carroll County, Virginia, wherein I was a defendant. Clerk White handed me the stack of nine files and said there wasn't another paper in his office with my name on it. I knew that this wasn't proper of him to be handing me all of the original files and not so much as keep copies for his own records. But, I thought, what the hell, as much as these people have done wrong in this courthouse in Carroll County, they could go to hell and suffer the consequences of whatever problems might arise from their mistake here.

Within three days of the time I picked up the files from White's office, I received orders from three different lawyers who had been representing the people in the various cases dismissing every one of the cases with prejudice. With prejudice means the case cannot be filed again once it's entered into the court record.

Chapter 45

"Lets celebrate, Michael. This is a big old victory that we both needed."

Being a couple and living together, Jean and I decided to go out to Winston-Salem's finest restaurant, Leon's Café. We both ordered their New York Strip and both drank our usual Budweiser. On the way home, Jean mentioned that somebody was still holding over two-hundred-thousand dollars of our money. As a matter of fact, this was money that we intended to split the profits from the festival, and we needed to pay our quarterly tax on our profits. Otherwise, with penalties and interest, the state and federal government would eat up all our profits and Jean and I would be left with nothing.

"I assume the federal judge will look at the file and see that that's an open matter and enter an order."

"Don't you assume anything, Michael."

"Let's prepare a motion to get our money back."

We prepared a motion and an order for the judge to sign and sent copies of both for the Federal Judge and for Francis Wyclif, who had represented the dairy farmer and seized our money. Again, I made an assumption that turned out to be wrong. Since the lawsuit had been dismissed with prejudice, there was no reason whatsoever for our money not to be returned to us. However, in a few days, I received a motion from lawyer Wyclif asking that our money be held and asking the court to allow him to re-file the dairy farmer's lawsuit. Wyclif's motion was accompanied by an affidavit that said that he had inadvertently dismissed the original lawsuit with prejudice, which he had intended to dismiss without prejudice. Judge Long, the Federal District Court Judge, sent me notice that he would be hearing my motion for the return of my money and Wyclif's motion to allow him to reopen the lawsuit. I couldn't imagine any judge allowing that lawsuit to be reopened. Jean and I drove up to the Federal Courthouse for the hearing. When I got to the federal courtroom, an attorney named Brandon Jones introduced himself to me and said he would be representing Wright, the dairy farmer. Attorney Jones told me, "I've already talked to Judge Long, and he suggested this motion to correct attorney Wyclif's mistake."

Judge Long opened the hearing.

"Your honor," I argued, "there is no pending lawsuit, so there is no basis for the court to hold my money."

Judge Long responded, "Mr. Spears, this court isn't holding your money; it's that court over there in Hillsville. And I don't have the authority to order a state Court to do anything other than send a case over here."

To my surprise, Jones actually spoke up in my behalf. "Actually, your honor, you do have the authority to order that court to release that money, or, as I'm asking you, you have the authority that the money be transferred up here to Abingdon pending the litigation that I intend to file in behalf of Mr. Wyclif's former client."

I couldn't believe what I was hearing. This federal judge was so dumb that he was claiming on the record that he didn't have the authority to order a state clerk of court to release money wrongfully held.

"But what about this other motion you've got here, Mr. Jones? You and I have talked about this, and I don't see any reason why I shouldn't amend lawyer Wyclif's mistake and let you re-file that suit up here in federal court and let a jury of good people from Western Virginia decide whether or not Mr. Spears owes that dairy farmer any money."

This judge is actually telling me from the bench that in an ex-parte conference he and attorney Jones decided they were going to reopen Wyclif's suit and let old lawyer Wyclif off the hook.

"Your honor," I said, speaking up. "There is no basis whatsoever for my money to be held. As Mr. Jones has said, you do have the authority to order the state court over in Hillsville to turn that money over to somebody, and since there is not a lawsuit pending, regardless of what you do concerning amending the order, I'm entitled to my money back."

How does anybody as dumb as this man get to be a federal judge? I felt a compromise coming. Judge Long was gonna throw me a bone and give my money back since there was no way in hell it could be legally held from me, but he was going to grant attorney Wyclif's, now attorney Jones's motion to amend the dismissal with prejudice and allow Jones to file a new suit against me here in federal court. It would be a suit that would have no legal basis. It would be making new law if it went so far as to go to a jury, but it would still be a lawsuit that would consume my time, energy, and mental stability. I just was getting to a point where I didn't know how much more abuse from the judicial system I could take. There was no way in hell that I could have filed the motion to amend that lawyer Wyclif, now Jones was going to prevail upon. If I had filed that motion, I would have been the laughing stock of everybody in the courthouse and would have been sanctioned by the judge for having the stupidity or audacity to have filed the motion. I was becoming totally sick of the practice of law, but like Brer Fox, or was it Brer Rabbit; I was into this tar baby with both hands and both feet.

Here it came. Judge Long began in that twangy high-pitched West Virginia way of talking. "Mr. Spears, I am gonna give your money back. And, Mr. Jones, I am gonna grant your motion, too. So you file that lawsuit anytime you want to, Mr. Jones.

Chapter 46

Jean and I were more pleased then unpleased. She had begun to think we weren't gonna get our money back, and our money was running short. We needed the money we'd made from the music festival. My law practice was suffering badly from the time I was taking on these cases that weren't producing any income, and I guess you could say we had gotten at least half a loaf from the federal court in Abingdon, Virginia. On the way back, I discussed with Jean whether or not I should file a counter-claim if Brandon Jones re-filed the ridiculous suit over the beer tops destroying the dairy herd. We both felt we could not lose a suit concerning the music festival. We also felt we could not pay any amount, even a few hundred dollars, in legal extortion to anyone up there who filed a frivolous suit. Everybody up there in Carroll County knew everybody else's business, especially mine since I had started holding the music festivals. There would be no way to pay any extortion demand without everybody else in the county finding out about it. And once that dam broke, we knew there would be so many vultures swarming down to get a piece of our carcass that there wouldn't be anything left.

I had consulted my attorney friend, Winston Peeler, after the ministers began their attack and the multitude of suits had been filed against me. I had asked Winston to represent me before we moved the cases to federal court.

Winston had said, "I couldn't charge you enough money to justify what I'd lose by representing you, the way you are under attack. Have you ever seen the movie *Elmer Gantry*?"

"Yea, Winston. Burt Lancaster is the star of that movie. As I recall it, Elmer Gantry was a shoe salesman who became an evangelist touring the mid-west in the movie."

"That's the movie I'm talkin' about," Winston said. "Michael, you remember how Elmer Gantry one day was everybody's hero and he couldn't do no wrong and then the next day he'd done something simple, like been caught with a hooker, and everybody hated him and he couldn't do no right? What I'm saying to you is, I ain't never seen anybody in Carroll County, Virginia, who went from be'n everybody's hero in the papers, the churches, and the civic groups one minute and then the next minute, just cause you had a bunch a, maybe it was a few thousand, naked women splashin' around at Pot Rock in Crooked Creek, become the evil Satan responsible for everything wrong in Carroll County. Did you realize that there was an earthquake in Carroll County the week after your festival?"

"Yea, Winston, I read about that in my hometown paper. The paper said it rattled a few dishes and windows, but nobody knew of any damage it did."

"That's right, nobody knows of any damage it did, but I heard that Sunday after that earthquake, there was preachers tellin their folks from the pulpit that that was God punishing the people of Carroll County for the Sodom and Gomorrah situation you'd brought up here."

As it turned out, I damned sure didn't wanna be in the state courts in Carroll County, and as bad as things were shaping up to be in the federal court over at Abingdon, at least I was in my own environment with my experience in civil rights cases in federal court.

"Jean," I said as we prepared for bed at night, "I'm gonna call Reggie tomorrow morning and tell him about what happened over in Abingdon."

"I bet he'll get a real hoot out of that," Jean said.

I walked into Reggie's office.

"You busy?" I asked.

"Of course I'm busy. Don't you ever practice law yourself? Sometimes I feel like I've kicked myself in the butt for not staying with you on that New River Jam festival, but I am mak'n money as a lawyer, and I do enjoy practicing law, except when you walk in the door," he said, laughing.

"Reggie, you're not gonna believe what happened in federal court up in Abingdon, Virginia."

"Michael, if your name was written on the file in any capacity, I don't believe I would be shocked at anything that happened. Look, you're good at buying and selling land. You have a knack for that that most people would kill for, no pun intended. Your festival up there is going like gangbusters, and for eleven months out of twelve, you and that beautiful woman you've got with you now get to enjoy that festival site and that pristine stream without anybody else around unless you want'em there. If I were you, I'd take that cute little woman with me and go up there and forget about practicing law. You don't really like it that much anyway, or, let me rephrase that, losing, which you've been doin' a whole lot of lately, takes so much out of you that it's just not worthwhile to you anymore. And let me give you one piece of advice from this older, more experienced lawyer: most everybody is going to win half the time and lose half the time. That's the law of averages because on that other side is going to be another lawyer who is also going to win half the time and lose half the time, and if you're going to continue practicing law, you have to learn to accept that."

"Well, Reggie, let me tell you what happened in federal court in Abingdon, Virginia. I'd told you about how a whole slue of lawsuits were filed against me in Carroll County relating to the festival, and all I had to do to get every one of them dismissed with prejudice was to move them to the federal court in Abingdon where those Carroll County lawyers didn't have any connections, leaving them one-on-one against me, which somehow they didn't think was a fair fight. Well, anyway, one of the lawyers up there had seized our bank account as part of his lawsuit, and when I petitioned the federal court for our bank account back, the old devil filed a motion with the federal judge saying that he had mistakenly signed a dismissal with prejudice and asked the federal judge to change the dismissal with prejudice to a dismissal without prejudice so his client could sue me again to get a chunk of that money they'd seized."

"There's no way a federal judge would grant a motion like that," Reggie said.

"That's what I thought, too, Reggie. But I'll be Goddamned if the judge didn't grant it while Jean and me were up there yesterday morning."

Reggie lost it. He began bending over with laughter and was laughing so hard, he couldn't talk or even catch his breath.

"Reggie, I didn't see the humor in it, myself."

"Nobody, nobody, nobody but you could find himself in a situation like that. I have never heard of a judge doing that, and I doubt that I ever will again. You know the character Pigpen from Charley Brown? I think Pigpen's the one. Anyway, I'm talking about the character from Charley Brown who's always walking around with a dark cloud over his head. That's got to be you. I don't see how you take it, and I may as well go ahead and tell you that in three weeks, we're set for oral argument in the North Carolina Supreme Court and opposing council will be the right Honorable Jessie Smith, former chief justice of that same court."

"Do you think we have a chance to win, Reggie?"

"I'm not gonna hold my breath, and I'm not gonna put any money on our side. I think it's reasonable to assume their Honorable Jessie Smith has already discussed the case at length with the eight associates he used to supervise on the Supreme Court up until only weeks ago. It'll take a miracle for us to win, and I do believe miracles happen, but I believe it's very rare."

"If this doesn't work, then what?"

"It's your call, but we are pretty much through if we don't get this motion. That plea bargain Henrietta made with the Abner Stitt case basically fried us. I hate to say it, Michael, but without the letter, we will have nothing."

"In that Virginia case, I stand a chance at losing everything I have."

"I know, and my law practice is dying from Linstrom doing everything he can to get back at me."

Reggie and I stood there for a second, afraid to say the obvious. We had both worked so hard and sacrificed so much; we would almost rather die than give up. But like I said, this was obvious.

I turned my head and slowly said, "I guess we are agreed then, this is our one last shot."

Chapter 47

Three days before Reggie, Jean, and I drove down to the Supreme Court; the bad news came by certified mail from Brandon Jones's law firm. At least we'd been served with the complaint this time. It was a little more polished, but essentially it accused me, the owner CEO of New River Jam, Inc., of negligently failing to provide enough space for all of the anticipated campers and knowingly not providing for them once they got to the site, thus forcing "unwashed hippies" to take over most of Northwestern Carroll County, including and not limited to the dairy farm of plaintiff Wright. The complaint went on to say that the dirty unwashed hippies had so frightened farmer Wright's dairy cattle that their milk production was drastically cut and would probably never resume the level it had previously been. Among the acts that were alleged to upset farmer Wright's cows were nude dancing around campfires and the prolific use of illicit drugs. There was the usual allegation of extreme emotional distress, lack of sleep, headaches, and anxiety produced by my wrongful actions. Apparently, the grievous act or the one that caused the most damage was the leaving of untold numbers of beer tabs, and those were the days when beer tabs were torn directly off a can of beer and often discarded at the feet of the beer drinker, and that these beer tabs were such a great danger to farmer Wright's cows in that when munching on the grass in the pastures now abandoned by the wild hippies, the cows could consume those beer tabs which would lacerate their innards and render them dead. I really hadn't needed this blow just before going to Raleigh for our appearance before the North Carolina Supreme Court.

The governor had not yet chosen anyone to replace Chief Justice Jessie Smith after he resigned from the Supreme Court, so this left only eight justices to hear our case. They were Justices Haywood, Hayes, Benton, Becton, Wilson, Riley, Choate, and Anderson. Justice Hayes was acting chief justice and probably was to be appointed chief justice, even when the Governor appointed a replacement for Justice Jessie Smith. All eight of the justices were Democrats. However, they varied in background and philosophy, going from Justice Haywood, who had been, early on, a George Wallace man, to Justice Anderson, whom I believed to be the most liberal of the group and had a history with the American Civil Liberties Union and some experience with civil rights activities prior to taking the bench. Reggie and I knew that they didn't have to consider our case but had accepted our petition for cert for reasons a supreme court did not have to disclose, and they had also granted oral argument, although they did not have to grant oral argument, and again for reasons they did not have to disclose. Justice Hayes, as acting chief justice, began the session by announcing for the record what case was before the court and who the opposing attorneys were.

Justice Hayes went on to say, "Justice Smith, it's good to see you with us again here today. It feels strange to me, and I'm sure it does to all of my colleagues, to welcome you here today as just another attorney arguing a case. Now, I believe this appeal was come to us from Forsyth County by way of the court of appeals upon a unanimous decision by the court of appeals, with Judge Cletus Freedman writing that opinion. I believe it was Judge Anthony Case from the Superior Court of Forsyth County who made the original ruling that is on appeal before us today. Is that correct, gentlemen?"

Again, Reggie, because he had been here many times, was speaking with his experience for our side. Reggie and Smith both acknowledged the history of the case as presented by Judge Hayes.

Judge Hayes went on. "Judge Case's ruling as affirmed by the court of appeals was that this document was not to be admitted or used in evidence because the chain of evidence had been broken, making it difficult, if not impossible, to insure that 'the document' had not been altered. Is that correct, gentlemen?"

Reggie and Smith both acknowledged that that was the ruling of Judge Case as affirmed by the court of appeals.

"In addition, gentlemen, we're on appeal today from Judge Case's gag order sealing this document forevermore as affirmed again by our court of appeals. Is that correct, gentlemen?"

"It is, your honor," Smith and Reggie both said.

"Now, I'm going to instruct both of you gentlemen in your arguments not to discuss the contents of the document. Is that understood?" he said roughly and loudly.

"It is, your honor," Reggie said.

"Yes, your honor," Smith answered.

"You may begin your argument, Mr. Scott."

"May it please the court my colleague and I attempted to introduce 'the document' as a part of a deposition of Armand Chandler, president and CEO of the Chandler Life and Casualty Insurance Company."

Judge Hayes interrupted Reggie. "Mr. Scott, I don't believe the issue has been raised either by Mr. Saits before Judge Case or at your hearing before the court of appeals, but the record here to me indicates that your colleague there, Mr. Spears, tried to slide one over in that deposition by handing 'the document' directly to Mr. Chandler without even giving Mr. Saits an opportunity to review that document. Isn't that correct, Mr. Smith?"

Smith responded, "That is correct, your honor. Mr. Saits told me that that is what Mr. Spears tried to do. And I was outraged by such conduct, but you know how Mr. Saits and I don't like to ever question the integrity of members of the bar, so we haven't really raised that issue up to this point."

I'll be a son-of-a-bitch here. They knew that was an oversight on my part. I apologized to Saits; the record shows that. And he grabbed the damn letter out of my hand. All he had to do was to just ask to see it and I would have been glad to have handed it to him for his review anyway.

244

"Your honor," Reggie tried to continue, "that was an oversight by Mr. Spears, and Mr. Saits certainly was able to see it and to review it, and I think you'll see that the record reflects it was never officially handed to Mr. Chandler by anyone."

"I don't see it that way, Mr. Scott," Judge Hayes retorted. "It's clear to me there was an attempt to get this evidence in the record by whatever means possible, and I don't know that this court here shouldn't sanction your colleague here for his wrongful conduct, but we'll hold that in reserve right now. Go ahead, Mr. Scott."

The old son-of-a-bitch just continued to beat that dead horse. He knew what he was doing. He was taking up Scott's time with that red herring so that the record wouldn't show any substance at all when anybody reviewed it in the future. Go ahead, you old son-of-a-bitch, I thought. You old hack, you got to sit there where you are for kissing ass and towing the party line, and now you're demanding respect.

Scott went on. "Your honor, all we were asking and all we ask now is that we have an opportunity to present this document to Mr. Chandler and let him tell us whether he's seen it and signed it and if he has any objections to the contents of it. We welcome giving him an opportunity to explain and point out anything that might be in error. There's a dead man at issue in this case, your honor, and there's an insu..." Scott wasn't even able to get out "insurance."

Hayes was determined that the real issue in this case, whether or not Chandler Insurance Company had contributed negligently or otherwise to the death of Harold Stennis Rains, was not going to be discussed.

"Mr. Scott, your time is up. I'll hear from Mr. Smith, I'm sorry, Judge Smith, at this time."

"Well, hold on, Justice Hayes. You're not the only judge up here. Maybe some of the rest of us have a question," Judge Haywood, who was sitting to Justice Hayses's far left interjected.

Judge Hayes looked over the top of his glasses down toward Jessie Smith with that "oh, shit" look on his face. Jessie Smith had this whole thing wrapped up and here was this George Wallace conservative who'd somehow gotten on this court who was just about to rewrite their movie script.

"Justice Hayes, I'm not bound by any gag order and you know that. What four judges below us have called a document is a letter, and it is a letter saying that a one million-dollar insurance policy on the life of one human being, Harold Stennis Rains, was canceled, and yet the pleadings in this case, which are before this court as part of the record, indicate that that one-million-dollar policy was paid on the life of that same Harold Stennis Rains after he was found brutally murdered nearly one year after this policy was supposedly canceled. Now, this case came to us before Judge Smith stepped down as our chief justice, and I'm going to assume," he said, the bitterness showing in his voice, "that the fact that Judge Smith is arguing before us today has nothing to do with the fact that this case was on the way to be heard by him and us and now by just us. Now, Judge Smith, I wanna ask you what the problem would be with Mr. Chandler answering the questions about this letter."

Smith stammered. It was obvious that he had never been dressed down by a judge in the manner that he was now, "Well, we, ah, we ah, believe, believe, ah, this, this is a forgery, judge."

"Do you now, Judge Smith?"

"Well, well, yes."

"Well, now, Judge Smith, explain to me what basis there is in the record for you to claim 'the document,' which I'm gonna call a letter, is a forgery?"

"Well, well, it's obvious. You must not have read the record, Judge Haywood."

"Show me what part of the record you're referring to, Judge Smith."

Judge Hayes was showing disgust in his face and even shaking his head. "Do we need to treat a former colleague like this?" Judge Hayes asked.

Judge Haywood began, "Judge Hayes, I should not have to remind you of this, but Judge Smith, although a colleague of ours, is now employed by the most prestigious and powerful law firm in our state, and he has no more, and should have no more, standing before this court than opposing attorneys Scott and Spears there."

Judge Haywood had been leaning over in his seat so he could look past his colleagues towards Judge Hayes. It was Judge Hayes he was addressing. Judges Benton, Becton, and Wilson had their heads bowed. Judges Riley and Choate sat stone-faced, staring straight ahead. I couldn't read Judge Anderson's face except that he appeared to be in deep thought.

"Judge Smith," Judge Haywood again began, "what would it hurt for your client, Mr. Chandler, to check his files and see if maybe he did write this letter?"

In typical lawyer style, Jessie Smith didn't really have an answer, so he went off on a tangent. "Your honor, at first the plaintiffs attempted to question my client with a copy of 'the document.' And then they broke and violated our sacred rule of the chain of evidence and the Honorable Anthony Case of Forsyth County, North Carolina, used his power as a superior court judge and ruled, and that ruling was unanimously upheld by the North Carolina Court of Appeals."

"I wish you would answer my question. A man has been murdered here and maybe your client has no negligence, but if we affirm the court of appeals opinion, we will never know, no one will ever know whether or not your client and his company were guilty in any way for the death of this man."

Judge Hayes spoke up. "That's all the time we have for this case. We're going to have to go on to our next case, gentlemen. The court will take a fifteen-minute recess."

Two weeks later, which was really rapid time, we received the order from the Supreme Court. They affirmed Judge Case and the court of appeals in a 6-to-2 decision. Their decision simply said, "Affirmed without comment." There was a twenty-page dissenting opinion written by Judge Haywood. Judge Anderson concurred with Judge Haywood without comment. Judge Hayes, as chief justice, directed that the opinion be an unpublished opinion, discouraging lawyers or anyone else from ever finding it or reading it. If I had ever felt victory in defeat, it was a victory to me to hear Judge Haywood put the real issues on the line and challenge these go along/get along judges.

Chapter 48

For the next week after our appearance before the North Carolina Supreme Court I couldn't leave the house. I would start each morning with a Budweiser. I didn't really care to eat, but Jean would go out for fast food or takeout of one kind or another. Sex was about the only thing I looked forward to in the day, and I couldn't stop thinking it was Jean's way of showing a little sympathy for me. I wasn't shaving or brushing my teeth or even bathing every day. Jean and I occasionally went to a bar, and there I had decided to let Chandler Corporation kill me in their legal way: I had taken up smoking.

With the beginning of a new week, Jean was up with the sun. I'd lay in bed while puffing on a Chandler listening to her first showering and singing in the shower. It was incredible how many of those old mountain songs she had picked up. I could now hear her singing "Rocky Top." I thought about getting up and joining her in the shower. I considered myself to be in a pretty sorry state of affairs when I wouldn't even get up to join a pretty girl in a shower, but that was the state I was in. She finished her shower and walked into the bedroom with her hands on her hips. The state of affairs I was in, I couldn't even look her in the eye. I turned and gazed at the opposite wall. Jean wasn't going to be stopped. She crawled right on top of the bed, bounced up and down a couple of times, then flopped down on top of me and sat cowgirl style on top of me. She then took the cigarette out of my hand and put it out, at the same time grabbing my jaw to force me to look her in the eyes.

"You know I have never asked you for anything."

"Uh huh," I mumbled.

"I never really asked you to do anything."

"Uh huh," I mumbled.

"Well, I'm asking you to do something now."

I sort of grimaced and looked at her out the corner of my eye.

"What?"

"I want you to get your sorry, lazy, pitiful, depressed ass out of this bed and to go in there and take a shower and shave and brush your teeth, and I'll even help you. And then when you're cleaned up, I want you to put your cleanest, nicest suit on and unwrap one of those nice new white shirts you must be saving to be buried in. I want you to put that white shirt on, and a tie, and that suit, and drive down to the courthouse, and I will go with you. I want you to go to the register of deeds, and I will go with you. And I want you to get, and I'll help you get it, a marriage license, and then we will go across the street to the Xion jewelry and get a couple wedding rings, and then we will come back to the Court house and get the clerk of court to marry us. I think it's about time you made me an honest woman.

"Since we got that money back from Virginia, we've got over two-hundred-thousand dollars in the bank. We've got your nice sports car, the Cadillac, the Jeep, the house here, and the farm in the mountains, and we don't owe anybody squat.

"It hurts to get beat down time and time again. It hurts me to see you getting beat down more than it hurts you to get beat down, but there are a whole lot more people in this world who are a whole lot worse off then we are, and I want you to get up from here and you and me are gonna get married, and then we're gonna take a week or two off for our honeymoon, and for our honeymoon, we're gonna go down to the Outer Banks of North Carolina and spend a week with your old friends, Jane and Brock, and you're gonna regain your energy, and when we get back from the beach, we're gonna file that answer to that complaint from that lawyer up in Abingdon, Virginia, and you're gonna use that skill as a lawyer that I know you got and we're gonna file a counter-claim that's gonna rock that dairy farmer's world."

It was in this moment that I realized I couldn't feel sorry for myself anymore. If I picked fights, I was going to lose every now and then, but I knew I had to still keep fighting, not for myself, but for the person I love and OUR future. It is needless to say, I never touched a Chandler cigarette again.

Jean jumped off the bed, pulled me out, and within three hours, we were a married couple on our honeymoon headed for Okracoke Island off the coast of North Carolina.

Jean had already called Jane and Brock to tell them we were on our way, and all we had to do first was to get married.

Jane was my oldest and dearest friend. We'd been friends since the 9th grade. We had been the nerd activists in our high school and had always walked to the beat of a different drummer. The sad thing about walking to the beat of a different drummer is you're always out of step with everybody else, but Jane and I had always been in step with each other, and that had been what mattered most to both of us. I had gone off and become a lawyer. Jane had gone off and become a veterinarian. Jane had been among the first women admitted to North Carolina State University, where she had studied in the pre-vet program before being admitted to the University of Oklahoma School of Veterinary Medicine with a full scholarship. Jane had married the summer before she was to enter the University of Oklahoma. She had sent a letter to Oklahoma stating that for their information, she would need to change her living arrangements since she had gotten married and would need married-student housing. Oklahoma had sent her, by return mail, a letter advising her that since she had gotten married and would thus be a housewife and not a serious practicing veterinarian, they were revoking her scholarship and her admission to their veterinary school. They said they needed serious veterinary students, not housewives. Jane had quickly applied to, and been admitted to, veterinary school in Brisbane, Australia. The next time I saw her, she was on TV being pulled from the top of a telephone booth where she was making an anti-Vietnam war speech as Lyndon Johnson's motorcade drove by on it's way for Johnson to meet with his lap dog, the prime minister of Australia. A few months later with the students on the streets of America shouting, "Hey, hey, LBJ, how many kids did you kill today," Johnson announced he would not run for a second full term. The big joke around at the time had become "People told me if I voted for Barry Goldwater in 1964, by 1968 there would be half a million Americans in Vietnam. Well, I voted for Barry Goldwater, and, sure enough by 1968, there were half a million Americans in Vietnam and over thirty thousand dead."

Jane and her first husband had divorced in Australia and she had met Brock, who had followed her back to the United States in 1970.

Jean had never met Jane and Brock, but she had heard me talk about them many times and had talked to them over the phone. I knew they would love her as much as I loved her.

"So this is little Jean who I've heard so much about," Brock said in that cultivated and sophisticated English accent of his as he opened Jean's door.

"Why the hell did yawl get married?" Jane yelled as she jumped up and wrapped her arms around me.

"Why did yawl get married?" I said to Jane and Brock.

"We got married because immigration was going to ship Brock back to Australia as an undesirable alien because of all those arrests in Brisbane and Sidney and the anti-Vietnam demonstrations. We had to. Don't tell me Jean's pregnant and yawl had to."

"No, not that we know of anyway. No babies on the way so far as we know. I just felt sorry for him, I knew he couldn't manage without me and I guess you could say I married him out of pity mainly."

"Bullshit," I said. "She made me get married. Before I met her the cops all warned me she carried a gun and I was afraid not to."

We went inside their house and talked and talked about how we had ended the war, about how we'd gotten rid of Lyndon Johnson, about how we'd gotten rid of Richard Nixon, and about how our generation had invented sex.

"Have you ever been to the Outer Banks?" Brock asked Jean.

"No, to me the beach has always meant Myrtle with the shows and the pavilion and the crowds. Until I met Michael, I had never been to the beach in the winter. We came down this past January and it was snowing. I'd never seen that before, snow falling on a beach. And you know what, those crazy Canadians were out there swimming at night in the ocean with the snow falling. The Canadians say the chances of being bitten by a shark are much less when it's snowing."

We all laughed with this obvious reference to the movie *Jaws*. It was after 2:30 before we got to bed. Jean and I were not up until nearly 12, and we felt guilty for keeping Jane and Brock up so late before a workday.

The village of Okracoke is very small, and you can ride bicycles just about any place you would want to go. Jane and Brock had told us to feel free to ride their two extra bikes anywhere we wanted. We rode the bikes over to Jane's office to take her for lunch.

"There's one thing I always wanted to do. That's to build a bonfire on the beach and camp there all night. Could we do that, Jane?" I asked.

"Sure, we'll do that. Brock and I have decided since this is such a special occasion, we're gonna take off a couple of days to be with you two honeymooners. That is, unless you two have private business you need to attend to."

Brock was home by 3 o'clock, and Jane closed her office early. She said it was no problem for either of them as they both worked on "Okracoke time." She explained that Okracoke time meant that if you had something you wanted to do other then work, you simply did it. And since everybody followed Okracoke time, when they found an office closed early, they always chalked it up to Okracoke time. The island was so sparsely inhabited that you could drive on the beach. There were more than twenty miles of beach to drive on, and you could always find a secluded spot where no one would bother you to pitch your tent and build your bonfire. Jean, Brock, and I all three loved shellfish, so we got a bushel basket filled with clams and oysters. This was freedom, I thought as we came to a stop in Jane and Brock's Jeep. We threw our tent up, and I mean threw it up. We all hoped there wouldn't be a storm because no more mechanically minded than any of us were, that tent we put up couldn't stand up to much wind. By the time we had the tent up, we were all soaking wet from the hot sun. Just like a bunch of hippies, we all stripped off all of our clothes and ran into the water. The water was actually kind of chilly.

"I think this water's as cold as at Pot Rock," Jean said as she crushed her body against mine.

In a few short minutes we were all cooled off, so we ran back to the tent and got a couple blankets to spread out in the sun. I oiled Jean up, she oiled me up, Brock oiled Jane up, and Jane oiled Brock up. This had to be the way the beach was where the Garden of Eden met the ocean.

"Isn't this better than Pot Rock?" Jane asked.

"If it weren't for the company, it wouldn't be," Jean and I both said simultaneously.

"Jinx, you owe me a Coke."

"Would a Budweiser do?" Jean asked.

Jean crawled over to the cooler and started passing Budweisers around. Until dark we would heat by the sun, then run into the ocean and cool off, then come back and be heated by the sun.

We walked all up and down the beach gathering driftwood and old tires for our bonfire. By the time dark came, we had three tires and a pile of driftwood four feet tall. We lit our fire with charcoal lighter. We had put our shellfish under the edge of the fire so we were able to pull them out with a rake when they were good and hot and had cracked open. Brock and I began to discuss Watergate. This was the first time we'd seen each other since '74, when impeachment pressure had forced Nixon to resign.

"You know, you Americans are so backward when it comes to democracy. You haven't improved at all in two hundred years. What you did in 1776 was a hundred years ahead of everybody else in the world, but then you haven't made any progress since that time. As a matter of fact, you've moved backwards while we English have steadily moved forward with our democracy."

"So you believe a parliamentary system is superior to what we have, Brock?"

"Oh, certainly. With the Nixon fiasco in a parliamentary system, there would have been a vote of no confidence in parliament of the prime minister's conduct, and Nixon would have been out of office a year before he was. You Americans believe you elect a king. In 1776, you threw the yolk of King George III off your backs for your George I."

"But, Brock, George Washington clearly refused to become an American king."

"I know he did, and that's the real irony of what happened to American democracy. You Americans in 1776 could not live with a king, and you Americans in 1974 could not live without a king. Don't you see what I'm saying? A king can do no wrong. A king derives his power from God. You Americans believe your president can do no wrong. Most of you believe your president derives his power from God. We English know the people grant our Prime Minister's power. Look at the difference in press conferences that are held by the Prime Minister of England or the President of the United States. Most reporters knew that Lyndon Johnson was lying about the Gulf of Tonkin affair, but it was years before any reporters would say that Johnson had lied about the Gulf of Tonkin. In England, or in Australia, reporters don't hesitate when they are lied to, to point it out to the prime minister and to get right up in his face about it. But your American reporters don't dare question the lies of a sitting president. I do hope the result of Nixon's disgrace with Watergate will be that you Americans no longer consider your president to be the divine king who must be supported, right or wrong, for the four years he's in office."

"Brock, I think the true test of Watergate will be if a Democratic president gets himself in trouble, will the Democrats in the end do the right thing and remove him. After all, it was when Republican Senator Barry Goldwater led a group of Republicans to tell Nixon that it was over that Nixon finally resigned."

Jane and Jean had been talking to each other while Brock and I were talking. It was a beautiful full-moon night.

"Look at the white caps as they come into shore. They look like they're lit up. How does the moon do that, Jane?"

"It's not the moonlight. The crashing waves actually are lit up. Let's go down to the water."

We all walked down to the edge of the water and gradually waded out until the water was above our knees. You could actually see that as a wave would crash, it would actually light up. I had seen this before.

"What's making this light up?" Jean asked.

"There are millions of tiny little algae," Jane began, "that when excited turn chemicals inside their bodies into light."

"Like a lightning bug," I said.

"What did Michael say?" Jane asked.

"Michael said it's comparable to fireflies," Brock said in that high fluting English accent.

"Brock," I said, "when are you ever gonna learn the language? Jane, why don't you send him home with a book so that he can learn how to talk and he can learn the customs, then bring him back. I said, 'lightning bugs,' not 'fire flies.'"

Jean reached her hand down into the water and spun around. She was completely encircled by light for a moment. I splashed water over Jean's body. When the water smacked against her skin, her skin lit up. We all began splashing each other.

Over our splashing, Jane yelled, "This is more like what you mountain people call 'fox fire' than it is like lightning bugs or fireflies. The fox fire of the mountains is a similar algae with the ability to produce light."

Brock and I were enjoying splashing our wives and watching them glowing in the dark. The light would trickle down their bodies, gradually losing its brilliance. The light remained in their hair much longer.

"Brock, don't you think they look like a couple of angels?" I asked.

"I wouldn't go that far," Brock said.

It was a wonderful week. Jane and Brock needed to get back to work. Jean and I had needed the break, and both of us were now rip-roaring ready to take on the judicial system of southwestern Virginia.

Chapter 49

Someone once said your ability to withstand challenges is directly proportional to your support base. I'm not exactly sure what they're talking about, but I kind of think Jean is my support base, and with her behind me, there isn't any challenge I can't overcome, and together we were going to take on the corruption we saw in the judicial system of southwest Virginia. I had a feeling Jean could do anything. Her way with people was absolutely amazing. We went back up to Carroll County, Virginia. We had an underground support base that was far beyond what we had imagined it to be. It seemed that the people up there, as opposed to the people in Winston-Salem, felt themselves to all be touched by the corruption of the judicial system. Whereas in North Carolina, although the tobacco company controlled everything, the tobacco company was in fact very benevolent, and after their fight with the commi union, they saw to it that their workers were well cared for and relatively well paid, and jobs in the tobacco family were passed from father to son to grandson. Whole families, including both husbands and wives, would work in the tobacco factory until retirement, and retire well. The tobacco business, not unlike a drug cartel, was making enough money for everyone to share in the profits, and the direct result of the commi unions coming to town had been to convince the family who owned the tobacco company that they'd better share their profits with their workers.

On the other hand, up in southwestern Virginia, there was limited good. There was just so much wealth to go around. So in that situation, some people had to be poor and powerless, no matter how hard they worked, if some were to live in mansions on huge estates.

It was all but done that Jean and I would be moving permanently to our farm up in the mountains. We had an old farmhouse there. We began spending more and more time at our old farmhouse. We joined a Baptist church.

Both Jean and I had grown up in conservative Baptist churches, so when we went looking for a church, it was natural for us to seek another Baptist church. To us, it wasn't so much the words themselves that came out of a preacher's mouth, but it was the charisma and a spiritual feeling that we saw in the church. At the time I met Jean, I had been active in a large Baptist church with a very active class for single adults. With the rising rate of divorce, even in the South, the churches had seen the need to give a place to single adults, whether divorced, never married, or widowed. The churches up here in Carroll County didn't minister to single adults, but that wasn't a problem now since Jean and I were married. One thing that did bother me was that the classes were segregated by sex, and I had wanted to be in a married class with my wife. Jean, on the other hand, was a much more social person than me and enjoyed her women's class. I had been baptized, but Jean never had, and within a few months without my pushing her, Jean had gone first to her Sunday-school teacher and then to our minister and been baptized.

Although my church back in Winston-Salem had been one of those Baptist churches founded and strengthened up until the 1960s by it's fundamentalist belief in prohibition, by 1975, there was an unspoken tolerance for alcohol; of course, not in the church, but it was accepted in members who were social drinkers. Jean had been out of the church since her early teens and told me her old church probably would still have put her out because of her love for Budweiser. Although our beloved Baptist church had been founded upon the concept of prohibition, neither of us believed that to be Biblical, and we determined that we might cut back drastically with our Budweiser, but for the time being, we were not going to become teetotalers. We weren't going to hide it, but we weren't going to flaunt it, either. If a fellow member of our church should be in line with us at Piggly Wiggly and we were buying a six-pack of Bud, we intended to treat the incident ourselves as if it were no more than a six-pack of Coke.

Most all of the men in my Sunday-school class seemed to be hen-pecked, but they didn't seem to be bothered by it, anyway. Jean said the women in her class ran the church. She also said the women in her class seemed to admire her for being the kind of strong woman she was and even admired her for the role she had assumed, taking control of our music festival.

There is something known as the "women's circle" in the southern Baptist churches. These women's circles become the social life of the women of these churches. They are the garden club, the bridge club, and the country club all wrapped into one for these women, and the circle consists of the women of each class. Jean's circle met on Tuesday nights. It's always seemed to me that the main purpose of the circle is gossip, or, as the women in Jean's circle would call it, "information sharing." It was through Jean's circle that Jean learned a lot about what had happened after our festival that stirred up so much trouble.

"I ain't supposed to tell nobody this," Mable said as all the ladies sat around in their circle, "but, Jean, what happened to you and Michael was them lawyers over at that Pentecostal Holiness Church that most of 'em goes to was jealous on account of Michael and that Scott feller had come up here to Carroll County and was mak'n' so much money. Well my cousin who goes over there at that Pentecostal Holiness Church she says that since them lawyers would'n getting nuthin out of it, they pushed preacher Jim Bob over there to stir up all that trouble against you, and they figured that if they was to get all that trouble started, people would file suits against y'all and their judges would see to it that them lawyers and their clients would get some money outta y'all. They been so used to controlling everything in the county that they never even thought nuthin 'bout Michael might make a 'Federal case' out of it."

"Mable, Michael and me come up here after we heard he's sued and they'd seized our money, and they wouldn't even let us see the court files. Now, that was wrong."

"Oh yea, oh yea, that Wyclif lawyer, a whole lotta people says he owns Judge Demarkus. And, by the way, Jean, that assistant clerk over there, Denice Morley, everybody says Wyclif is, you know, with her."

"That Wyclif, ain't he bout eighty years old?"

"Oh yea, oh yea, and Denice, she's 'bout forty. That'd make her about forty years younger than him."

All the other ladies in the circle were just leaning forward, trying to hang on to every word between Mable and Jean. And Mable, she was just thoroughly enjoying the attention and authority she was getting from sharing this inside information her cousin had given her on the Pentecostal Holiness Church.

Mable went on. "My cousin says that something has been a-goin' on between Wyclif and Denice since she's twenty and he's sixty."

"It's just a disgrace," interjected Rhonda.

"Yea, that Denice was the first one of them clerks to come over there and tell us we couldn't see the files, and then the other two clerks came over there and blocked our way."

Mable went on. "Well, my cousin says the reason they didn't want y'all to see them files was because they knew every one of 'em was just made up stuff so that they knowed they could get Judge Demarkus to give em some money outta all that money yawl had. And my cousin, she said that Wyclif and Judge Demarkus worked that up together to take that money outta y'all's bank account and Demarkus was in on the whole thing. I don't know if he was or not, but I will tell you this. Now, you aren't gonna let this thing get out, are ya?"

"Oh, no, what's said in this women's circle stays in this women's circle."

"You see, Judge Demarkus got to be a judge because of Wyclif. When he's a lawyer, he always stayed drunk so he couldn't make a live'n'. So Wyclif saw to it that he became a judge, and, of course, Demarkus knows Wyclif can take it away anytime he wants to 'cause the Republican Party controls everything up here in Carroll County, and Wyclif controls the

Republican Party. Even been times when Judge Demarkus would be sittin' up there so drunk that he would pass out and fall over, and Wyclif would threaten any of them sheriffs if they didn't say that Judge Demarkus fell over on account of his high blood pressure. And, Jean, you know it's hard to get a job up here. There don't nobody get a county job less'n Wyclif approves it, whether it's Sheriff or somebody work'n' down at the tax office."

All the ladies in the circle were just falling over themselves to get home and tell their husbands, and everybody else, what Mable had shared with them, and Mable knew it, and she felt like a star. And one of those ladies, of course, was my wife, Jean, who came on home and shared it with me.

"Jean, this is dynamite. I'm gonna go to Wyclif' office tomorrow and carry me this little tape recorder I've got and just talk to him and see how much he'll admit to. I'm also gonna ask him about this affidavit that he says he mistakenly put without prejudice and then got it changed."

The next day, I went to Wyclif's office. I waited until after lunch cause I figured he would be busy in court until after morning. As I parked my car a block or so from Wyclif's building, of all people, I saw coming out of his doorway one Denice Morley. I walked up the stairs. The door to the office was open. Wyclif's secretary was not yet back from lunch. I walked over to Wyclif's office door. On the way, I clicked my tape recorder inside my jacket to record.

"Mr. Wyclif, you got a minute?"

"Just a minute, I'm a busy man. Common in."

"Mind if I have a seat, Mr. Wyclif?"

"Sure, go ahead."

"Mr. Wyclif, I'm confused. Are you representing that dairy farmer, Mr. Wright?"

"No, sir, I referred that case to Mr. Jones over in Abingdon."

"I did get my money back, Mr. Wyclif."

"Well, that's a damn shame. I just don't understand why the judge didn't keep that money 'til the lawsuit was over so he could give it to Mr. Wright."

"But, Mr.Wyclif, you did file the papers that seized my bank account."

"That's right, and if you check the file, I seized your farm, too."

"Mr. Wyclif, one thing that really bothers me is the clerk over there wouldn't let me see the files."

"I told em not to let you see the files, Mr. Spears."

"Well, Mr. Wyclif, any citizen is entitled to see the public records."

"We do things differently up here in Carroll County, Mr. Spears. I asked Judge Demarkus to send down an order to Denice and the others in the office to tell you that you were not allowed to see those files, or any of the files in the courthouse of Carroll County. That ruckus you caused over there, you could smell it all the way up to the Pentecostal Holiness Church out there I attend, and all them naked women over there just splashin' around in Pot Rock, that Pot Rock is a hell hole. It's a den of sin."

"Well, now, Mr. Wyclif, due process demands that when I'm a defendant in a law suit, I'm to be allowed to see the lawsuit filed against me."

"You must have not heard me the first time. I'm gonna repeat. We do things different here in Carroll County, Virginia."

"Mr. Wyclif, just one other thing. Let me ask you. You do know when a dismissal is taken with prejudice what it means, don't you?"

"Of course, I do. That means it cant be brought up again."

"And you knew when you signed the original dismissal with prejudice that that was supposed to end everything and it could not be brought up again."

"I just told you that."

"Well, what about that affidavit that you signed that said the order with prejudice was a mistake?"

"Mr. Jones sent that over here for me to sign, and I looked at it and I read it and I signed it."

"And that affidavit said that it was a mistake, didn't it?"

"That's what the affidavit said, but Mr. Jones prepared that. Well, I tell you, Mr. Spears, the only mistake was I thought when I signed the order with prejudice that Judge Demarkus had already distributed that money I'd seized."

"You mean my money."

"Yes, sir, I thought I told Demarkus to go ahead and distribute that money, and he didn't do it, and now you got it back."

"Well, that's pretty clear, Mr. Wyclif. I appreciate you talkin' to me."

"You're welcome, Mr. Spears."

I could not believe what I had gotten on tape. This lawyer, who had the very highest rating of any lawyer in Carroll County, Virginia, in the Martindel Hubble directory of lawyers, a rating that was earning him hundreds of thousands of dollars per year, had just admitted doing everything wrong I knew he'd done. As soon as I got home, I told Jean about the tape. Before we even played it, we placed two more tape recorders to record it so that if anything happened upon the first playing, we would have two copies. And then we sealed the original in an envelope and hid it away and made a written transcript of what was on the tape.

The next day, Jean and I prepared a motion to reverse the order from Abingdon that had allowed the suit to be reopened. We didn't wait for the mail for it to be delivered. We hand-delivered it to the federal clerk of court and to Jones's office. We had a hearing set for three weeks later.

Chapter 50

Before the hearing in federal court, Brandon Jones called me. Butter would not have melted in the man's mouth.

"Michael, why don't we just go ahead and dismiss both these claims? There's no use in us fighting over this matter. I've already talked to Judge Long, and he suggests that I dismiss and you dismiss and everybody just accept the costs that they've suffered."

"Well, now, Brandon, I could've agreed to that, or, let me say, if you just hadn't filed that last suit after you and Judge Long got together and made it possible to file it, I wouldn't have filed anything, but I've got a lot of work into my counter-claim. And what about that affidavit? Way Wyclif talks tells me, you and him agreed to commit perjury. It would appear to me that he's guilty of perjury, and I believe that would make you guilty of subornation of perjury."

"How dare you accuse me of subornation of perjury."

I was having fun with this

"Well, Brandon, Wyclif tells me that he told you the truth that he told you that he had intended that order be with prejudice and that you made up that affidavit that he signed anyway."

"Well, Michael, we don't have anything to talk about, Goodbye." Click.

Jean and I got to the federal courthouse for the hearing. Jones was there already. I looked around. I did not see Wyclif.

The judge began in his whiny tone, "Mr. Spears, Mr. Jones and I have talked. He said that he thought y'all could settle this case, now what is it?"

"Your honor, I'm never gonna say that a case can't be settled, but I'm here for my motion. Could we hear that, your honor?"

"I've got your affidavit, Mr. Spears, and your motion, now you go ahead."

"Your honor, I have a complete transcript of the tape. I have one copy for Mr. Jones here." I handed Mr. Jones a copy. "Your honor, May I approach the bench?"

"You may."

I handed the judge a copy of the transcript of the tape and walked back to my table. He took his time examining the transcript. He looked over his glasses occasionally at Jones. He looked over his glasses and said, "Go ahead, Mr. Spears."

"Your honor," I said holding up the small cassette tape in my right hand as I held up the small cassette recorder in my left hand. "Your honor, I have in my right hand the original cassette tape. In my left hand, I'm holding the recorder I used to make the tape. I'll go ahead and put them together. Your honor, this tape and tape recorder have been in my possession at all times since I made the tape recording of my conversation with Mr. Wyclif."

I was not going to be beaten again by the assertion that the chain of evidence had been broken, as ridiculous as I realized what I was doing might appear to be.

"Your honor, I am speaking as an officer of the court, and under such duty, I am bound to say the truth and nothing but the truth, but if your honor so chooses, I will be sworn."

The judge whined out, "That won't be necessary, Mr. Spears."

"If your honor desires, I will turn over the original tape and/or tape recorder to the court or to the U.S. Marshall if that would be helpful for the court to understand my motion."

Again, the judge whined on, "That won't be necessary, Mr. Spears."

"Your honor, I have here a copy of the Wyclif tape, and on a full size cassette recorder, which with the court's permission, I will play it for the Court."

"Go ahead, Mr. Spears."

"Your honor and Mr. Jones may follow the tape recording with the transcript you have before you." I then played the tape. It was loud and clear and but for possibly two words out of the fifteen-minute tape, everything could be understood and coincided with the transcript. "That's my evidence, your honor."

"Mr. Jones, I'll hear from you."

Jones began, "Your honor, that transcript and that tape recording may be of Mr. Wyclif, but he was not under oath at the time he made those statements, and that's all I have to say."

"Mr. Jones, I have to agree with you. Mr. Wyclif was not under oath, and I'm going to disregard the transcript and the tape recording."

I couldn't believe it. This judge is so dumb. Of course, I was going to appeal to the Fourth Circuit Court of Appeals.

Within three months, the Fourth Circuit Court of Appeals in Richmond reversed the district court order, admonishing the district court judge that "It is the oath that transforms the statement into perjury and the district court is ordered to consider the transcripts provided by Mr. Spears."

Without granting a new hearing, the whiny judge drafted a new order saying that this Carroll County, Virginia, lawyer with the highest rating of Martindel Hubble was clearly too old to know what he was saying and doing, so he wasn't going to find perjury and he was not going to reverse the order that allowed the dairy farmer's suit against me.

Chapter 51

Jean woke up one Sunday morning sick to her stomach. I got up to see what was wrong, and she said she felt just a little nauseated. I walked into the kitchen and yelled back to her while she was still standing in the bathroom, asking if she would like me to scramble some eggs, at which point she began puking into the toilet. She didn't have symptoms of cold or flu, so we had a good idea what her problem was.

Monday morning, Gene went to see Doctor Andover. I had the drier pushed out and was cleaning lint from behind it when Jean walked in with sort of a sheepish grin on her face. I was sitting on the floor looking up at her, and she said, "I'm pregnant."

It took my breath away. I had always wondered what it would be like to be a father, but at thirty-two, I'd kind of given up on ever being one. It put a whole new meaning into life. I had taken out a one-million-dollar insurance policy on my life just after Blaine Cromer had warned me to be careful around the people in the Rains case, including Jean, by the way. I made the one-million-dollar life-insurance policy payable to my estate and directed that in the event there should be question about whether my death had been a homicide, that one-hundred-thousand dollars of that insurance policy was to be placed into a trust to go as a reward for information leading to the arrest and conviction of the person responsible for my homicide. Blaine had made me believe that these people, including Jean, just might want me dead, but since our marriage, I had made Jean the owner and beneficiary of the policy on my life. I couldn't help but reflect that with a baby on the way, it was a good thing that that policy would be two years old and uncontestable within a few months.

I stood up and walked toward Jean. We held each other for a while.

"Are you gonna be okay for the festival? It's less than six months away. I can cancel it if you're not. You and now our baby mean more to me then anything in the world and more than anything ever has."

"No," she answered. "I'll just wear big pants when I'm on the stage, and if I have to waddle, I'll waddle."

A few days later, a notice came from the court in Abingdon. Our trial was scheduled for the week of July 4 of the summer of '77. Our festival would be only a few weeks after that. This would mean tremendous pressure on both Jean and me. We talked about whether or not we should consider Jones's previous offer and see if we could still get a dismissal on the complaint if we have a dismissal of our counter-claim. We both decided that the time had come for us to stand up and fight. We needed a miracle; we'd needed a miracle many times before, and we really needed one this time. We met in Abingdon for the trial on Monday, the first week of July.

I looked at the pool of potential jurors. They were people just like the people in our church. They were people who believed in justice and believed it was wrong to seize somebody's property without just cause. If I could convince these people that the dairy farmer had conspired to seize our farm and our bank account wrongfully, then no matter what the judge did, there was a possibility of winning. Jean and I didn't need the money, but we knew a loss could take everything we had. It was only property, but it was our property and we loved it, and someday we wanted our unborn child to enjoy Crooked Creek and Pot Rock as much as we did, and there was that possibility that the judge and Brandon Jones and the dairy farmer would take it from us.

The judge called Jones and me back into his chambers.

"Mr. Spears, you can't win this suit. You know I'm not gonna let that evidence come in on Wyclif. Now, that jury that's sittin' out there, that's my people, I know those people, and I'm not gonna let them hear any evidence that don't belong before them."

The judge was flat-out telling me I was going to lose, he was going to see that I lost.

Jones began presenting his evidence. He was accusing me of fraudulently misleading all of the people of Carroll County, Virginia, and asking this jury to not only grant his client actual damages for a few gallons of lost milk, but for punitive damages that would take away everything Jean and I had so that that would serve as an example to anybody else who would come into the county to defraud the good people of Carroll County, Virginia.

The judge let in all of the evidence that Jones offered. He allowed Jones to lead the witnesses. At one point in frustration, I stood and objected. Jones was so flagrantly leading his witness that I asked the judge if it wouldn't be better for Mr. Jones to take the stand and testify himself, so at least I could cross examine the real witness in the case, who was the lawyer himself. Of course, the Judge denied my motion and threatened me with contempt in front of the jurors. When it came time for me to present my evidence, the Judge himself made motion after motion limiting the evidence that I was able to present and hurrying me on so that I didn't possibly see how the jury could understand my position at all. The only point that I was able to make was when Jones questioned me about a document submitted to the Virginia Department of Health in Richmond describing the anticipated crowd as far smaller than it turned out to be, the document purported to have my signature. But it clearly was not my signature, which I was able to point out to the jury, and when Jones handed the jury the health document with the other documents with my signature on them, it clearly showed the jury the one from Richmond did not have my signature.

Jean had been sitting right beside of me throughout the entire trial and had helped me by keeping all of the documents that I at least attempted to present in order. She had kept me calm at moments when I felt I was going to explode in rage against Jones and the judge. We made final arguments to the jury. Jones repeated how I had come up and taken advantage of these poor country people and was a rich lawyer and made so much money and therefore the jury should find not only the damages for the lost milk, but also the punitive damages to make an example of me to discourage anyone ever again from coming in and taking advantage of the poor people of Carroll County. Jean and I knew that all of the people in our church were praying for us and knew that our trial was being held this week. Many of them had offered to come to court. But I really felt that it was hypocritical to have our church members sitting there in court, so we declined their invitation. However, one of our fine church members, Miss Fanny, had suggested to me a new prayer. I had always prayed before to the father. She said, "No, Michael, pray to the son. Ask Jesus for help." Throughout Jones's closing argument to the jury, I had continued to whisper under my breath, "Dear Jesus, please help me; dear Jesus, please help me," and I knew that Jean was also praying. I didn't know what she was saying, but I knew she was praying. I made my final argument to the jury.

I said to them, "Remember what has happened to me could happen to anyone. Anyone could have their property seized, but you, the members of the jury, have the power to send a message that its wrong to seize somebody's property, at least until the jury has determined they owe money and must pay." I concluded my argument but didn't really feel good about it and started to walk back to my seat, and then I turned to the jury and looked directly to all of them. I still had plenty of time to talk; I had not used all of my time. I stood there for a moment and looked at the jury and said to them, "Mr. Jones will tell you there is fraud here. Yes, there's fraud here, you know there is fraud here, you've been here for a week and heard the evidence and you members of the jury know where that fraud is." And then I took my seat.

Judge Long began his instructions to the jury. He summarized the evidence in a way that was mostly favorable to the dairy farmer and Jones, and then he got to the point the first point, where Jones had argued to the jury I had committed fraud, and I knew exactly how Judge Long was going to say it. I knew exactly what he was going to say. He was going to tell them I had committed fraud, and just as he started to mouth the word fraud, lightning struck that court house and everything went dark; the emergency lights didn't come on as they should have, or at least they took a while, but even with the emergency lights, it was still dim. The courtroom was in the very center of the building, so it was impossible for any outside light to come in. The time was around 6 in the evening, and we waited for probably thirty minutes and then the lights came on again, and the entire time, I had been praying "Dear Jesus please help me; dear Jesus, please help me." And Judge Long began his jury instructions again, and he used the word fraud, but, of course, its impact after the lightning was much less. And then he built again and he built his crescendo and he built to that second point where he was going to accuse me of fraud, and just as he got to the point where he was going to mouth the word fraud and before he could get the word out, lightning struck the courthouse again.

I had continued to pray, "Dear Jesus, please help me; dear Jesus, please help me." If you pray, you know there are times when, for whatever reason, you're simply not in touch. This was not one of those times. I knew I was in touch with God. I had felt the presence of his spirit in that courtroom. With the lightning strike this time, the lights did not come back on for hours. Gradually, the security lights came up around the walls of the courtroom. The judge ordered candles and kerosene lanterns be brought in. By this time, it was becoming late enough that it was dark outside the building. After about an hour without electric lights, he began again with his final instructions to the jury. I don't think anybody in the courtroom heard a word he said during the darkness. As the judge read his jury instructions, he stumbled and more or less just spoke the words. The jury was then sent out to begin deliberations.

It was a very eerie sight as we waited later and later in the darkness. If you walked at all, you had to be very careful and feel your way to avoid chairs and desks and other objects in the courthouse. During the jury deliberations, the court personnel brought in supper for the jurors. I continued to pray, "Dear Jesus, please help me." Suddenly, about 11:30, the lights came on. Apparently, the jurors had reached their decision at the same time the lights came back on because they knocked to alert the bailiff that they had reached their decision immediately. We all assembled in the courtroom; clearly everyone present was thoroughly and totally emotionally drained. The jurors came filing back in. I had never seen a jury look that way before. They appeared to be at peace with themselves.

"Mr. Foreman, has the jury reached a decision?"

"We have, your honor."

"Mr. Foreman, pass your decision to the clerk."

The clerk took the folded piece of paper. She handed it to the judge. He looked over his glasses at Mr. Jones. The color appeared to drain from his face.

"We, the jury, find Mr. Spears," he said, pausing. "They found for you in the amount of ten thousand dollars."

"Thank you, father," I whispered.

Jean clasped my right arm. I looked over at Mr. Jones. He was so stunned he said nothing. His young associate grabbed him by the arm and started jerking him.

"You've got to make a motion," the associate said.

Jones stood up. "Your honor, I move to set the jury verdict aside."

The jurors stared in disbelief. As with most laymen, these jurors were shocked after being told all their lives how important the jury system was. Now they were being brought to reality that their solid verdict could be set aside.

I started to walk around my table to thank the jurors but stopped myself, realizing they had not yet been dismissed. The jurors were given a polite dismissal and thanked for giving their time in jury service. They then hurried out of the courtroom. After all, it was after midnight.

I had never been so happy with a jury verdict before in my life. The main part of it, of course, was that I had won. The money didn't really matter. I shook everybody's hand in the courthouse, and my pregnant wife and I headed back to our home in Carroll County, Virginia. The next day, papers all over Virginia and North Carolina reported my victory. They even embellished it by indicating how I had represented myself against a powerful Virginia law firm. Jean and I felt secure that at least in Virginia, we would no longer be harassed by a corrupt judicial system.

Chapter 52

We only had three weeks to get ready for our festival. There were so many things to do, and there was so little time to do it. We enlisted the aid of a lot of our church people, especially the ones who we felt might take a sip of cough medicine every now and then and wouldn't be as offended by the drinking at the festival. Jean would be seven months pregnant and showing by the time she would act as master of ceremonies and run the stage. Our advertising this time had made clear there would be limited tickets. We were confident from the previous year we would have a crowd that would give us a profit, so our advertising was much more limited than the prior year. Jean was healthy as a horse and didn't have any problems at all throughout the festival. She had leased hundreds of additional acres as backup land should the crowd be too great. We were better prepared with our Port-A-Jons and garbage collection. There were fewer incidents of trouble this year than there had been the prior year. The community and Jean and I had learned from prior mistakes. Our church people suggested we add an annual gospel festival and that the church sponsor that since the site could easily be used two, three, maybe even four times a year without creating any burden on the community. Jean and I thought it was a great idea and a great way for us to give back to the community that we were becoming so much a part of.

Needless to say, with so many people encouraging me to quit the practice of law, I arrived at the decision that this was indeed best for me. However, I determined that I would keep my North Carolina law license active. I considered getting a Virginia law license, but I met a teacher in the Carroll County school system whom I had known and who had been a very successful and honest (I know it sounds like an oxymoron) lawyer in Mount Airy, North Carolina. He advised me to do as he had done so that he wouldn't be tempted to take on cases in Virginia when he moved there to become a teacher. He kept his North Carolina law license active, which always gave him the option of using comity to quickly get a Virginia law license if he really wanted one. He explained that it was easy to refuse friends and family legal cases here in Virginia when he told people he wasn't licensed in Virginia and it would thus be illegal for him to represent them.

I returned to Winston-Salem to say goodbye to many friends in the legal community and to make sure that Reggie was keeping up with the last cases I was turning over to him. I stopped by to see the Sage. The Sage had followed closely my case in Virginia and knew full well that it distressed me almost as much as the Rains case.

"How did you ever pull that off, Michael?"

"Simon, it was a miracle."

Simon, although ethnically very Jewish, always emphasized to me that religiously he was an atheist, which really disturbed me. I consider myself open-minded enough to believe that Jews, Hindus, Muslims, and other believers in God would someday meet me in heaven, but it's hard for me to believe that an atheist could find a place in heaven.

I told Simon of the prayer that Miss Fanny had told me to use. I went on to tell him that not one, but two lightning strikes had occurred. I told him that the lightning strikes had occurred exactly where I would have placed them if I had the power. I told him it was that miracle that I had prayed for many times in court.

"I don't know whether it was a miracle or not, but it certainly was amazing, Michael."

Jean and I stayed in Winston-Salem for a couple of weeks. We said our goodbyes to many of our friends. We decided to keep our Winston-Salem house, at least for the time being. She was getting really big. I kept telling her she looked like a pregnant guppy. I quit telling her this once when it made her cry. My strong woman had become so fragile while pregnant. As short and slim as she was, she appeared to be all belly. We decided to return to Winston-Salem for the birth or our baby, since we both believed the medical facilities of the larger city were much better.

We had a beautiful baby girl.

Chapter 53

Early spring, 1978, Jean and Michael's home at Potrock, near Galax, Virginia.

Jean and I had gotten up early in the morning. Baby Jena always got us up early in the mornings. It was a beautiful Indian summer day with the temperature in the high 70's. Jean had been pushing me to do what I knew I had to do. I had to call Lynda and Harry and tell them there was no hope. Sometimes when you have been beaten, you have to accept it and go on. We had gone up against the richest and most powerful people in North Carolina and had lost. The kids had told us they trusted Reggie and me at every point. It broke my heart, but I knew, as Jean told me, that I had to be honest with the children.

Jean and I were sitting in the front yard in the swing with baby Jena talking about how Reggie and I could tell the children it was over, when a huge black Mercedes pulled into our driveway. It was Malcolm Saits. I had no idea what brought Malcolm up here. I knew it wasn't a courtesy call.

Jean and I stayed in our swing as baby Jena cooed at the pretty black car Malcolm was driving. Malcolm was dressed as sharply as ever in a two thousand dollar suit and carrying an expensive black leather briefcase.

"Malcolm, what on earth brought you up here to the mountains today? As you see, the leaves are still real pretty, but I bet you're not up here to enjoy the beauty."

Malcolm began to speak in his usual business manner: "I'm up here on business. I want to make you an offer. But first before we discuss anything, I must have your promise that nothing that is said here today will be used in any way against me or my clients. I know you to be an honest man from dealing with you for the past two years and I know I can take your word as your bond. I also know I can put full faith and trust in the word of your lovely wife, Mrs. Spears."

Jean spoke up. "Malcolm, you have our word that nothing you say here will be used in any way against you or your client."

Malcolm began to explain his visit: "My sources have advised me that an investigative reporter for the *New York Times* is working on a story intended to expose the power of the tobacco interest in North Carolina and what he intends to portray as a corruption of the North Carolina Judicial System by tobacco money. My sources tell me that he intends to use the Harold Stennis Rains case as the foundation for his story. My sources tell me that you know this reporter but that as of now, he has not contacted you for the support he will need if he is to publish his story. If this story is published, it will cost my client and his companies and the people who work for his companies in your hometown far more than the generous offer I am prepared to make you. Shall I go on?"

"Go ahead, Malcolm," Jean said.

"What I am asking of you is that your clients bind themselves by prepared statement that I hand you now saying that they do not believe my client or clients contributed in any way to the death of their father. I will hold this statement in my file for eternity, if necessary, or to be used at the time of my choosing in defense of any statement that reporter may make. I also insist that you and your clients sign a document that from this day forward none of you will speak of the death of Harold Stennis Rains or the circumstances of the death of Harold Stennis Rains, upon forfeiture jointly and severally as liquidated damages of all funds to be paid to you and/or your clients by this business agreement."

"In other words, if the kids or Doris or Michael or I speak again about the death of Big Head, everything you're paying today, you get back."

"That's correct, Mrs. Spears."

"Big Head's kids are minors. This will have to be court approved. A new file will have to be created and a trust fund and all the tax considerations will have to be completed before this can be done, Malcolm."

"Michael, if you've learned anything about me over the past two years, it's that I know how to take care of the paperwork. Believe me, all of the appropriate judicial authorities have pre-approved what I'm asking and at the end of this day, with your cooperation, a legally sealed record will end this matter. I have sources who assure me that you can contact Reggie, the children, and their mother and this matter can be completed in Reggie's office by the end of this day. However, time is of the essence and I only have authority to give you and your lovely wife forty-five minutes to give me a yes or no answer. Here is the check that I am authorized to offer your clients for their cooperation."

Malcolm handed a check to Jean in the amount of ten million dollars.

"Malcolm, let Michael and me take the baby down to Potrock and discuss this."

Jean and I walked down to Potrock and sat down on the beach that just two years earlier I had shown her for the first time.

"Michael, what would the children accept if you called them right now without this offer?"

"You know they're living from hand to mouth. They would probably consider fifty-thousand dollars to be fair, maybe even ten."

"What would they get if we went to court?"

"I would say at best half a million dollars."

"What will this give them after taxes?"

"It's a wrongful death action, Jean. There are no taxes. The kids share six million dollars. Malcolm has taken care of all the paperwork."

"You have to remember. The case is not yours. The case belongs to your client. Let's call Reggie and follow Malcolm back down the mountain."

Within two hours, everything was signed and Malcolm had left Reggie's office. Doris and the kids were crying for joy and couldn't stop thanking Reggie, Jean, and me.

Thus ended the case of Harold Stennis "Big Head" Rains.

Chapter 54

Now here we are in 2005 with our baby girl, Jena, graduating Magna Cum Laude from Virginia law and given the stage to speak on the quad of the University of Virginia, the school founded by Thomas Jefferson. Every parent prays for a normal child, and God had given us a super child. She had been first in her grade, not just her class, from kindergarten through high school in the public schools of Carroll County. She had been a high-school athlete on the track team and the cross-country team, and her favorite sport had, of course, been wrestling. She was just a little bit of a person, a clone of her momma, and never backed off from a fight. And here was our little girl, speaking to the graduating class of 2005 at the University of Virginia. She had graduated from UVA undergraduate and then taken a course similar to mine, teaching chemistry in an inner city high school where she taught black, hispanic, and poor white students almost exclusively. I had warned her that things had changed; that kids were meaner then they had been in the '60s when I had taught at an all-black school. She had said, "Don't tell me that, Daddy. How many times have you told me when you were teaching chemistry in that high school and you would need a knife to cut something with and you would ask one of your young black students, 'Got a knife I can use, Leon?'"

"Yea, yea, Jena," I said.

"Okay, Daddy, what would he say?"

"He would say, 'Mr. Spears, you askin' me have I got a knife? Have I got my pants on?' And then he'd pull out a eight-inch stiletto and hand it to me."

"Well, now Daddy, they got cops and metal detectors and they don't allow knives in schools, so I figure it's got to be safer then it was when you were there."

I could hear her speaking to the crowd here in UVA: "Jerry Falwell, Charles Stanley, and Pat Robertson turning the Prince of Peace into the warrior God Christos. These so-called preachers of the gospel telling us on TV that Christ would have supported Bush's war on Iraq as a 'just war.' Give me a break. Gentlemen, you ought to be ashamed. That's blasphemy and heresy, and Satan has a special place in hell for people like you." She paused, and then went on. "I supported George Bush in the 2000 election. Especially when he called 'foreign intervention' and 'nation building' an 'arrogance of power,' but now, Mr. President, you're building an American empire in the Muslim world that is the very picture and definition of 'arrogance of power.'

"It's one thing for you to have made yourself the most hated world leader since Adolph Hitler. But I cannot forgive you for making the country I love the most hated nation on Earth since Nazi Germany.

"President Bush, you keep making these speeches to laid off mill-hands at technical schools telling them they have to 'retrain' in the new economy.

"Let me ask you, President Bush, what jobs can those technical schools train those mill-hands to do that you and your big buddies can't ship to communist China?

"Come down here to southwest Virginia or northwest North Carolina and talk to these third-generation mill-hands who are laid-off because of NAFTA. Come to Galax, come to Marion, or come to Mount Airy, North Carolina. Find them living in their cars along the rivers. Tell them how they are benefiting from your 'new economy.'

"Yes Mr. President, I close with these few lines from a document written by a great man; "But when a long train of abuses and usurpations, pursuing invariably the same object evinces a design to reduce them under absolute despotism, it is their right, it is their duty, and, I repeat, it is their duty to throw off such government and to provide new Guards for their future security.'"

I heard a woman say, "Somebody ought to arrest her. That's something a terrorist would say."

She just quoted the Declaration of Independence, lady.